THE REINVENTION of *Jinx Howell*

a pine bluff novel

NANCEE CAIN

Serrated Edge Publishing

Serrated Edge Publishing
PO Box 969
Jasper, AL 35502
www.nanceecain.com

First published February 2019

ISBN: 978-0-9995362-5-4

10 9 8 7 6 5 4 3 2 1

Editor: Jessica Royer Ocken
Line Editor: Coreen Montagna
Cover Design by Shannon Lumetta
Interior Book Design by Coreen Montagna

Printed in the United States of America

*For Christina Santos and Stephanie Phillips.
It's a tough job, but you both have kept me relatively sane.*

Chapter One

Three years ago

Mark MacGregor stormed out into the dimly lit back alley. A couple of rats scurried out of the way, disappearing behind the dumpster, and he scowled, displeased with the world at large.

A band? The Highland Hangout was barely operating in the black, and Derrick had gone and hired a live band?

Touching a flame to his much-needed cigarette, he damn near jumped out of his skin when a soft southern accent asked, "May I bum a light?"

Out of the shadows, a petite woman approached him in the hottest fuck-me boots he'd ever seen. The flame of the lighter revealed whiskey-colored eyes rimmed with black liner. Red lips parted in a soft smile. She seemed quite young, which was jarringly incongruent with her heavy makeup.

"Thanks."

"Come here often?" he joked. He let his gaze roam down her body, liking what he saw.

Damn if she wasn't hotter than a firecracker with her spiky black hair, piercings, and dominatrix-meets-schoolgirl outfit.

Her musical laugh echoed down the alley. "No, my first time." She swept her eyes up and down his body in return as she blew a perfect smoke ring.

I wonder what else that mouth can blow…

"So is it true?" She tilted her head.

"Is what true, love?" He crossed his arms and leaned against the doorframe.

"I'm doing research on sexual clichés. Do you mind?"

"Mind what?"

"If I check out what a man wears under his kilt?" She wiggled her fingers.

He chuckled; she wouldn't have the nerve. "Be my guest."

His breath caught in his throat as her hand slid up under his kilt and grasped his cock, which immediately stood at attention.

Hello, I'm Mark's cock. Pleased to meet you.

"I'll be dog-goned." She stroked him once, and he sucked in a ragged breath when her delicate finger whispered across the head of his penis.

Then she removed her hand, much to his dismay.

"Well, now I know. Thanks for the light." With a wink, she turned and sashayed away. Her sweet ass beckoned him like a neon light outside a strip club.

What. The. Fuck? No way in hell he'd let her get away. This chick had just captured his attention like no other in recent history. *Also, did she really just say "dog-goned"?*

He caught up to her and caged her against the brick wall. When she attempted to duck under his arm, he caught hold of her wrists with one hand and held them above her head. She looked up at him and laughed as he stared into her huge amber eyes. She wiggled her hands in his grasp but didn't try to get away. Their ragged breathing seemed to echo in the silent alley.

"Better be glad I gave consent. Some would file a sexual assault charge after that stunt."

She shrugged. "Some would. But you won't, Two-Time MacGregor."

He frowned. "Do I know you?" *Have I fucked this chick before?*

"Everybody knows you."

"I think turnabout, fair play is in order. I don't usually have strange women fondle me without at least learning their name." His free hand slid up her thigh above her killer boots, easing over her silky-smooth skin.

He watched her closely to gauge her response. He'd stop if she resisted. Her nostrils flared as she took in a sharp breath, but her eyes never left his. His hand slipped higher and squeezed her ass. He leaned in, capturing her lips, and tasted cigarette smoke and mint. To his surprise, she didn't pull away, but instead kissed him back, finishing with a nip to his lower lip.

"My name is Jinx, and unless you have a condom hidden somewhere on your person, I'd appreciate it if you'd get your hand off my butt." Her voice sounded breathy.

He wouldn't blame her if she slapped his face when he let go of her wrists. Removing his hands, he placed them on the brick wall on either side of her shoulders, still making it difficult for her to get away. "Your name is Jinx?"

"That's what I answer to, yes."

"Mark MacGregor, but you already know that." Again he took in her sinfully sexy body. "So are you channeling a young Britney Spears with this outfit?"

"I suppose. Are you channeling Jamie Frasier? Nice sword, by the way."

He threw his head back and laughed. *Damn. Cute* and *witty.* "Touché. Look, I work in the bar behind us. Got time for a quickie? I have plenty of condoms inside. Plus, I can get you in without a cover. I'll ply you with free drinks, and then we can hook up when I finish my shift. Sound like a plan?" He nibbled her earlobe, flicking her earrings with his tongue. The resulting shudder of desire and slight moan from those kissable lips jacked up his interest one-hundred percent.

"I have to go to work, too. Sorry."

Was that disappointment he heard in this sweet voice that curled around him like Spanish moss on the bayou?

"Really?" He sighed. "Too bad. Let's get together after we both get off—"

"Get off? Here?" she teased.

He chuckled. "Our shifts, smarty pants. Although I wouldn't be averse to getting off here." He waggled his eyebrows. "Seriously, I've got thirty minutes before duty calls. Let me walk you to your car, or to work. You don't need to be walking alone; it isn't safe." He didn't want to let her go. He wanted to get to know her.

Who the hell am I kidding? I want to fuck her, now or later. Preferably both.

"True. Some guy might want to stick his hand up my skirt and cop a cheap feel," she replied with a small laugh. "I promise I'm perfectly capable of taking care of myself. Thanks for the offer, though. See ya around." She ducked under his arm.

He liked her sense of humor. No way he'd let her get away that fast. Mark grabbed her elbow to stop her. The unexpected sharp pain in his side and kick to the back of his knees had him doubled over and hitting the ground before he knew what had happened. He gulped when he realized a wicked, six-inch stiletto heel hovered over his rapidly shrinking package. His balls had moved to take up permanent residence in the pit of his stomach.

She wasn't even breathing hard, dammit.

He let out a long, slow breath when she flicked open a switchblade.

"Hey, I'm sorry. Please, remove the weapon of sperm destruction. I'd like to have some little MacGregors someday. While you're at it, you can put away the knife. It's a bit of an overkill." He prayed he sounded more confident than he felt.

She laughed—without moving her foot. But she did snap the blade shut, shoving it in her jacket. She stood with her hands on her hips. "Just showing you I can take care of myself. Now, kiss my boot," she instructed saucily.

He raised an eyebrow. "What? No fucking way." He grimaced as the toe pressed into his groin and his nuts receded even farther.

He swore he heard them begging, *Kiss it! Kiss it now, dumbass.*

With a grin, he answered in a feigned falsetto, "Okay, Mistress Jinx." She moved the boot to hover over his face and a sliver of fear zipped through him. She truly held his life under her shoe. All it would take is a kick to the throat to send him straight to hell. His cock hardened. *Stupid fucker.*

With a loud smacking noise, he kissed her boot and chuckled. Damn, this little pixie entranced him. He'd submit to her in a second, and he didn't normally swing that way.

Jinx turned with a flounce and headed into the bar through the back door. He jumped to his feet and followed like a dog after a cur bitch in heat.

Who the hell is she? Wait just a fuckin' minute—she just walked into my *bar!*

Striding toward the stage, Jinx stopped to speak to the acne-prone guy strumming a guitar. She must be a groupie or the guy's girlfriend. Pity, she was the first girl to truly pique his interest in a long damn time.

Mark returned to his post and finished setting up the bar, watching her the entire time. She never gave him a second look, which annoyed him more than he cared to admit. Usually women fawned all over him when he wore his kilt. Although she'd started it, maybe he'd pushed her too far by groping her in the alley. She'd known who he was, so she more than likely knew his reputation for being a sonofabitch. He made it a policy to be upfront from the get-go that he was in it strictly for the sex, and it wouldn't happen more than twice. That way there were no misunderstandings regarding his intentions. And he never, ever pushed for sex. He didn't have to.

Derrick walked by, and Mark motioned him over. He nodded toward Jinx, who stood with her back to him, chatting with the band members. The lilt of her musical laughter filtered across the room.

"Band broad or one of the girlfriends?" Mark asked.

Glancing over his shoulder, Derrick grinned. "Jinx? She's the painter I told you about. As the band plays, she dances and paints. Sometimes they convince her to sing, but only in practice. I swear, just watching her paint is almost an orgasmic experience. She's the main reason I hired them. She gets the guys riled up and drinking when she does her artsy-fartsy stuff. Just wait and see."

An orgasmic experience? Watching a girl paint while some doofus band plays covers? Yeah, right.

Mark shook his head, both amused and irritated by his best friend and business partner's latest hare-brained idea to draw patrons.

Customers began wandering in, and Mark dove into filling drink orders. The crowd was a combination of regulars and green wristbanders — underage college kids getting in one last party before going home for the Thanksgiving holidays. Tips would be non-existent tonight; damn college kids were always broke. But he preferred busy to twiddling his thumbs.

The band started playing, and Mark paused, pleasantly surprised. Their cover of Rob Zombie's "Pussy Liquor" was spot on, and the crowd went wild. He watched out of the corner of his eye as Jinx took up her paint palette and went to work on a canvas. Her hips moved seductively to the music as she danced around and painted in those fantastic fuck-me boots.

Surveying the packed bar, Mark realized Derrick hadn't been kidding about Jinx getting the men hyped. He'd bet there wasn't a limp dick in the place—his included—and he listened with growing irritation to the whistles and lewd suggestions. Appearing oblivious to the audience, Jinx concentrated on her abstract painting while she seduced the crowd. She positively reeked of sex, sin, and self-assurance—an enticing combination, especially with her killer body and arresting face.

He had to have her. No question about it.

A little while later, as the band finished playing Nine Inch Nails' "Closer," Jinx put her paintbrush and palette down and moved with the music, her eyes closed, her hands running down her body. She shed the jacket and danced in her red, lacy cropped top, skirt, and boots, and Mark wished to hell there was a pole up on the stage. Not that she needed it, but damn, seeing those legs wrapped around a pole would be the stuff of fantasies. The only thing better would be her wrapped around *his* pole.

He served drinks, refilled popcorn bowls, and surreptitiously watched her until the set ended and the band took a break. She headed toward the bar with her jacket slung over her shoulder. Her aloof manner seemed totally opposite her stage persona. Several men and women tried to strike up conversations, but she kept walking until she arrived at the bar. With a crook of her finger, she motioned him over.

In no hurry, he moved toward her and smiled. "What can I get you, Mistress Jinx? On the house, of course."

She gave him a big, gusty laugh. "May I slip behind the bar to wash my hands?" She wiggled paint-stained fingers at him.

"Sure." He let her in, and she flung her jacket over the stool by the cash register. Trying to hide his interest, he covertly watched her glide to the sink, where she proceeded to scrub her hands.

When she turned around, drying her hands, a drunk at the bar yelled, "How about a beer and a kiss, sweetheart?"

She smiled, but it didn't quite reach her eyes as she shook her head. "Not my job."

"Which? The beer or the kiss?" the drunk asked with a leer.

Mark shook his head. "If you value your balls, I suggest you apologize to the lady. She's liable to castrate you." He winked at her.

The drunk snorted. "She couldn't hurt a fly."

"Trust me, the girl's packing a wicked blade."

Ignoring the jerk, Jinx reached for her coat. The drunk leaned over the bar, grabbing her wrist with his beefy hand. "C'mon, one little kiss."

"Let go," she ground out, tugging on her arm.

Mark acted fast, gripping the asshole's arm until he howled and let her go.

"Hey, calm down," Jinx shouted above the noise in the bar. "He's just a drunk jerk."

Mark released him with a shove and turned to face Jinx. "That's still not okay. But help me out and put your jacket back on before we have a goddamned riot in here. I don't have time to play Prince Charming and rescue your ass."

She rolled her expressive eyes at him and stood with her hands on her hips. "Didn't we already establish the fact that I can take care of myself?"

Her resistance sparked his anger. "Put the jacket on," he roared.

"Frog you," she screamed back. "You're not my boss, Prince Chauvinist."

Frog me?

Mark motioned for Derrick to take over bartending. Grabbing her hand, he shuffled her into the storage room that also served as the office.

"What is your problem?" she huffed. "Jealous?"

He'd be damned if he knew. But for some reason, he felt protective. He slammed the door shut and stood glaring at her.

"Jealous? Of course, not."

"Uh huh." Her grin widened.

Tension crackled between them. Her breasts heaved with her breathing, and her tongue snaked across her lower lip. That did him in. Protectiveness slipped into lust. With a yank, he pulled her into his arms and crushed his lips to hers. Jinx's moan inflamed his passion, and he deepened the kiss. She dug her nails into his shoulders, pulling him closer. He growled into her mouth.

When he broke away, she gasped for air.

"I want you," he rumbled. "Now."

"Ditto."

Deftly, he bent her over the desk as he reached into the drawer where the condoms were. One hand held her by the back of her neck as he yanked up her skirt to reveal a black satin thong on one of the prettiest asses he'd ever seen. He pulled the thong down and smacked her hard on her round cheek. She made a sound like a kitten mewling in response, and he smacked the other one hard enough to leave a red handprint. He quickly got himself sheathed, ready to satisfy his burning desire, but he paused when he looked down at her.

She had a death grip on the edge of the desk, and she'd gone eerily quiet and still. He leaned over her, his hard cock brushing her red bottom and peered at her, kissing her temple. With her eyes squeezed shut, her breathing sawed, and her cheeks had flushed bright red against the pallor of her face.

He frowned. "You sure about this?"

"I think so. I-I mean y-yes. Hurry up. I have to get back to work." She opened her eyes but appeared strangely disconnected.

Fuck! What the hell am I doing?

He eased his grip on her neck, tore off the condom, and put her thong back in place. Gently, he helped her up and straightened both of their clothes. He peered into her flushed face for a moment, and seeing no recrimination there, he kissed her forehead. Hugging her close, he realized she was actually a tiny girl, compared to her big personality. He rubbed her back.

"Why did you stop?" Her voice sounded as flat as her affect.

"Geezus, Jinx. I'm sorry. I thought you wanted this; I totally misread the signals. I promise, if you'd said *no*, or *stop*, I would've—in an instant."

"I didn't say stop. I do want it. I, uh, it's j-just that I have to be back on stage in a few. I didn't take you for a minute man, but if that's what you like, fine." She shrugged as if it was of no consequence. "Later, maybe?"

Her bloodless face contradicted her bravado.

Something isn't adding up—except my guilt. It's multiplying.

He'd kill any sonofabitch who treated Claire, his adopted sister, this way. Technically, he should be in the back of a police car for assault, and yet here she was acting like this was no big deal.

"I'm sorry, Jinx. While I'm not a hearts and roses kind of guy, I'm also not a rapist. I just…misread the signals." He ran a hand through his hair, loosening his ponytail. Blowing out a breath, he rewrapped it. "Again, I'm sorry. Don't ever let a guy treat you like that if it isn't what you want. Use that damn switchblade."

She placed a finger over his lips. "It's fine. There's no need to apologize. I have to go back to work, and so do you."

Cupping her face in his hands, he brushed his lips over hers, once again murmuring his apologies.

She smiled up at him and winked. "Later, 'kay?"

He nodded and watched her straighten her shoulders and swagger back into the bar.

Rubbing his face with the palms of his hands, he tried to process what the hell had just happened. She hadn't looked scared, just detached, and she hadn't told him to stop. The girl was a paradox of vulnerability and self-assurance all rolled up in a hot, sexy body.

Fuckin' asshole, he berated himself.

Mark went back to work, filling drinks and ignoring Derrick's questioning looks. He scanned the room until he found Jinx talking to some guy. The painting Mark wished *he'd* bought lay on the table in front of them, and the guy pulled several bills out of his wallet. Jinx took the money and put it in the inside pocket of her jacket. Giving Mark a wink and what seemed to be a genuine smile, she strolled back toward the stage as the band prepped for the second set. He rolled his head on his neck and tried to relax.

Chapter Two

Absofrogginlutely nothing was the answer to the age-old question: what does a Scotsman wear under his kilt? And when the Scotsman was as drop-dead gorgeous as Mark MacGregor, it caused a girl's heart to race in triple time. Jinx managed a smile as she remembered the stunned look on his face when she'd grabbed his formidable appendage. She'd considered dropping to her knees to take a closer look, but he would've expected a whole lot more than a look-see.

The rumors about him were not unfounded.

Phew. Her pulse hadn't quit hammering since she'd stumbled upon him in the alley. Guilty of amateur stalking, she knew he worked at the club because she'd overheard him talking to Derrick at the campus library where he worked during the day. His partner had just put the notice up on the bulletin board about needing a band, and she'd immediately torn it down to give to Will. It didn't hurt that her best friend, Ava, also worked at the bar and put a good word in for them. She'd met Ava working at a fast food joint when she first moved to New Orleans. A few years older, Ava had taken her under her wing.

Mark MacGregor had held her attention—and that of every other breathing female on campus—since she'd transferred here. The first time she met him was at the library. She'd stumbled upon an amorous couple going at it in the stacks like they were in the privacy of their own home. Peering through the shelf, she'd watched them until she heard a soft chuckle behind her.

"Again? I ran them off last week," he'd whispered. "Interested in seeing the grand finale, or can I end it now?"

Her cheeks had flamed, and she'd shaken her head no, unable to meet his eyes. Using two fingers, he'd whistled shrilly, and the couple had stopped, straightened their clothes, and hurried away, laughing.

"Did you need help finding anything?" he'd asked her with a smile in his voice.

Tongue-tied, she'd shoved her glasses up her nose and scurried away. No way was she going to face him as a blushing schoolgirl. She knew she needed to be in control when she met him. And tonight was that night.

Not that she felt very in control after the desk episode.

Dammit, why? What's wrong with me? That was precisely what she'd wanted…But the encroaching darkness had interrupted her plan. She could never predict when it would happen, and the random lapses in her memory always freaked her out.

Fanning her jacket to get some air, she blew her bangs out of her hot, flushed face. She downed half a bottle of water and peered at Mark from under her lashes. The guy sitting across from her took out his billfold to pay for the painting. She'd already shut down his flirting. With a fake smile, she thanked him and stood to leave, still feeling Mark's gaze on her.

Mark had been staring at her all night, and she found it a little disconcerting, but not in a creepy way. She'd pretended to ignore him so she could concentrate on her job. But he was her target. If anyone could help her, it had to be him. If her plan didn't work, she'd just commit herself to a hospital for the mentally insane and admit defeat. She had her mother's genes, after all.

Mark slid a drink down the bar, laughing at something someone said. She loved his wide, easy smile and the way his eyes crinkled when he laughed. He had to be well over six feet tall, because even in these boots, she had to look up to take in those compelling sapphire eyes. A desire to pull his dark auburn hair loose from the ponytail and run her fingers through the amazing waves overtook her. And the muscles she'd felt underneath his shirt…*Holy shitake.*

She let her imagination run wild, thinking about him naked. He had a tattoo on each wrist, and she wondered if there were any more. She had every intention of exploring to find out after the bar closed…if her courage held up.

He glanced her way again, and she gave him a wink, smiling in anticipation of the night ahead as she walked back to the stage.

"Hey, Jinx, need one of us to walk you to your car?" Will shouted from across the bar.

The lead singer of the Spellcast Socialists was like the brother she'd never had and as protective as a pit bull. They'd been friends since meeting in an English lit class. When he'd asked her to join the band, she'd been flattered and excited. He pushed for her to sing more, but her voice didn't hold a candle to his sultry sound.

"No, thanks." She glanced over at Mark, who was drying and putting away glasses.

"I'll make sure she's safe from the bogeyman, although the bogeyman might need protection from her," Mark replied with a chuckle.

"Got that right," Will conceded. "She took her self-defense class very seriously." He waved and followed the rest of the band out the door, leaving them alone.

"I'll be done in a moment." The smile Mark flashed was full of promises.

She crossed her legs, wishing she'd had a drink earlier, to take the edge off her nerves.

Derrick walked by with a money bag and paused. "You were fantastic, Jinx. I think the Spellcast Socialists are just what this place needs. I'm glad you all agreed to play again next weekend."

"Thanks."

"You gonna lock up, Mark?"

"Got it. See you later." Mark held her gaze as Derrick left. The front door closed, and he leaned on the bar, his face a mere two inches from hers. "So, love, your place or mine? Or right here on the bar?"

The husky timbre of his voice made her toes curl. She couldn't answer, her mouth suddenly so dry her lips seemed stuck together.

He grinned. "Or all three places—four, if you want to take it back out to the alley as well."

"You're pretty doggone sure of yourself. I doubt you can last that long," she replied with a shrug. "I need to go home first, but I'm not bringing some stranger there on a first date."

"I assure you, I can last as long as you want me to. And who said anything about a *date?*" Leaning into the bar, he raised an eyebrow and rested his chin on his hand. "Well, I suppose I *could* buy you breakfast in the morning."

Thrown off her game, she didn't know how to respond. He was right. *Date* didn't sound like a love 'em and leave 'em word. Her plan was to emulate him. And she knew from campus gossip that Mark MacGregor never dated. He'd see a girl twice before dropping her like a hot dish. This was precisely why Mr. Two-Time MacGregor, king of the hook-ups, fit her criteria. All she wanted was sex—to feel connected for a brief moment in time without the emotional entanglement that went with a relationship.

Hopping off the barstool, she shrugged into her jacket. "Where do you live? I need an hour or so."

"For?"

"Shower, feed the dog."

"You can shower with me," he purred as his thumb rubbed a circle on the sensitive spot between her thumb and index finger.

Her heart pounded, and she held her breath. "True, but I need to feed my dog and let him out to take care of business."

Mark sighed. "Wow."

"Wow, what?"

"I didn't take you for a cocktease. For what it's worth, I prefer honesty. Just say you're not interested; it's no big deal." He pulled the towel off his shoulder and tossed it under the bar. "I'll walk you to your car." His voice was clipped, his face impassive as he turned off the lights behind the bar.

"I'm not. Tell me where you live, and I'll be there. There's no need to walk me to my car." She raised her chin. "I can take care of myself."

"I have a need to walk you to your car. Security's already left, so humor me." He placed his hand on the small of her back, propelling her toward the entrance. After locking the front door, he held her hand as they walked through the practically empty parking lot. He let out a low whistle of appreciation as she unlocked her red Mustang. "You get this from painting?"

"No, my parents. It was my high school graduation present."

"How old are you?"

"Twenty-one."

She opened the car door and stood with her hands in her jacket, shivering. Illuminated by the diffuse light in the parking lot, he looked like a Celtic warrior. "Where do you live?"

He thumbed over his shoulder to a staircase on the side of the building. "Up there, above the bar. You're really coming back? What's your number?"

She sang the phone number refrain from the old Tommy Tutone song.

"Funny girl."

His lips teased across her jaw until they found hers. He smiled against her mouth before his tongue slipped inside, tenderly at first, but growing more persistent. It was the best kiss of her life, and she grabbed hold of his firm biceps for support. When he pulled away, a long, slow breath puffed between them in the cold night air. She blinked out of her kiss-induced fog. The man sure knew how to use his mouth.

Maybe he'll be the one…

"An hour or less," Jinx purred. She opened the car door and sat on the ice-cold leather seats with a shiver. She didn't bother turning the seat warmer on; she needed to cool down.

He nodded and closed her car door. As she drove away, she could see the burning ember of his cigarette in her rearview mirror. *Winston better take care of his business fast.* She hit the accelerator a little harder.

Home in ten minutes, she sprinted up the front stairs as quickly as possible in her stiletto boots. She rented half of a shotgun house just outside the French Quarter in New Orleans. As she opened the door and deactivated the alarm, she knew to brace herself for the exuberant doggie hug from her two-hundred-pound, fawn-colored mastiff. Winston wrapped his paws around her neck, and she wrinkled her nose as he licked her face. She gave him a quick hug and snapped her fingers. Well trained, he sat, quietly, wagging his tail. Her phone vibrated, but she ignored it. She'd already missed two calls, one from her mother and one from her father. If they couldn't bother to get in this century and leave a text message, or at the very least, a voice mail, she couldn't be bothered returning the call. It would invariably be a lecture, anyway, or the obligatory birthday wishes—neither of which she cared about.

After she fed Winston, she went to the bathroom for a shower. The hot water felt good on her tired muscles. Quickly, she re-shaved her legs, and other places, so she'd be silky smooth. She grinned at her reflection in the mirror while she dried her hair. Mark might be a bit surprised to see her in a few minutes, but oh well. Masks weren't always visible. Her eyes stung, and she removed her contacts. Shrugging into a pair of jeans and a sweatshirt, she shoved her feet into her favorite tennis shoes and grabbed her glasses off the bathroom counter. She whistled for Winston, who met her at the door with his leash in his mouth.

"Such a good boy. Now no playing; you need to hurry. Mama has plans," she cooed.

They walked across the street to the park. Shivering in the cold night air, she took him off the leash to run for a few minutes. The silly dog inspected every tree. There was very little traffic at this time of night, and the park was deserted, but she felt perfectly safe. Lonely parks and dark alleys didn't scare her. Only the lapses in her memory did.

Jinx glanced at the time on her cell phone and rolled her eyes when she saw another missed call from her mother. This wasn't uncommon. Her mother would call for no reason umpteen times a day, and she had decided after moving to New Orleans to only answer her every other day. Today wasn't that day. Calls from her father were less frequent, but tonight's was probably just the obligatory birthday wish, coupled with a lecture about ignoring her mother's calls. Shoving the phone back in her pocket, she whistled for Winston.

On the short drive back to The Highland Hangout, she mentally checked off her to-do list. She'd showered and brushed her teeth. In her purse were clean underwear, cigarettes, and condoms—although, she was pretty sure Mark would have a gazillion of them.

Pulling into the lot, she parked under the light and leaned her head against the steering wheel, closing her eyes for a moment. *You can do this. It's what you want, what you need.* Nerves steeled, she surveyed the parking lot and surrounding area before exiting her car.

Trembling, she lit a cigarette. She paused when she saw Mark sitting on a step outside his apartment at the top of the converted warehouse. His orange ember glowed. She couldn't see his face, but she could see he'd also changed into a pair of jeans and a sweatshirt. Tossing her head and squaring her shoulders, she walked up the metal steps toward him.

He spoke when she reached eye level, though with the shadows and where he was seated, she couldn't see his face.

"I wasn't positive you'd show, but I'm glad you did." Flicking his cigarette over the railing, he stood and offered his hand.

"I told you I'd be back." *The man has some serious trust issues. We're a match made in heaven.* "You shouldn't litter."

"I'm the one who cleans the damn parking lot, so it doesn't matter."

She took a final draw off her cigarette and followed suit, sending it over the rail. His huge hand enveloped hers, and she felt strangely safe, considering the circumstances.

"You get the dog fed?"

"Yes. And walked."

"You don't need to be walking a dog this late at night. You really have no sense of danger, do you?"

She heard the frown in his deep voice. "Guess not. I'm here, aren't I?" Stranger danger was the least of her problems.

"Ah, Mistress Jinx, I think I'm probably the one who should be afraid," he teased. "Although I don't think your tennis shoes will do as much damage as those fuck-me boots." He pulled her up the steps, pausing on the stoop. Tipping her head back, his warm breath fanned across her neck. "But someday I'm going to fuck you while you're wearing those boots. They're hot as hell when not lodged over my prized possession." His voice held promises of smoldering sex. "I like the glasses."

She giggled—whether from what he said or nervousness, she couldn't be sure. "You would. You're a librarian, after all."

"I just play one during the day. I'm working on my masters in accounting, and the library helps pay the bills. I'm also a bartender/ bar owner and sex god by night."

She draped her arms around his neck. "Sex god by night? You're pretty doggone sure of yourself."

"Just stating the facts, ma'am." He grabbed her ass to lift her, and she wrapped her legs around his waist. Leaning her against the front door, he kissed her, taking his time. His mouth tasted of fine liquor and cigarettes. She deepened the kiss, her tongue dancing with his. One of them growled, though she had no clue if it was him or her. After fumbling with the doorknob, he managed to get inside and carried her into his living area. The room was lit by a lamp on the end table, next to a long couch with tan upholstery.

He kissed her neck, and his forehead met hers. Smiling, his eyebrows rose when he reached up and pulled off her ball cap. With a grin, he tousled her short blond hair.

"You're just full of surprises, aren't you? You're not at all what I expected. You're a mystery, Jinx."

She liked the way his blue eyes seemed to twinkle. He was everything she wanted. Surely this time would be different…

"I'm not so complicated," she lied, pulling the elastic from his hair, loosening his ponytail. At last, she fulfilled her fantasy and ran her fingers through his dark auburn waves.

He sank on the couch with her straddling his lap. Feeling his erection through his jeans, she rubbed against it, causing him to lean his head back. He moaned and grasped her hips, moving her to rock slowly and deliberately. He opened his eyes and gave her short hair another tousle.

"You're really a blonde?" he asked with a bemused grin.

"Yes, with a little help," she confessed. Towheaded as a kid, she now lightened her honey blond hair to platinum.

"You look younger with a scrubbed face, glasses, and no wig," he murmured. "Are you sure you're twenty-one? Wait, do I know you?"

"Yes and no. How old are you?" She didn't mention that today was her birthday, and she'd appointed him her present.

"Twenty-eight." He frowned. "You sure? You look fifteen and strangely familiar…"

"I'm very strange and about to get really familiar. I'd show you my license, but then you'd know my full name and where I live, and I'd have to kill you. Gosh, this feels good…" She continued to rock, liking the control.

"Kill me? Why?" His eyes sparkled.

She kissed his smooth, freshly shaven cheek. The liar — he'd anticipated her visit, despite his expressed doubt. Or perhaps he'd made other arrangements in case she was a no-show.

"Because only my parents use my given name. It *sucks*," she whispered suggestively into his ear. She smiled against his jaw when he grew harder underneath her.

"You certainly know how to try a man's patience," he muttered.

"What do you mean?"

"I mean, I had good intentions to make nice before I fuck your brains out. You know, pretend like I'm a good guy and all that shit." He grinned. "But it's *hard* to think with you in my lap, pun intended." Smacking her on the butt, he attempted to shift. "Hop up and let me get you something to drink."

"That would be great," she replied, frustrated and yet relieved. She promised herself not to get drunk this time; she just needed to take the edge off.

Mark stood and walked to the kitchen, returning with two clean glasses. With a steady hand, he poured them each two fingers of scotch, neat.

"I usually drink beer…"

He raised his glass to hers in a toast. "Try it. *Uisge Beatha*, the water of life." He took a sip and smiled.

"It's my birthday. Go big or go home." With a grin, she threw back the contents of the glass. The burn seared her throat, and she gasped as her eyes watered. She hadn't had hard liquor since she was a teenager sneaking it out of her father's stash.

"Fuck, Jinx. You don't chug Macallan like cheap beer."

The horrified look on his face combined with the heady rush from the alcohol made her giggle.

"Sorry. Give me some more; I'll sip it this time."

She held out her glass, and he poured her more. She took a sip and glanced around. Small, the room appeared somewhat overwhelmed by the massive tan couch and big screen TV. The end table held an empty, but unwashed ashtray, a lamp with a tilted shade, and a copy of *Sports Illustrated* upon which she placed her glass of scotch since there wasn't a coaster.

A bookcase with books haphazardly shoved in it and photos on various shelves completed the living area. She wanted to take a closer look at the titles of the books and the pictures but didn't want to appear nosy. His laptop sat on the floor with the TV remote on top of it. She wondered what secrets his browsing history harbored. Probably lots of porn.

Furtively, she peeked over at the kitchen, which was barely visible in the dark. There didn't appear to be any garbage, beer cans, or empty pizza boxes, just open cupboards. It was fairly clean for a bachelor's place. She assumed one of the doors behind them led to his bedroom and nervously twisted her fingers together.

"Does it pass muster?"

"Pardon?" She drew her attention back to him, feeling flustered.

"I emptied the ashtray and did the dishes. I even changed the sheets on the bed." He smiled, tilting his head to the side.

She wondered how those lips would feel when he kissed her in more intimate places. Would she allow it? Or freeze up? Would her self-imposed aversion therapy work?

"I thought you weren't expecting me to show. Did you have someone else lined up?"

"Are you asking me in a roundabout way if I'm a man-whore?" He reached over and stroked her cheek with the back of his fingers, making her insides turn to mush. They were so close she could see the different shades of blue in his irises.

Jinx shrugged, praying he couldn't hear her pounding heart. "Rumors say you are. Are you?"

"Pretty much, yeah."

"Thought so." She summoned all of her courage to grin at him. "Been checked lately for STDs?" She flicked a spot of paint she'd missed off of her thumbnail.

"Every three months. I'm clean, and I cover up. You?"

"I'm good. So, uh, here or the bedroom?" she asked, peeling off her sweatshirt.

Chapter Three

Momentarily struck speechless, Mark stared at her gorgeous breasts. They were round, perky, and just right: not too big and not too small. *What was the question?*

Jinx's dusky-rose nipples hardened, and goose bumps danced across her skin as she flushed a delicate shade of pink. The silence grew awkward and she folded her arms, covering herself.

She shook her head and moved to slip her sweatshirt back on, plainly embarrassed. "Sorry. I know I'm not much."

He captured her hands in his. "Wait. Sorry…I, uh, shouldn't stare, but damn, you're beautiful, love. Perfect."

"Quit calling me that."

"What?"

"I'm not your *love*. This is just two people scratching the itch." She paused and shrugged, not meeting his gaze. "You know."

"Scratching the itch?" Damn, she piqued his curiosity. Bold, yet shy at the same time.

"You know — the *f word*." She chewed her lower lip.

"Fucking?" He laughed. "As audacious as you are, I'd think you'd cuss like a sailor."

He stood and turned out the light. Taking her hand, he moved toward the bedroom, grabbing his glass and the scotch with his other hand.

"I don't cuss." Jinx threw back the contents of her glass, still holding her sweatshirt to her chest.

She wasn't a discriminate drinker, either. What a waste of a beautiful scotch.

Mark turned on the lamp by the king-size bed. Her breathing hitched, and she hesitated before meeting his gaze. He pushed her blond bangs out of her face and tried to remember why she seemed so familiar. She reminded him a lot of Harley. They were both sassy blondes, sexy and intriguing. Removing her glasses, he placed them on the bedside table and leaned in to kiss her closed eyelids. When she caught her breath and hummed in the back of her throat, he smiled against her forehead. She dropped the sweatshirt and pressed her pebbled nipples into his chest.

He yanked his shirt over his head and threw it on top of hers. Her hand shook as she set her empty glass down and sank to the bed, her eyes now wide open. His skin heated from her stare.

"Holy shitake. You look even better without a shirt. Are those pecs and abs for real?"

He laughed. "Um, yeah? Why don't you find out for yourself?"

She reached out and softly ran her fingers across his chest, flicking her thumbnail over his nipple. She blushed as her fingers explored his chest down to his stomach, just above his jeans. It took every ounce of control he possessed to stand there and allow her to do this instead of ravishing her.

"Definitely not airbrushed," she whispered. "The art department would go nuts over this definition. You should model for them."

"You approve?"

She nodded. Her warm breath bathed his skin, and he pushed her back on the bed. His lips slanted over hers as his hands brushed along her soft, smooth skin, exploring the planes and dips of her supple body.

He trailed kisses across her jaw and whispered, "Mmm, baby."

Jinx stiffened and shrugged away. "Don't call me that."

"What? What did I call you?" He truly couldn't think. This chick's hot little body was fuckin' with his mind.

"*Baby.*" The venom in her voice gave him pause.

"O-*kay*," he replied, not understanding. "I'm sorry." He pressed a kiss to her lips, and her body relaxed. Slowly, he teased her neck and ear with his tongue as his hands stroked her skin, playing her like a beautiful instrument.

The mewling sound she made when he deepened the kiss inflamed him as he licked, kissed, and nibbled down her neck and across her collarbone. Her body arched toward him. Taking one nipple in his mouth, he lapped it with his tongue, and it hardened even more. Her hands grasped his hair and pulled. Bit by tasty bit, he worked his way back to her neck as one hand roamed down her ribcage and dipped just under the waistband of her jeans. With a soft gasp, she gripped his bicep almost to the point of pain and moved his hand back up to her waist. He smiled against her skin. Nothing turned him on more than a challenge.

"My God, you are so fuckin' hot, love."

She giggled. "Thanks, Thurston."

He pulled her up so they were both fully on the bed. Propping his head on his hand, he grinned down at her. "I know you don't cuss. But what's with calling me Thurston?" Unable to resist, he grazed her hard nipple with his teeth.

"You keep calling me Love, short for Lovey." She started to laugh and couldn't seem to stop, pulling her knees up to her chest and wiping the tears from her eyes. "I want some more of that stuff to drink. It's good."

"Who the hell is Thurston?" Grabbing the bottle, he poured them each another glass of scotch. He frowned as she once again took a big gulp. He placed a gentle hand over hers before she threw back the rest. "Sip it, love."

Jinx's whiskey-colored eyes looked slightly unfocused. "Call me Lovey," she slurred.

"Sip it, Lovey." He kicked off his shoes and socks, and she did the same.

Jesus, if she doesn't slow down she'll be drunk off her sweet little ass in no time. He took the glass from her hand and placed it out of reach. Before he knew it, she had him flat on his back, straddling his waist.

"Didn't you ever watch *Gilligan's Island?* You're Thurston, and I'm Lovey Howell."

"The old couple?" He chuckled. *Fuck, she's drunker than I thought.* "I wish we had the Howell's money." For some reason, this made her laugh even harder, and her breasts bounced with her giggles.

"Nah, I wish I had Ginger's body." She leaned forward and kissed him, her bare breasts brushing his chest. Currents of sexual electricity coursed straight to his already hard cock. He rubbed his hands down her warm back and up her sides, causing her to fidget.

"Your body's slammin' hot, Lovey. Ginger hasn't got a thing on you."

She squirmed again when he brushed her breasts. "Ticklish?" he murmured with a smile. He captured a nipple in his mouth and tugged.

"Yes, terribly." She repositioned herself on top of him, and he pulled his mouth from her breast to kiss her deeply, their tongues mating until she purred. Possessive and aggressive, her kisses made him wonder what other magic her mouth could perform. When she sat up and arched her back, he groaned at the visual torture. She unbuttoned his jeans and lowered the zipper. *Soon…*

A loud squeal made him open his eyes.

"Oh my gosh! Look at the size of that sword!"

"Why, thank you," he murmured and then grunted. She stood on the bed, her foot trapping him by his hair. He gazed up at her, confused. *Why isn't she naked yet? Why aren't I?*

"Not *your* sword, *that* sword." She laughed as she pointed to the antique highland sword mounted above the bed. "Is it real?"

"Well damn, I thought you were complimenting *me*," Mark teased, grabbing her by the foot and pulling her down with a thud on top of him. "And yes, it's real." He nudged her with his hard dick. "So's this one." Soft breasts and hard nipples pressed against his chest. He wondered if he'd ever get enough of her body. Something moved against his erection.

"You're so fuckin' hot, your pussy's vibrating against my cock." Mark frowned and wondered if he was drunker than he realized. Surely her pussy wasn't vibrating.

Jinx laughed, her eyes hooded with desire. "Hello? I think my vajayjay's calling you."

Realizing it was her phone, he glanced at his watch. "It's a little after four in the morning, who's calling you this late? Please God, don't say your husband." He took off his watch and placed it on the bedside table. Sitting up, she pulled the phone from her pocket and glanced at it with a frown.

"No, it's my parents. This is, like, the fifth time they've tried to call me, doggone it."

"Maybe you should answer."

"Now? Are you kidding me? They're probably just mad that I ignored their call earlier. I don't want to listen to the lecture. My parents don't think I'm capable of taking care of myself. The whole reason I'm going to school out of state is to get away from them and their control issues." The phone stopped vibrating. "Yay! Now frog me, Thurston." She tossed the phone on the bedside table next to his watch.

"Froggin'? You really say *frog* instead of *fuck?*" Laughing, he sat up, positioning her so she straddled his lap. He wrapped his arms around her and kissed her neck. "You fascinate me, Jinx. You're an old soul with child-like enthusiasm. It's been a long time since anyone has interested me as much as you. I want to know what goes on in that crazy head of yours."

"Can we stop talking now, so we can at least catch a nap before sunrise? I have to work tomorrow."

Goddamn, what's wrong with me? Marcas Ian MacGregor, man-whore extraordinaire, wants to get to know what's in a girl's head and not just tap what's between her legs? *No way.*

All rational thought left his mind when she maneuvered him onto his back. She moved down his body, trailing kisses over his abdomen and quickly divesting him of his jeans and underwear. He ran his fingers through her hair, loving its silky softness and the way it made her amber eyes stand out.

A sudden, terrifying thought occurred to him. *What if she's some insane man-hater about to make off with my pride and joy?* When her pink tongue licked him like a goddamned ice cream cone, he groaned and closed his eyes. Even if she was insane and killed him right now, he'd die a happy man. He relaxed and took pleasure in her warm mouth as it slid up and down.

"Shiiiiiit," he ground out as she continued her relentless, delightful onslaught.

"Did I do something wrong?" She paused and crawled up his naked torso until they were nose to nose. With an impish grin, she kissed him and tugged on his lower lip, her hard nipples crushed against his chest.

"Hell no," he managed as he flipped her onto her back. "Where'd you learn to do that? Never mind—I don't want to know."

"Porn, of course."

He laughed and reached into his bedside table, pulling out a condom. She rose up on her elbows to peer into the drawer and laughed. Her sultry come-hither look made his need to fuck her almost painful.

"I knew it, and yet *you* still surprised *me*." She grinned as she helped him slide the condom down his shaft.

"You knew what? And how did I surprise you?" he rasped, trying to control his raging need. Burying his face in her neck, he inhaled her clean citrus scent.

"I knew you'd have a box of condoms, but I rather thought you'd have porn in your nightstand, not a thesaurus."

"Ah, well, it's so I can offer you any number of descriptions for your delightful pussy."

She moaned with pleasure when he captured her hardened nipple in his mouth again and unzipped her jeans.

"So hit me," she murmured, eyes closed, her hands fisted in his hair.

"What?" Mark paused and looked down at her quizzically, wondering what kind of kink this girl was in to, and was he up for it? Hell, he'd try—no doubt about it.

"Tell me the different names for my hoo-ha—and none of the familiar ones," she said with a smile.

He relaxed. "Let's see." He worked her jeans and thong off and threw them on the floor. "Delectable, scrumptious?" He licked up her wet slit and flicked her clit with his tongue.

"Oh!" Her hips bucked, but her body stiffened. "You don't have to do this…"

"Shhh, let me make it up to you from earlier." He gentled her with soft strokes and kisses. She gripped the bedspread. "Mmm, succulent," he teased.

"You make me sound like a pastry or something." She gasped, attempting to wiggle away as he worked her closer and closer to the edge, tormenting her with his slow attention.

"You're better than chocolate cake." He continued nibbling, blowing, and licking. Over and over he'd take her just to the edge and stop, chuckling at her apparent impatience as she writhed beneath him. *Not yet, love.*

"I hate chocolate. Stop," she croaked.

Something in her tone of voice unnerved him. He maneuvered his hair from her grip and kissed his way up her stomach to her neck.

"You okay?"

"Yes, just…stop with the foreplay and do it. Now. I don't like this part." She closed her eyes.

"What part?"

"You down there. Just do it…now! Or I'm leaving."

"Your wish is my command." Puzzled, he entered her swiftly. She was tight, but ready. *God, it feels good.*

"Oh, baby," he groaned in her ear.

Her body went lifeless, and he looked down to see her eyes scrunched shut as if she were in pain.

She was slick and ready, but perhaps I was too forceful? "Hey, Jinx?" He brushed the hair from her pale face. With his thumb he pulled her lower lip from her teeth. "What's the matter? Fuck, honey…"

Mark moved to get off her, but she gripped his arms. Her lower lip quivered, and when she opened her eyes, they shimmered with unshed tears.

"No! Please d-don't stop. I-I'm sorry." Her voice sounded strangled, and she sucked in a deep breath.

"No, something's wrong. What just happened here?"

"I'm okay. Just do it." She moved beneath him as she pulled his face to hers, kissing him frantically. "Please?"

"I don't know…"

"Please, Mark. Make me feel something. I'm okay."

Mark slowly moved inside her and watched her face, which showed no emotion whatsoever. He used one hand to stroke her breast and tried to move it between them, but she grabbed it and moved it back to her breast.

"Do you want on top?"

She shrugged, meeting him stroke for stroke, yet she seemed detached, just going through the motions. Her lips curved into a sad smile. "It's okay. It isn't you; it's me." She brushed his hair out of his face and wrapped her smooth legs around his waist with her arms around his neck.

"I can make this—"

"Just shut up and frog me."

"Ribbit?" He smiled down at her and stroked her cheek, gauging her response. She closed her eyes and moved with him, encouraging him to continue.

He held off as long as he could before exploding deep inside her.

The relief was so powerful his arms shook, and his jaw clenched. She blinked up at him and smiled, totally relaxed and…unfulfilled. As he gasped for breath, he felt like a shit for not bringing her a similar release. Mark rested his weight on his arms, unable to move for a moment. Their bodies were slick with sweat.

Brushing her damp hair out of her face, he smiled down at her. "I'm sorry. Whatever I did wrong, I promise I'll do better next time." He kissed her tenderly and tried to process what the hell had just happened. It was a source of pride for him to always give his partner as much pleasure as he received. And here, he'd failed.

She smiled up at him and played with his hair. "Thank you, and please don't be sorry. It wasn't you; it's me. I'm probably just overtired, and I have a slight headache. Besides, now I know."

"Know what?" He kissed her again, feeling like he was in some sort of parallel universe.

"What a Scotsman wears under his kilt, and what the big stink about frogging Mark MacGregor is."

Mark sighed. "I'm afraid one of those ended up a disappointment."

She grinned at him impishly. "Nah, you did the kilt proud."

He snorted and pinched her nipple. "Thanks, Lovey." Kissing the tip of her pierced nose, he rolled off and headed to the bathroom to dispose of the condom. He grabbed a glass of water and the ibuprofen and returned to the bedroom. He scowled to find her sitting on the side of the bed about to pull on her thong.

"Where are you going?"

She gave him a perplexed look. "Home. I told you I have to work today. I need to shower and catch a nap."

"You're not going anywhere; take this for your headache so you won't have a hangover."

"Don't order me around." She glared at him.

"I'm not. I'm trying to be Mr. Sensitive Guy here. Trust me, I'm a bartender. You need to hydrate. Besides, I at least owe you breakfast. And you don't need to be driving, you've been drinking."

He gave her the medicine and water, but she swallowed the pills with the remainder of her scotch. With a defiantly cocked brow, she smirked. Taking the glass from her, he placed it on the bedside table. He handed her the water, which she drank.

"I'm sorry." He stroked her cheek.

"Quit apologizing. I'm fine."

"Stay with me." He took her hand. "Stay and I'll buy you breakfast. Please? Here, you can wear my T-shirt."

She sighed. "Okay, just give me a minute." Bounding off the bed, she slammed the door to the bathroom behind her.

He pulled on a pair of pajama pants and crawled back in bed. She wasn't fine, but he was at a loss. He covered his face with his hands. *What the fuck just happened here?*

She returned in a billow of steam, her skin bright red as if she'd taken the hottest shower possible. She shrugged into her panties and his T-shirt and climbed into bed. Switching off the bedside light, he spooned her butt.

"Cuddling really isn't necessary. I can go home," she murmured, lying stiff in his arms.

"Shut the hell up and go to sleep, Lovey." For some strange reason, cuddling *was* necessary for him tonight.

"'Night, Thurston."

Chapter Four

Mark rubbed his eyes as the incessant buzzing continued. Picking up his watch, he tried to focus his bleary eyes. Seven? The phone on the bedside table continued vibrating, and without thinking, he picked it up.

"What the fuck do you want?" He yawned into the phone. Anyone who knew him knew better than to call before ten on a Saturday morning.

"Who the hell are you?" an angry male voice demanded. "And why are you answering my daughter's phone?"

Oh shit. Mark looked at the phone again and realized it wasn't his. *Offense is the best defense.* "Why are you calling Jinx this early?"

Jinx stirred and stretched. "What?" She rolled over. When she realized he was on her phone, she snapped, "What the heck are you doing?"

"Talking to your father, love." He smirked and handed it over.

Jinx glared as she grabbed it. "Hi, Daddy." She sat up and reached for her jeans.

Mark watched her sadly, knowing she was about to head out. His morning wood had been hoping for some relief. Sitting up, he found his cigarettes, lit two, and handed one to her. She smiled an acknowledgement and rolled her eyes. Her old man must be raising hell about him. He felt responsible for subjecting her to the parental lecture.

Concern replaced his guilt when all the color drained from her face. Shaking like an alcoholic with DTs, she sank back on the bed.

"W-What?" she stammered.

She rocked with one arm clutching her stomach. "No, you're lying. No, no…Where's Mother? I want to talk to her!" Her shrill voice sounded like a scared child's.

Mark took the cigarette from her shaky hand before she burned herself, wondering what horrible news she'd just received.

"No, Daddy, I c-can't. I'll drive…I…God, I'm going to be sick—" Dropping the phone, she ran to the bathroom.

Mark picked it up. "Hello? What's going on?" Choked sobs came across the line. The sound of Jinx vomiting in the bathroom increased his uneasiness.

"She needs to come home right away," her father said. "She refuses to fly, and I don't want her driving. She *can't* drive. Goddammit, I've lost one daughter to an accident; I can't lose another."

Shit. A daughter lost to an accident? "I'll drive her. I'll get her home safely; I promise," Mark assured the distraught father. "I need to check on her. We'll be in touch when we get on the road." He hung up and threw the phone down.

Hurrying to the bathroom door, he found Jinx curled in a ball beside the toilet, not making a sound. Mark pulled her into his lap and held her tight.

"I got you, love," he crooned into her hair.

"I c-can't fly. I'm scared of flying. And Winston—" She clung to his neck. "Oh, God, why Karen? Why not me? I don't matter. She has kids…"

"Shh, don't say that. You *do* matter. No one can explain shit like this. I'm going to drive you home. Come on, hop up and get dressed while I grab a quick shower. We'll run by your place to pick up your things and your dog. I can catch a bus or a flight after I get you home." He popped her on the butt to get her up and moving.

Blank eyes stared at him as she stood, obviously in a daze. Her teeth chattered, and her body shook with a violence he'd only seen one other time in his life — staring at his own reflection in the mirror a week after his mother had left. He turned on the shower. With a firm hand, he stripped her and steered her into the water, where she remained motionless as her shivers subsided under the warm spray.

Mark peeled off his pajama pants and stepped in with her. He soaped her body, forcing himself not to think about the soft curves under his hands. She stopped him when he moved below her waist. As if a switch had been flipped, she mechanically finished bathing. In record time, he scooted her out of the shower and had her dried and dressed. He knew his dreams would now include visions of her wet body, and he kicked himself for being such a pig as he collected his clothes and toiletries, throwing them into a suitcase.

In less than twenty minutes, they were on the road. Jinx croaked out directions to her place and stared blankly out the window, no sign of emotion on her face. She'd shut down.

Ten minutes later, he parked her car in front of a beautifully restored shotgun house that had been made into two apartments, each with its own entrance.

Smiling, he squeezed her knee. "Hey, you need to pack, call work, and get your pup. I'll call Derrick, and he'll let the band know what's going on, okay?" It dawned on him, he had no clue where they were going, and for a second he regretted his hasty offer to help. "Where do your parents live? Would you be more comfortable if someone else took you home? One of the band members?"

"No, I can't ask them…I have to get to Pine Bluff, Alabama. It's about a seven-hour drive," she replied flatly, staring out the windshield. "She has kids. Elizabeth and Luke. They're just little kids…" Her haunted eyes were bright, but no tears fell. "I can't do this alone…"

"You're not. Let's go so we can get on the road and be there for them."

Escorting her to the front door, he opened it and found himself barred from entering by the biggest damn dog he'd ever seen. A menacing growl had him stepping back, uncertain. *What the fuck?* He'd thought she'd have a little girly dog, like a poodle.

Jinx crumpled to the floor and buried her face in the dog's neck. "It's okay; he's a friend." The intimidating animal gave her face a lick while eyeing him.

"C'mon, Jinx, get moving. I daresay you need to let this monster here go do his or her thing before we leave. What kind of dog is it?"

"Winston. He's an English Mastiff."

Mark lit a cigarette and looked around her messy place. They stood in a large front room that led into a small, but workable kitchen painted a sunny yellow. The bathroom had an entrance from the kitchen and a queen-size bed dominated the small bedroom. A rack of clothes stood next to a dilapidated dresser that appeared to have more clothes on top of it than in its drawers.

Judging by the hodge-podge of art supplies and canvases on easels, she used the front room as her studio. He examined her artwork while she flew to the bedroom to pack, talking into the phone tucked against her shoulder. She spoke to wherever she worked, telling them she'd be gone at least a week. Impressed with her talent as an artist, he perused the paintings. Her artwork leaned toward abstracts, but mixed in were delicate watercolors of flowers and street scenes evoking the essence of New Orleans. He wondered if he could commission her to do one of the bar.

She picked up a leash and a pair of sunglasses. "I'll be back in a few minutes; do you mind putting my suitcase in the car?"

"Not at all. Are you done in here? Why don't we walk him together and then leave?"

She nodded, and he followed her, putting her suitcase in the trunk while she walked across the street to a small park with the dog that was almost bigger than she was. Although he was no longer growling, Winston didn't stray far from Jinx's side. It actually made Mark feel a little better about her living alone.

Whoa, why am I concerned? Fuck, this girl had somehow wormed her way under his skin. He justified his feelings as sympathy, that's all. He dialed Derrick and gave him the lowdown about Jinx's sister. Next, he dialed his supervisor at the library.

The library. That's where I've seen her.

Walking back across the street, he knocked on the door at the adjoining apartment next to Jinx's. An elderly woman answered with the chain blocking the entrance. Mark explained that there'd been a family emergency and pointed toward Jinx and Winston. The woman clucked like a hen, assuring him she would check Jinx's mail and offering her condolences. As he walked back to the car, his phone beeped with an incoming text.

Call me. We need to talk. H

Harley. He ignored it; he didn't have time to deal with her right now.

Returning to the car, Jinx opened the door, and Winston lumbered into the backseat. Throwing her shoulders back, she offered a wan smile. "Thanks for everything. I-I'm better. It was just the shock. I'll, uh, be fine driving to my parents."

Her lower lip trembled, and she looked anything but fine.

"I'll drop you off at your place and be on my way." Jinx held out her hand for the keys, staring at his chest. She looked like a lost little girl.

"No. I promised your father I'd bring you home safely, and I'm a man of my word."

She sighed, her shoulders sagging. "I can't do that to you. It's too far. Plus, I won't subject you to my family, especially my father. It wouldn't be fair. We have a terrible relationship, and it's bound to be not only a sad visit, but uncomfortable as well." The resigned look she gave him made his heart lurch.

"I'm a big boy. I can handle disgruntled parents. End of discussion." He walked her to the passenger side of the car. "Besides, a red Mustang? Damn, girl, what man wouldn't want to drive this car?"

To his surprise, she twined her arms around his waist, hugging him tight.

"Thank you," she mumbled into his jacket.

He kissed the top of her head, pleased by her spontaneous embrace and humbled by her gratitude. He opened the door for her.

"Besides, I owe you breakfast, remember? We'll catch some fast food on the way out of town."

She nodded and buckled up, instructing Winston to settle down in the backseat. Mark walked around the back of the car and chuckled as he got in on the driver's side. Only Jinx would have a custom license plate that read FROG U. As he pulled out, he asked her to dial her parents, putting it on speakerphone.

Her father answered with a shaky "Hello?"

"This is Mark MacGregor. Jinx and I are leaving now and should be there this afternoon. Should we come to your house?"

A tired sigh came through the line. "Call when you're about an hour away. Things aren't very good, so I have no idea where we'll be. Karen and Elizabeth are gone. Luke remains in critical condition."

A small cry escaped Jinx's lips, and she crumpled in the seat, covering her head with her arms. "No, not the kids…"

Mark reached over, rubbing her back. "Yes, sir. I'm sorry. I'll get your daughter home as soon as possible." He hung up the phone, at a loss as to what to say to the broken girl next to him. "I'm sorry."

She rocked for a few minutes before sitting up, her arms wrapped tight around her stomach. Her throat bobbled up and down, and tears again glistened in her troubled eyes, but none fell.

"This can't be happening. Elizabeth's only twelve. Luke is three, I think—just a baby." She turned to look out the window, hiding her grief. "I don't know how to deal with this. Oh God, poor Matt…" She took a deep breath and held her fist to her mouth as if it could contain her emotions.

"It's okay to cry. Let it out." He held her free hand, wishing he could do more.

"I'm fine," she replied. Her hands shook as she put on her sunglasses.

They'd driven in silence for four hours, aside from ordering their breakfast, which she hadn't eaten.

Beside her, Mark said something. Jinx pulled her mind back from organizing her paints by color. She'd been doing mental games so she wouldn't cry. Crying was unacceptable.

"I'm sorry, what?" she asked.

"Do you want to talk about your sister? Or anything?"

"Not about my family. I c-can't."

"Okay."

They drove in silence for another fifteen minutes.

"What happened last night?" Mark asked, his tone gentle. He chewed on a toothpick since she didn't allow smoking in her car.

Winston picked his head up and peered at her over the seat. She scratched his ears, and he settled down, content for the moment.

"W-What?" Her heart pounded, and she dug her nails into her sweaty palms. Dark spots danced in her peripheral vision.

Mark navigated through the traffic, his eyes on the road. "Last night you kind of freaked out on me and then just went through the motions. And the incident in the office…Um, not to be insensitive to your situation, but I need to know what I'm walking into when I get you home. Are you truly twenty-one? I mean — you're not jailbait or anything, are you? I don't relish facing an angry father or going to prison for statutory rape."

She rolled her eyes and breathed a little easier. "Like I said, I was just tired. And yes, I'm twenty-one. I told you last night it was my birthday. You were my birthday present."

He blinked before he responded. "Happy belated birthday. Sorry. I'm afraid it wasn't much of a present."

"I told you, it was *me* not you," she sneered. "*Men.* You always think it's about you and your performance."

Chastised, he thankfully kept his mouth shut for another ten minutes. She knew it was too good to last.

"Talk to me, love. What's your favorite ice cream? Best childhood memory? Tell me why you didn't answer your phone last night when your folks called. Or you could tell me about your sister and her kids. Talking helps with the grief process."

"I don't need your pop psychology. Most people would leave me alone and not push at a time like this." Thank God her dark sunglasses hid the tears welling in her eyes. She didn't want to talk. Once she started talking about her loss, she'd never be able to stop crying, and crying was a sign of weakness. She hadn't cried in years.

"I'm not most people. Tell me about you, then. Anything. We can make it a game. You answer my questions, and I'll answer yours."

"How many women have you been with?" she shot out.

He chewed on the toothpick before clarifying, "At one time or total?"

"At one time?" She swung around in her seat and stared at him.

"Three." He grinned and gave an exaggerated sigh of happiness. "A blonde, a brunette, and a redhead walked in to my bar…"

"Wait, that wasn't my question." She wrinkled her nose.

"Too bad, my turn. Hmm…A gentleman would never ask how many guys you've been with. *Sooo,* why me for your birthday present?"

"I didn't want to be alone on my birthday." She shrugged and stared out the window. "I wanted to banish the bad birthday memories. Do you remember the blonde, brunette, and redhead's names?"

"No. What bad birthday memories?"

Jinx looked at the passing scenery for a few moments, collecting her thoughts. "I grew up in a very small town. Jeremy Turner was three years older than me and kept pushing me to do more than I wanted to. When I refused, he spread rumors about me on social media. He said I'd done things I'd never done."

She dug her fingernails in her palms, her anger toward Jeremy simmering close to the surface.

"My parents believed the rumors. They convicted me without hearing my side of the story." Jinx didn't attempt to keep the bitterness out of her voice. She let out a slow breath. "I survived high school as the girl with the worst reputation."

"And?" Mark glanced at her, worrying his lip with his teeth.

"I decided to just go with it. I became the girl everyone said I was. In a way, it freed me. It became a choice *I* made. You obviously didn't grow up in a small town where everyone knows your business better than you do, or they *think* they do. Truth didn't matter, so I made the lies the truth."

She left out the part about how easy it had been in high school to hook up with boys who didn't give a shit about her. What was it about college that made guys decide to pursue relationships? She also didn't mention that it always took alcohol to steel herself for sex.

"Look, it's my turn for a question," she said instead. "Why don't you ever do a girl more than twice?"

"I don't like girls who cling, so I don't give them a reason to. So, why *me* last night?"

He searched her face for the answer. She decided to just be straight with him.

"You know every girl on campus has a crush on you, right? I mean, you're seriously hot. Do you really think that many girls are interested in the stupid library?"

She rolled her eyes when his chest seemed to expand, and his grin widened.

"Your reputation precedes you. It's rumored you've been with more than six hundred and fifty girls."

The car swerved, and he glanced over at her with a furrowed brow. "Six hundred and fifty? Jesus H. Christ, that's kind of disgusting." He pulled at his lip, lost in thought.

Probably doing a quick tally to see if the number was in the ballpark.

Jinx shrugged. "That's the conservative estimate. Anyway, I just wanted to see what the big deal was."

"Have you ever been in love?"

She snorted. "You're joking, right?"

"Well, some girls claim they only do it with guys they're in love with."

"Or they do it because they're drunk and stupid."

Again, the car swerved, and he looked stunned. "Shit," he hissed.

He reached for a cigarette but stopped and got a piece of gum instead.

"I'm not like most girls, or hadn't you noticed? Love is overrated. I think it's a figment of the imagination."

Mark's shoulders relaxed, and he laughed. "Damn, you *are* the girl of my dreams: cynical, smart, sexy, and self-assured."

"You sure love alliteration."

He chuckled. "It's a game I used to play with a, uh, friend. She got me started doing it."

Jinx watched his mouth working the gum. "If you want to pull over and smoke, I'm good with that. Do you like having a bad reputation?"

"I'm okay. Do you want to stop?"

She shook her head. "Have you ever been in love?"

"That's two questions, and yes to both." He shifted in his seat, staring at the road. "Why didn't your parents believe you when you were in high school?"

"Jeremy Turner circulated incriminating photos throughout the school, and someone sent them to my father." She clenched her jaw and stared at her folded hands.

"Did you know you were being photographed?"

"Of course not. I passed out after drinking hunch punch. It was my own dumb fault." She shrugged, though it still made her sick to have been that gullible. "Daddy had the visual evidence. Case closed, verdict guilty, no need for a fair trial. It is what it is."

Frowning, Mark shot her a look, and his knuckles whitened as they gripped the steering wheel. "Did he hurt you?"

"Who?" she croaked, her throat feeling strangled.

"Jeremy."

It was her turn to squirm in her seat. "Look, it was a long time ago. I don't want to talk about it anymore. I'm done with questions. Pull over; I think I do need a smoke and a bathroom break."

Mark pulled into a convenience store. After he pumped gas and she peed, he pulled out two cigarettes and lit them, handing her one.

She grinned. "Just like the movies."

He chuckled. "Yep, but it doesn't impress many anymore. Hardly anybody smokes. Pity. Hungry?"

"No, but if you are, we can stop."

"I'm good."

"I thought you were a bad boy."

He laughed, and she smiled. They smoked their cigarettes in silence, watching the traffic go by. She found him easy to be with. Unlike most people.

Once they were back on the road, Mark reached over and, to her surprise, took her hand and held it. Hers looked tiny in his. She liked the fine dusting of dark auburn hair on the back of his hand, and his nails were neat, trimmed. In comparison, she'd chewed her nails to nubs and missed removing some paint flecks. His thumb rubbed her hand, and she looked up.

"I have a very serious question that needs to be answered."

Jinx sighed. "Please, I'm not up to it."

"Tough shit, sugarbritches. DC or Marvel?"

"That's your serious question?"

He nodded, staring at the road, but a smile teased the corner of his mouth.

"I don't know Marvel from DC."

"Woman! Have you been living under a rock?"

She giggled. "Okay, Wonder Woman, which one is she?"

"Good choice, DC. Chocolate or vanilla ice cream?"

"I'm not much of an ice cream girl, but nothing chocolate. I loathe it…"

"Are you even human? Who the fuck doesn't like ice cream or chocolate?"

"Me. It makes me gag. My turn. Thin crust or thick crust pizza?"

"Thick. Bet you like thick, too," he teased with a leer. "Lots of meat."

"I do." She bit her lower lip, and heat rose in her cheeks.

"Why don't you close your eyes, maybe catch a little nap?"

She shrugged. He didn't push, which made her like him that much more.

An hour passed in silence. Jinx stared at the passing countryside, struggling to suppress the rising sense of panic as each mile brought her closer to her past. Family visits were difficult and rare by choice. Yet here she was on her way home to bury Karen, her niece, and possibly her nephew. She thought about asking her brother-in-law, Matt, if she could stay at his house and then felt bad for being selfish. He had enough going on. She could put up with her parents for a few days. But life sure sucked.

Jinx closed her eyes and tried to suppress the memories, but they surfaced anyway. *Karen…*A lone tear spilled down her cheek, and she wiped it away, grateful Mark either hadn't seen it or chose to not acknowledge it.

She remembered being dressed up for Easter in a pale blue smocked dress, one her mother had labored over for months. Karen, who was nine years older, wore a beautiful pink dress and, in Jinx's eyes, looked like a model. Jinx had been so excited sitting in front of the mirror while Karen meticulously curled her hair. She remembered thinking maybe Daddy would love her looking like this, and she could be his princess instead of the baby.

"You look beautiful!" her sister had assured her with a sunny smile.

"Can I wear lipstick, Karen?"

"Don't tell Daddy. We'll let him think it's just lip balm." Karen had slicked some clear lip gloss over her seven-year-old lips. She'd smacked them in the mirror and smiled at herself, amazed at the transformation. A tomboy who hated dressing up, she'd much rather have been in shorts and a T-shirt. But Karen had made her feel special and pretty. Together they'd descended the stairs to greet their parents, who'd been waiting in the foyer. Daddy had been tapping his foot with annoyance, but Jinx knew he'd look up at her and see a princess and be happy.

"There's my princess!" Her father had smiled widely, and she'd blushed with happiness — until Daddy gave Karen a kiss on the forehead. He'd turned and looked at her, frowning.

"Straighten your shoulders, don't slump, and wipe that lipstick off, *baby girl.*"

"It's not lipstick. It's lip balm," she'd replied with a smug smirk and sly glance to Karen, who'd given her a conspiratorial wink.

Her father's face had turned red, and he'd snapped, "Don't be impudent; do as you're told." As usual, her mother had stood there like a silent, beautiful statue. Mother never stood up to Daddy.

She'd angrily marched to the sink in the kitchen, wiping off the offensive lip gloss. Seeing a black permanent marker in the basket by the phone, she'd grabbed it and drawn a moustache on her upper lip.

Livid, her father had marched her upstairs and locked her in the dark linen closet until they returned from church. Being locked in the dark was her most feared punishment.

Her mind snapped back to the present when Mark rubbed her shoulder. Reassuring doggy snores from the backseat helped her relax a bit. She wondered why Mark was here, helping her. And what would the cost be? Turning, she caught hold of his hand and rested her cheek on it with a tired sigh. She knew she had it in her to be strong and to survive, but a tiny part of her liked having someone else to rely on for a change, even if she didn't trust him. Why did life have to be such a struggle?

Chapter Five

Mark held her hand as they entered the hospital room. The bright lighting added to the harsh reality of a child fighting to live. The beeping of machinery was rhythmic and constant, and a distinct smell of blood, fear, and anguish hung in the air. At first, she couldn't see the small, fragile boy. Her nephew was almost unrecognizable with all the bandages, tubes, and bruising on his battered little body. Matt, her brother-in-law, sat next to the bed holding his son's hand. Matt appeared to have aged twenty years since she'd seen him last, mere months ago when her sister's family had taken the train to New Orleans for a weekend visit. His dark, unruly hair was uncombed, his strong, square jaw covered in dark five-o'clock shadow.

Eyes wide, she covered her mouth in an attempt to contain her shock, but a pitiful, anguished sound escaped nonetheless. Matt appeared shell-shocked as he stood and embraced her.

He held his hand out to Mark. "Matt Tyler." He nodded sadly toward the bed. "My son, Luke."

"Mark MacGregor. I'm sorry to meet you under these circumstances."

Jinx took Luke's small hand in hers. Leaning forward, she kissed his forehead. "Aunt Jinx is here. You need to hurry and get better so you can ride the train and come play with Winston." She ran her fingers through his dark hair.

She turned back to Matt. "Is he going to be okay? Are you okay? Do you need anything? A cigarette, a break, both?"

"They're hopeful he'll make a full recovery, but he'll need some rehab…" Matt's voice broke, and he rubbed his swollen, red eyes, unable to speak for a moment. "I'll be okay. I don't want to leave his side. I have to be here when he wakes up."

Mark shifted uncomfortably and motioned that he was going to step out of the room.

Jinx nodded and turned back to Matt. "What happened?"

"Apparently Karen ran a stop sign and an eighteen-wheeler wasn't able to stop…She took the full impact. The kids…Elizabeth made it to the hospital, but…" His face twisted, and his eyes filled as he struggled to retain his composure. "I can't lose Luke. I just can't…" He broke down.

She held him, rubbing his back. "He'll be okay. He has to be," she said. "I mean, they would've sent him to Children's Hospital if he wasn't."

"That may still happen, once he's stable."

They looked up as a nurse in cartoon character scrubs came in to tell them Mr. and Mrs. Howell had arrived. She went on to check the machinery and examine Luke. Matt stepped out of the way and let out a slow breath, as if preparing for another disaster. Jinx understood his anxiety. Her parents had hated him since the day he and her sister had announced Karen was pregnant and they were marrying. They'd tried every way possible to stop the wedding. The local bootlegger's son hadn't been worthy of their daughter.

Matt looked over at his son and whispered, "Let's do this in the hall. Not in here."

Taking her own fortifying breath, Jinx nodded and followed Matt out the door.

Mark stepped into the hallway, needing air like a drowning victim. The pain blanketing Matt and the little boy was damn near unbearable. The memories it triggered of another hospital, another child fighting desperately for life were still raw.

A nurse brushed passed him and went into Luke's room. Mark rubbed his burning eyes and plastered on a smile as the door opened. Jinx stepped into the hallway, looking exhausted. Matt stood behind her in the doorway, his gaze darting from his son to down the hall. The tension in the air became palpable when a distinguished-looking older couple rounded the corner. Ignoring Matt, the attractive woman embraced Jinx, tears spilling down her perfectly made-up face. It wasn't difficult to deduce she was her mother. A slender woman with honey blond hair, she looked like an older version of Jinx.

"Eugenia, thank God you're here and safe," the woman said, pulling away. She captured Jinx's face in her hands, giving her a kiss on the cheek. Jinx held her mother close before stepping back.

Eugenia? Jinx didn't look like a Eugenia.

Jinx stiffened and appeared surprised when her father also reached for her. "Baby girl, why wouldn't you fly? You would've been here much sooner." Her father's tone was brusque, as he hugged her, brushing a light kiss on her forehead.

Mark raised an eyebrow and winked at Jinx, silently mouthing, "Eugenia?"

Bright eyes in a pale, pinched face met his when she pulled away from her father. "I don't like to fly, Daddy. And I go by Jinx. I've told you this." She sounded detached and robotic.

Mark attributed it to fatigue and stress.

"Don't be ridiculous," her father countered. "You've always had the most unfounded, nonsensical fears. And you have a beautiful name. It was your grandmother's. Your mother and I have made the arrangements for Karen and Elizabeth. Visitation will be tomorrow evening. The funeral will be held the following day at the church at ten." He pulled his handkerchief out of his pocket and mopped his eyes.

Mark looked over at Matt, who stood slumped against the doorframe, his hands stuffed in the pockets of his frayed jeans. He wondered if the poor guy had willingly turned over the final arrangements for his wife and daughter, or if his in-laws had railroaded him into their plans. Matt slipped back in to his son's room, closing the door behind him. *Definitely railroaded.*

"Matt looks exhausted. Has anyone helped him? Is Leroy here?" Jinx reached behind her and grabbed Mark's hand.

Her father ignored the question, but her mother answered, "Matt refuses to leave Luke's side. Leroy has visited…" Her voice trailed off, and she darted a look at her husband.

"Just say it," Jinx's father said. "He was drunk. Leroy Tyler is *always* drunk." He pressed his lips together.

"I brought Matt some lunch earlier, but he didn't eat it. I have a sandwich for him from Mae." Her mother drew her eyes toward Mark, staring with frank curiosity.

He moved to introduce himself, holding out his hand and feeling a little self-conscious. His shirt was rumpled and stained, he hadn't shaved, and his hair was pulled back in a messy ponytail.

"Mark MacGregor. I'm very sorry to meet you under these circumstances."

"Lila Howell. And this is my husband, James."

Jinx's mother offered a cold, manicured hand, which he shook. Mark smiled as he looked down at Jinx. *Eugenia Howell. Lovey Howell. Silly girl.* Jinx elbowed him in the side and rolled her eyes.

"Mrs. *Howell*, Mr. *Howell*."

James Howell gave him the onceover with his icy blue stare. Judging by the grim expression on his face, he was less than pleased to make *his* acquaintance. Mark lowered his hand when it became obvious James wasn't going to sully himself by shaking hands with a non-entity.

"Thank you for bringing Eugenia home. It was very kind of you." Jinx's mother paused barely long enough to take a breath. "How can we help you get back? I'm sure your schedule has been disrupted." Her smile lacked warmth as she waited for his reply.

And away from our daughter as soon as possible, Mark added silently. He glanced down at Jinx. She bit her lip, casting a furtive look at her father before lowering her gaze to the floor. She seemed to shrink into herself.

"I'm not leaving. I'm staying here. For Jinx."

Jinx looked up at him, and the relief in her sad, shadowed eyes assured him he'd made the right decision.

She squared her shoulders. "Mark can stay with me in my room."

Mark's brow shot to his hairline, and he swallowed nervously. That wasn't at all what he'd meant. By the thunderous look on her father's face, Jinx had shocked him as well.

"I hardly think that's appropriate," her father said firmly. "You will be in separate rooms." He held up two fingers as he glared at them.

Mark wanted to hold one up in return but refrained.

"This is neither the time nor the place to discuss this," Lila whispered, looking around at the hospital personnel going in and out of rooms.

"I'm twenty-one, Daddy. I pay my own way, and I am not a b-ba—" She took a deep breath. "I'm not a child. Either Mark stays with me—*in my room*—at the house, or we'll both go to the dive motel on the county line," Jinx affirmed, but her gaze wavered just a bit under her father's cold scrutiny.

"Eugenia." Her father's eyes narrowed to two dangerous-looking slits, and his lips thinned into a tight line.

Mark damn near shivered.

"We're living together; we're practically married," Jinx blurted.

An excellent poker player, Mark contained his surprise as he suppressed the urge to run and never look back.

Without saying another word, Mr. Howell stormed into Luke's room.

Mrs. Howell gave Jinx a quick kiss on the cheek. "I wish you wouldn't push your father so, especially at this time. I'll talk to him. Mae's at the house to let you in and help you get settled. We'll be home in a little while." She gave Mark a wary look and followed her husband into the room.

Jinx took a deep breath and sagged against him.

"So, Eugenia, shall we head home? You realize Louisiana doesn't recognize common-law marriage, right?" he teased.

"Call me Eugenia again, and I'll be going to jail after I hand you your privates on a platter," she said, storming down the hall.

Mark followed her, not doubting it one bit.

"I beg your pardon?" Mae frowned, crossing her arms in front of her ample chest.

Mark shifted on his feet, looking as if he wanted to be anywhere but here under Mae's scrutiny. In a perverse, mean way, it was kind of funny. Mae presented herself as an intimidating tower of strength, but Jinx knew for a fact that she was a softie.

Mae's dark, disapproving eyes darted back and forth between them. "When did you get *married*, Eugenia?"

"You know I go by Jinx now. I'm *not* married, Mae. You need to move into this century. Mark will be staying with me in my room, or we're leaving."

"I'm her bae." Mark wrapped an arm around her shoulder.

Jinx rolled her eyes at the innocent choirboy look he offered.

"You gonna be dead, *boo,* if Mr. Howell doesn't approve." The housekeeper grunted and turned her back to him.

Jinx should've known she'd live to regret the hasty excuse she'd thrown out to get her father off her case. Feeling like a four-year-old under Mae's scrutiny, she shifted from foot to foot.

"Does Ms. Lila know about this?"

"Yes, ma'am." *Old habits die hard.* She wasn't about to risk Mae's wrath by forgetting to say *ma'am.* Good manners had been instilled in her from the first time Mae rocked her.

"*Hmph,*" Mae snorted. "You do remember your daddy has guns? And he isn't afraid to use them," Mae mumbled as she led them upstairs.

Mark raised his eyebrows at Jinx behind Mae's back.

"You best be getting married, little miss. Didn't I tell you men don't buy the cow if the milk is free?"

Mark snorted and motioned that Mae was scary.

Jinx smiled for the first time since arriving back home. Mark might have good reason to be afraid. Mae riled up was a sight to behold.

Mae opened the door to her bedroom, and Jinx's shoulders fell. The walls were no longer electric blue and covered with abstract art and posters of her favorite bands. Her room was now an insipid lavender color with white trim. A few of her early watercolors of flowers hung on the wall. *Lavender. Ugh.* Jinx placed Winston's special dog pillow next to the bed she'd be sharing with Mark.

"That dog is as big as a horse. Is he stayin' in the house?" Fists on her hips, Mae glared at Winston.

He wagged his tail, as if amused by the entire situation.

"Yes, ma'am. He's housebroken. When did my room get painted?" Jinx bit her lip as Mae muttered under her breath about spoiled animals and girls.

Winston settled on his ridiculously overpriced pillow with an indignant dog snort, unperturbed by Mae's disapproval.

"Your mother always hoped Elizabeth would spend the night. This is, I mean *was,* her favorite color. But your sister was overprotective. Those kids never spent the night anywhere." She wiped her tears away with her thumb.

Jinx looked into to the eyes of the woman who had loved her since birth. Her hair was now gray, and her kind face lined with sadness. Nostalgic for the comfort only Mae could provide, she threw her arms around her neck.

"I've missed you so much, Me-Mae." Mae had always been there for her—as much as she could be without overstepping her job boundaries. "They can't be gone. Not Karen, not Elizabeth."

Mae held her, stroking her back, and Mae's tears mingled with her own when she kissed her cheek. "The good Lord has them now. They're in good hands. I've missed you, too, Eugenia. This house will never be the same. Your daddy is crazy with grief and will regret some of the things he's said, and done, to that poor boy. He told Matt this was his fault. Now how could it be his fault? That boy wasn't even home when the accident happened. Your mama's handling it better, but Karen was your daddy's princess, and Elizabeth was the apple of his eye. I don't know what will happen if Luke doesn't make it." Her sobbing intensified. "My sweet little boy, he smiles so big when he sees me."

Mae pulled a damp tissue from her pocket and wiped her eyes. She gave Jinx another hug. "You get your boyfriend-soon-to-be-fiancé a towel and clean up," she said, barely sparing him a glance. "I'll be in the kitchen when y'all are ready for something to eat. We got more food than Carter's got little liver pills, even some of Mrs. Jordan's chicken salad. She's one of the few at that church who makes it right with just the white meat," she fussed as she left the room, closing the door behind her.

"*Who* has liver pills? And what's wrong with dark meat in chicken salad?" Mark asked with a laugh.

"It's just an expression. Apparently the church and neighbors have brought over a ton of food. It's what small-town Southerners do when there's a death in the family. And every Southern woman knows you don't use dark meat in chicken salad unless you want to be talked about like a dog."

"That sounds like something my sister Claire would say. Are you sure about me staying in your room? I could sleep on the couch or something. It wasn't my intent to upset your parents. I just wanted to be here for *you*."

"Yes, I'm positive. We'll conveniently break up when we get home. Daddy will be thrilled."

Mark chuckled. "I haven't dealt with an irate parent in years; I'm really not sure about this…"

At the thought of being alone right now, dark, overwhelming fear engulfed her. Her breath felt trapped in her chest. Her vision started to tunnel, and Mark's voice sounded far away. He eased her to the bed and bent her over.

"Breathe, Jinx. Slow and deep."

She managed somehow to pull in some air.

"Again."

He talked her through it until she no longer felt light-headed. She grabbed his hand.

"I don't want to be here alone. I, uh…" She swallowed and attempted to say the words that didn't want to come out of her mouth.

"You need me?" he finished for her, his eyes unreadable.

Hearing the words raised her hackles. "*Want* you," she amended, turning her back to him, feeling ashamed of her weakness. She didn't want to *need* anyone.

"I'm not going anywhere. Not without you. So, this was your room? What color did it used to be?"

"Blue. One time it was red. The worst was when I painted it black. Daddy was furious. I did those flower paintings in junior high for my mother. She…was sick at the time. They're awful."

She sank to the bed, emotionally and physically exhausted. She took a moment to compose herself. "Mark?"

"Yes, love?"

"Thank you for everything. You didn't have to do this for me. I know you don't like to have anything much to do with a girl after… um, you know."

"Yeah, I know. I'm a frog 'em and leave 'em kind of guy." He sat next to her, rubbing her back. "Rules are meant to be broken. And sometimes, things aren't what they seem. I have a feeling we're a lot alike. We're good. Don't worry about this. You have enough on your plate right now."

He stood and stepped over the sleeping dog. "What's the plan? I'm thinking a shower, a quick bite to eat, and an early bedtime. I, for one, am exhausted, and I know you must be, too."

Jinx stood and took a steadying breath. "Wait here. I'll get you a towel." She shuffled into the hallway and stood before the linen closet. Her heart hammered as she reached toward the doorknob, her eyes drawn to the lock on it. What kind of sick, sadistic bastard puts a lock on a linen closet?

Sweat broke out on her brow, and she wiped it away with the back of her trembling hand. She reached again, but stood frozen, hearing the echoes of the past as she attempted to reel in the wayward emotions brought on by being back in this house. *Please let me out, I have to pee! It's dark! Please, Daddy—I'm scared!*

She wondered if they'd ever painted over the scratch marks on the door. The first time he'd locked her in there, she'd scraped and scratched until her fingers were bleeding.

Mentally shaking herself, she squared her shoulders and threw the door open. Reaching in without looking, she grabbed a towel and washcloth before slamming the door shut. Slumping against the door with her eyes closed, she took a moment to steady her nerves.

When she opened her eyes, Mark stood in the doorway. Curiosity and concern creased his face. She tried to brush past him as she handed him the linens.

"You look like you've seen a ghost," he commented quietly, cupping her chin and forcing her face up. His thumb wiped sweat off her upper lip.

She bit it.

"Ouch, dammit." Mark dropped her face and shook his hand. Frustration replaced the concern.

Leaning in close to her ear, he whispered, "Do you like things a little rough, Lovey? If so, that's something we can explore later."

"Perhaps I just don't like being manhandled, Thurston." She shook off his hands and slipped past him into the bedroom to find Winston's leash. The dog rose to his feet, standing guard in front of her, hackles raised. The menacing growl he emitted made Mark back away.

"Whoa, call off your bodyguard. I'm not the enemy here."

"It's okay, Winston." Jinx patted the dog's head and walked out the door without looking back.

She needed to get out of the house to breathe and collect her thoughts before her father returned. Being home wasn't helping her already questionable mental health. And she didn't want to end up being "sent away to rest" like her mother and grandmother had been.

Chapter Six

After an uncomfortable supper with the Howells, Mark sat in the kitchen talking to Mae, drinking a cup of coffee and eating a piece of apple pie. Jinx had been summoned to her father's study.

Raised voices echoed down the hallway. Mark glanced up at Mae as she wiped down the white granite countertop. She shook her head and sighed.

"It's best not to get between them. They've fought like this since Eugenia was a little girl. Her daddy never did understand her non-conformity. She and Karen were total opposites. Karen was an easy child."

"I've never been one to listen to sound advice," Mark replied and threw down his napkin.

He stormed out of the kitchen, headed toward the shouting. A shiver ran up his spine. This house was cold, and not just because of the cavernous rooms and clinical white décor. It was the essence of the place. It reminded him of a museum, perfect on the outside and totally impersonal on the inside.

He stopped outside the closed door and found Winston pacing back and forth, obviously riled by the argument intensifying between Jinx and her father.

"What the hell is wrong with you? You've been a defiant little bitch since you were seven years old. Where is your brain? Hooking up with this tattooed deadbeat? It's disgusting. And you dare to bring him into my home to fuck him under my roof? Tell me you're not going to marry this man. Don't you see what happened to Karen when she ran off and married that loser Matt Tyler? Your sister and niece are lying dead on a cold slab because of him! How dare you do this to your mother and me? Have you no respect? No shame?"

Mark froze, stunned and angered by the vicious attack. Winston growled and nudged at the door.

"You know nothing about Mark, so just shut up, Daddy. I told you we could stay at the motel. The best thing Karen ever did was marry Matt and get out of this house. He adored her and has been a good husband and father. I know you're upset by their deaths, so am I, so is Mother. Please, I'm begging you, just stop. I'll be gone after the funeral, and you won't have to be disrespected by me ever again."

"You have the gall to tell *me* to shut up in my own goddamned house? Don't you dare light that cigarette, *young lady!* I'll teach you respect."

The sound of a slap sent Mark over the edge. He threw the door open, and Winston bounced in with a ferocious growl, coming to stand between Jinx and her father. The fur on the back of his neck stood on end. Mark felt hot anger surge through his body at the sight of the red handprint on Jinx's cheek, and he clenched his fists.

Gritting his teeth, he kept his voice low and as respectful as he could muster. "This conversation is over." He glanced at Jinx. "Come on, love. Let's go. We'll find some other place to stay. Hell, sleeping in the car would be preferable to having you listen to this shit." He held his hand out to Jinx, ignoring the sputtered indignations of her so-called father.

"James, calm down," her mother broke in.

Who knew she was even in the room?

"We're all tired. Eugenia, just apologize and everything will be okay. It will be okay, won't it, James? Please don't run Eugenia off… Not now. She's our only child now…" Mrs. Howell broke down crying, rocking back and forth on the white sofa.

Jinx stared at the floor. "S-Sorry."

James gave his wife a cursory glance. He pinched the bridge of his nose and hissed out a deep breath before speaking. His eyes shifted from Mark to Jinx.

"Fine. But only because your mother is upset enough as it is. We'll talk again tomorrow. Get out of my sight before I change my mind. And that damn dog better be housebroken." He marched over to the bar and poured himself a drink. "Lila, go take your medication. You're overwrought."

Mark grabbed Jinx's hand and escorted her from the room. Winston followed them out to the front porch. Her hands shook as he lit her cigarette and then one for himself. The red handprint still lingering on her pale cheek infuriated him all over again. To keep from storming back inside to knock the shit out of her asshole father, he paced.

"You didn't have to do that, but thank you," she murmured with a sad smile. "Karen used to stand up to Daddy for me; she could talk him down when he was angry…" She stared out into the yard with a faraway expression.

Mark brushed her bangs out of her eyes. "Come back to the present, Jinx. Don't dwell in the past. It will only bring you down. Trust me, I know. I'll go back inside and beat the shit out of him if it'll make you feel better. Or how about I let Winston do the dirty work?"

"I'm fine, and that's not necessary. Today was actually pretty mild. Grief and having company in the house tempered his anger. And to be fair, I tend to push his buttons." She shrugged.

"Was he often abusive to you and your sister?"

"Karen was his princess, although they had their moments. I was his *b-baby*. He was strict and inflicted more psychological punishment than physical. I mean, he didn't b-beat me or anything…" she stuttered. She didn't make eye contact.

Nice dodge. Mark wondered if she shivered from the bitingly cold air or her memories.

They finished their cigarettes and with Winston trailing behind them, headed straight for her bedroom. Mark brushed his teeth and changed into a pair of pajama pants. He stretched out on the double bed as Jinx took her turn getting ready. While he'd been in the bathroom, she'd changed into a tight white tank top that did little to hide her nipples and low-riding pink yoga pants that fit her body like a glove.

Mark threw an arm over his eyes. *Down, boy.* He thought about old people. He thought about old people having sex. *Ugh.* That did it. Exhaling a slow breath, he once again felt in control and turned out the light. Maybe if he didn't see her, he could just relax and go to sleep—although in this small bed, that was about as likely as Mr. Howell being cordial.

After brushing her teeth, Jinx left the bathroom light on and pulled the door closed until just a sliver of light was visible. Winston turned twice on his pillow before collapsing with a dog snort. The bed dipped, and Jinx lay down with her back to him, not saying a word. He wondered for a moment if she'd already fallen asleep, exhausted from the turmoil of the past two days. Then her shoulders began to shake, but she didn't make a sound.

"Jinx?"

"I'm sorry I disturbed you. I'll let you sleep," she whispered in a choked voice, shoving the covers aside. Mark wrapped an arm around her waist before she could get up and rolled her over to face him. She curled into his body, flinging an arm over his chest and her leg over his, and wept. Unlike Harley and his sister, Claire, who were both loud with their ugly crying, she was silent. He hugged her close, not saying a word.

There wasn't anything he could do but be here. He knew from experience, at this point nothing would fill the emptiness. After a few minutes her silent sobs stopped, and he thought she might've fallen asleep.

"Thank you," she whispered. She moved to turn away from him, but he held on.

"Cuddling is definitely needed."

Jinx nodded. A whisper of a kiss brushed his chest, and she held him a tad tighter before they both slipped off to sleep.

Mark woke up to a tongue lapping his face and frowned. "If that's your tongue, Lovey, I can think of better places for it."

He opened one eye and grimaced at the smell of the doggie breath. Jinx giggled. Rolling over, he licked her face in retaliation.

"Stop! Ugh, your breath is as bad as Winston's," she sputtered. Her eyes widened, and she squealed when his arm snaked over, pulling her close.

"Good grief, it's true," she gasped.

"Now what?" Yawning, he rolled on top of her and kissed her cheek.

"Guys wake up with woodies."

"It's a given. Haven't you ever experienced this before?"

"Nope. I'm a frog 'em and leave 'em kind of girl. Do you wake up with company often?"

He chuckled. "Not if I can help it." He brushed the hair out of her face. "Only when the girl is special. Now about my woody…It's very painful, and there's only one solution for it." He gave her his best lascivious leer.

A blond imp smiled up at him. "I didn't bring any condoms."

"You're in luck. I'm always prepared."

He jumped out of bed and made his way to the bathroom. In record time he'd brushed his teeth and bounded back to bed, tossing a handful of condoms at her.

"Five?"

"This should get us started," he teased. Sliding back on top of her, he trailed his lips across her soft cheek until he reached her plump lower lip.

"How long have you been up?" he murmured, kissing the column of her neck, tracing a blue vein with his tongue.

"An hour or so. I took Winston out and came back to bed. I know why you never spend the night with anyone. You snore."

"Sorry. It's my deep, dark secret." Kissing the tip of her nose, he smiled, taking in her tousled bed hair and pert nipples peeking through her tank top.

Jinx raised an eyebrow and snorted. "How can it be a secret? It's loud enough to wake the dead. I'm pretty sure the neighbors heard you, and they live a mile down the road."

"Because I don't usually spend the night with the girls I frog, remember?"

The light in her eyes flickered, and her lashes fanned out over her pale cheeks. A slight furrow creased her brow. She took a deep breath, and when she glanced back up at him, he didn't have a clue to the thoughts in her beautiful head.

"Guess I wasn't so lucky, huh?" She reached up to brush a strand of his hair behind his ear.

"Or you're special," he replied, realizing it was true.

The thought was disconcerting. For some strange reason, he wanted to know what made her tick. What was her story?

On impulse he blurted, "Tell me something no one else knows about you."

Jinx shrugged. "I'm a pretty open book."

Hardly. "Why are you scared of the dark?"

"I always have been…" Her voice trailed off as she stared at the ceiling, lost in the past until he nudged her. She smiled and whispered, "Sorry. You go first. Tell me one of your deep, dark secrets." With her index finger, she traced the tattooed lettering on the inside of his right wrist.

The tattoo was part of his deepest, darkest secret, but it wasn't his alone to share. He opted for one to make her smile.

"You already know I snore. Another one?"

She nodded.

"Okay. This one I'm truly ashamed of. Ready?"

"Ready."

"I'm terrified of spiders," he stage-whispered and ducked his head into her neck, kissing it.

She squirmed, sighed, and wiggled all at the same time. His cock stood at attention.

"No, seriously, tell me a secret." She continued to trace his tattoo. "What does this say?"

"Analiese." He gave her an affronted look. "I *am* being serious. I'll kick a damn snake out of my way, but a spider makes me scream like a little girl."

"Who is Analiese?"

He closed his eyes and wished he had a cigarette. "A part of my past and not open for discussion."

A soft hand rubbed his scruffy beard. "Okay. But your fear of spiders is open for ridicule. You can squoosh a spider with your shoe, Thurston."

He could hear the smile in her voice. Opening his eyes, he saw her curiosity, but she didn't press him for details. His admiration for her grew. She, too, had secrets, and he respected her right to keep them. He grinned.

"*You* can squoosh the spider with your fuck-me boots, Lovey. I'll stand aside and cheer you on." With a self-deprecating laugh, his gaze raked over her face, noting her hooded eyes and softly parted mouth. He nuzzled her neck again and sucked on her earlobe, his tongue flicking the three earrings.

"Jinx?" he whispered.

"Yes?" she replied, adding a soft moan when his hand crept under her tank and he kissed the pulse pounding in her neck.

"Um, are you on birth control? Condoms aren't always a hundred percent." He held his breath, waiting for her answer.

"Yes. Like you, I'm prepared."

"Good." *Thank God.* He rubbed her soft cheek with the back of his fingers where his beard stubble had abraded her skin.

"I'm also not stupid. I don't want to make the same mistake Karen did." She sucked in a ragged breath. "I'm not ready to be a mother."

He paused and laid his head on the pillow next to hers, stroking her neck. Her remark hit close to home. He couldn't afford any more mistakes, either.

"You never did answer my question. Why me the other night? Was it really just my reputation?" He removed her tank top.

"Pretty much. I had an itch. I heard you could scratch it. I don't want a commitment, and you're known as being commitment-phobic." She cocked her head and grinned. "Your reputation is legendary, Two-Time MacGregor." She tugged his sleep pants down, and he kicked them to the floor.

Her answer troubled him on some level, maybe because it was so true. Strangely, it bothered him to be on the receiving end of the fuck-'em-and-leave-'em cycle. Like Jinx, he'd always made it clear he wasn't interested in a long-term relationship. So why did her arm's-length attitude hurt?

Because everyone leaves me.

He attributed his conflicted emotions to exhaustion. After all, the thought of falling in love again terrified him—even more than spiders.

"So, where are we headed with this?" He pulled her yoga pants off and licked up her hipbone. His curiosity remained piqued, but he knew the answers would not be forthcoming. He'd have to work for them. The real question was, did he want to invest the time and effort? Yes, quite possibly he did. She fascinated him like no woman had in years. Not since he'd first laid eyes on Harley Taylor…

"Jeepers, Mark, you're acting like a girl. Just frog me, for heaven's sake."

"Why won't you say fuck?"

What the hell is wrong with me? She doesn't want a commitment, for Christ's sake. She's beautiful, intelligent—the perfect girl. Why the fuck am I pushing her for an answer?

"Would you believe me if I said because I'm a lady?" She twisted away from him when he tickled her slick parts with his tongue. "S-Stop." She went still, squeezing her eyes shut.

"Do you really want me to stop? Relax, Lovey. Trust me."

She opened her eyes and stared at him. Biting her lip, she whispered, "Okay."

He started with her feet, massaging one and then the other until she was practically purring.

"That feels good."

He worked up her calves and stroked over the outside of her thighs. Grasping her hips, he lowered his face and trailed kisses across her taut abdomen, his tongue flicking her belly button. Her hand reached for him. He held it and paused.

"We good?"

"Y-Yes…"

He took his time kissing her warm skin lower and lower, gentling her with soft strokes. His tongue flicked her clit. "Mmm, baby…"

"Stop!" This time panic laced her voice. Her eyes were no longer hooded. They were dark and unfocused. She slapped at his arm frantically, bucking to get away from him.

"I said s-stop." She scrambled away and reached under her pillow, pulling out her switchblade. She snapped it open with a wild, menacing look. He jumped off the bed, raising his hands.

"What the fuck is your problem?" he bit out, more frustrated than furious. Storming into the bathroom, he shut the door, needing a minute alone to check his emotions.

Goddammit. Did she have that thing under her pillow all this time? Why would she sleep with a switchblade under her pillow?

Nausea twisted his gut. Something was terribly wrong here. With a heavy sigh he leaned against the counter and forced several deep breaths. He wasn't sure if he wanted to shake her, kill her, or comfort her.

Turning on the faucet, he washed his face, taking the time to cool off before he confronted her. He found her sitting on the bed with her arms wrapped tight around her knees, her head resting on top of them. The switchblade hung loose in her open hand. She raised her face to his.

He squatted next to the bed. "Jinx? Talk to me. What's going on?"

As long as he lived, he'd never forget the gut-wrenching anguish in her eyes.

"I-I'm s-sorry," she stammered. "It's not you. It's me. I just freak out at times. I don't know why. I guess I'm crazy like my mother."

Mark took the switchblade and snapped it shut. "I don't understand. This is insane. I mean, you know I'd never do anything you don't want, right? I mean, fuck. I'm a prick, but I'm not going to hurt you."

Her silence twisted his gut. He stood and pulled on his pajama pants. Sitting on the bed with his elbows resting on his knees, he covered his face, taking the time to think for a moment before speaking.

"I keep misreading your signals," he finally said. "I shouldn't have assumed…well, anything. You come across as a tough girl. I like that about you. As I'm sure you've heard, I'm not a touchy-feely kind of guy. I like shit straight up. So tell me what the fuck I'm doing wrong, or I'm outta here."

The look she leveled at him sent chills down his spine. "Don't call me *baby*, and I don't much like foreplay," she said through gritted teeth. "I believe I've said both those things before."

"That's it?"

She nodded, and he shook his head with disbelief.

"Lovey, I don't mean anything when I say it…Wait. You don't like foreplay *ever?*"

She blew out a breath that ruffled the bangs in her eyes. "Never mind. It's me, not you. Just do it and be done." She rubbed her eyes, placed her cheek on top of her knees, and stared at him, looking lost and detached.

Is she fucking kidding? "No, I don't think so." *We're in her parents' house, dumbass. She's an emotional mess and doesn't need to give me any more explanation than she has.* He ran his hands through his hair, feeling like a dick.

"I-I…" She covered her face and shuddered.

"No, no. It's a crazy situation. I'm not trying to take advantage of you, please know that. We're friends first. Right?" He pulled her into his lap and held her, rocking and kissing the top of her head, feeling like an asshole. She'd just lost her sister and niece. This wasn't about his blue balls. For once, he needed to put aside his selfishness.

"I'm so fucked up. I'm frigid or something. I'm sorry," she whispered. Her use of profanity made him pause. He turned her face up to his.

"We're all fucked up, Jinx. Every last damn one of us. You're not frigid. You're stressed. We're in your parents' home, and I'm a prick. I get it, and I'm sorry."

She wrapped her arms around his neck and kissed him.

"Thank you, Mark."

Bringing her with him, he fell back on the bed, holding her tight. Softly, he traced lazy circles on her back until they both fell asleep.

A few hours later, he woke up and glanced at his watch. It was nine in the morning.

"You asleep?" he whispered.

"No."

"I'm sorry about earlier."

She moved and pressed a kiss to his cheek. "It's okay. Quit apologizing."

Foreheads touching, he gazed into eyes the color of good whiskey.

"Did I scare you with the switchblade?" she asked with a tiny smile.

He jumped when she nipped his earlobe with her teeth. "A bit," he admitted. "You looked scary as hell but totally fuckin' hot at the same time."

She kissed him and smacked his chest. "I need to get a shower; I want to go check on Luke and Matt." Rolling off him, she headed to the bathroom.

Stunned by her mercurial mood swings, it took him a moment to settle before he followed her.

"What are you doing?" she asked when he joined her in the hot, steamy shower.

"Saving time," he joked, running his hands down her soapy body. Damn, she was beautiful. Jinx giggled and flashed him a bright smile, pressing her firm breasts to his chest. When she gazed up at him with that pixie look, he knew he was in deep trouble.

"Fine, just don't call me baby." She slid down to her knees in front of him.

"Wouldn't dream of it," he murmured, closing his eyes when she stroked him from base to tip.

They were two fucked-up people headed down a rocky path. There was no question in his mind—someone was going to get hurt. It just remained to be seen who and when. And strangely, he hoped it wasn't Jinx.

Then her mouth followed her hand, and he quit thinking altogether.

That evening, Jinx stood in the hallway of the funeral home. She nodded politely at the condolences offered by people she didn't give a rat's butt about. She wished Mark would hurry with his cigarette. It scared her how dependent she'd grown on him in just over forty-eight hours. Despite her meltdown this morning, he'd stuck by her. She ran her dampened palms down the black miniskirt that had started World War III before they left the house.

While Mark walked Winston, her father had taken the opportunity to berate her "whorish appearance." Daddy thought a short black skirt, electric blue blouse, and four-inch heels were inappropriate for the funeral home. Considering this was a rural area and there'd be folks dressed in overalls and jeans, she thought his concern ridiculous. She wasn't even showing cleavage. Mother had fussed because her eye makeup was too dark, so she'd added bright red lipstick out of sheer obstinacy and wished she'd had her black wig. She would forever be thirteen in their eyes.

Once they'd arrived at the funeral home, her father had commenced holding court with the upper echelon in the county, ignoring her—and Mark—completely. Her mother had pasted on a brave smile and greeted people like she was at a charity event. Looking over at her now, Jinx wondered how many pills Mother had taken today to numb her emotions. Prescription meds had always been her mom's way of handling things. Judging by her pinpoint pupils and nervous chattering, she was flying high. Concerned for her mother's health, she vowed to fly under the radar this evening and not stress her more than necessary by arguing with her father.

"Eugenia, are you coming in to greet the guests?" her mother called.

Jinx had no desire to go into the room to see her sister and niece in their caskets. Lying dead in their coffins was not the way she wanted to remember them.

"Um…in a bit. Phone call." She took her phone out of her purse. She glanced at the texts from the band but called Ava. Her friend had called and texted several times, but Jinx hadn't had it in her to call her back.

"Jinx! How are you, honey?" Ava's voice was warm and sweet, like pralines from the Quarter.

"As well as can be expected. The flowers you and Derrick sent are pretty. Thank you."

"I wish we could be there. I'm so sorry. So many people at the bar have expressed how sad they are for you and your family. Do you need anything?"

"Just for all of this to be over."

"I know. I'm glad Mark's there for you. He's a good guy."

"Yeah." Talking was exhausting. "Look, I'll talk to ya later, 'kay? Thanks for keeping in touch."

"Sure, sure. I'm here if you need to talk. See you when you get home. Derrick sends his love, too."

"Thanks, bye." She hung up and edged away from the doorway to the viewing and prayed she'd develop magical powers and disappear.

No such luck.

"When did you get home?"

A large woman with beady eyes stared at her, anticipation written all over her sweaty face. Beside her stood her polar opposite: a bird-like woman with piercing eyes and the look of a hawk going in for the kill. Jinx inwardly groaned as she faced the two biggest gossips in Pine Bluff. Frances Kelton owned the Mug and Cone hamburger joint, and Lydia Meadows—Frances's best friend and cohort in misinformation—worked at Hudson's One Stop Grocery. Between the two of them, social media was entirely unnecessary to catch up on the county gossip.

"Yesterday."

"Are you still in school?" Frances asked, louder than necessary.

"Yes." Jinx looked away, hoping the nosy witch would get the hint she didn't want to talk. Unfortunately, there was no one available to rescue her.

"We were so sad to hear about your sister and niece," Lydia commented, as if programmed in funeral-home niceties. She spoke without looking at Jinx, scanning the hallway for someone. Her true intentions became clear with her next question. "Where's poor Matt? I'm here for him if he needs me."

Jinx wrinkled her nose, disgusted. Matt was mourning, and still in shock over the loss of Karen and Elizabeth. Lydia was older than him, and he was way out of her league when it came to class and kindness.

"He's with Luke." Jinx searched the room for a reason to get away. She'd even welcome her father's presence. Daddy had no qualms about telling people to get lost.

"Have you seen Jeremy since you got home?" Frances flashed a bloodthirsty, predatory smile.

Jinx felt bile in the back of her throat at the name of the boy who'd made her life hell as a teenager. "No. I'm not exactly home for a visit." She knew anything she said would become fuel for malicious gossip before these two left the funeral home. She opted to let them form their opinions unaided.

Finally, Mark sauntered toward her with the confidence of a man comfortable in his own skin. More than a few heads turned to stare. With his hair in a neat ponytail, and wearing gray pants, a white shirt, and a maroon paisley tie he'd bought this morning, he looked more like a model than a bartender. Her father walked by, glaring at them before smiling at the minister by his side.

Lydia's eyes narrowed, and Frances raised an eyebrow when Mark placed a protective arm around her waist.

"You holdin' up okay, Lovey?" He kissed her temple.

"Fine." Jinx sagged against him, despite her best effort to be strong on her own.

"Aren't you going to introduce us to your *friend?*" Frances was practically salivating.

"He's not my friend," Jinx snapped.

"He's not?" Lydia asked.

"I'm not?" Mark asked.

"He's actually my pimp from New Orleans. C'mon, let's go." She tugged on his arm.

"I thought I was your boyfriend," he argued.

"You're both, Mark. Now let's go."

They left the women with their mouths hanging open. Jinx calculated it would take less than a minute before the gossip spread to the other side of the county.

"Wanna explain that?" Mark murmured as he followed her to the front of the funeral parlor.

"It doesn't matter what I say or do, it'll be twisted—"

Jinx stopped cold in her tracks, and Mark ran into her from behind. *Shoot!* She relaxed her features as she faced the boy—now a man—who had ruined her reputation. As if sensing her unease, Mark reached out and held her hand.

Jeremy Turner was taller than she remembered, and his once athletic build was now soft in the middle, showing signs of excess. She supposed he was still what some would call handsome, with short, highlighted blond hair and teeth that were too white not to be veneers. His green eyes raked up and down her body, probably mentally undressing her at this very moment. His wolfish smile and leering gaze made her want to throw up. The snake in a suit straightened his tie as he approached her, stopping on the way to speak to those he knew.

Jinx rolled her eyes and turned to slip out before he reached her, but she was too late. He spun her around and raised his eyebrows in fake surprise.

"Well, well, well, Genie. Long time no see. You've changed a bit, baby doll. I liked your hair longer."

Jinx stood ramrod straight. "Don't call me that," she ground out. "And maybe I'll shave my head."

"Which? Genie? Or baby doll? You used to love those names." He turned his attention to Mark and held out his hand. "Jeremy Turner. Me and Eugenia used to connect in high school."

"I meant nothing to you, Jeremy, and you know it." Her cheeks burned, and she twisted her hands as she stared at the floor, wishing she could sink through it. How she wished she had her wig and stage makeup to hide behind. She took a deep breath, channeling her I-don't-give-a-shit persona.

Mark wrapped an arm around her waist, his hand resting on her hip. "It's *Eugenia and I,* you illiterate bastard."

She looked up, feeling the tension wound in him. He was like a viper, ready to strike. Her confidence soared, but she didn't want a scene. Her father would kill her.

"He isn't worth it, Mark."

"I don't know who you are, but Genie and I have history. We go way back, right, kiddo?"

Beside her, Mark hissed. He drew back and clenched his fist, his body shaking with fury.

Jinx placed herself between the two men. "We're leaving. We're not doing this *here.*"

She tugged on Mark's sleeve. He shrugged her off and grabbed Jeremy, shoving him into an empty room. Jinx followed, whisper-begging him to stop while she scanned the crowd for her parents.

She shut the door behind them. "Please, Mark, don't."

Mark took Jeremy by the throat and shoved him against the wall. "You sick motherfucker. Do you get off on tormenting women? If you ever say another word, or so much as breathe the air she's breathing, or harm her in any way, I'll come after you. And make no mistake. *I. Will. Find. You.*" Mark spoke softly through clenched teeth.

Jeremy's eyes widened to the point that the white became visible all around his irises. Jinx watched with fascinated horror as his face turned red and then purple. It reminded her of a catfish flopping on the bank of the lake.

"Mark, stop." She tugged on his arm. *Dear God, if he kills Jeremy…*

"I'll slit your throat and not think twice about it. You can thank your tax dollars for the education I received in thirteen different fuck-ing foster homes. Taking you down will be the least of my many crimes."

Mark loosened his grip slightly. "Did I make myself clear?"

When Jeremy nodded, Mark let go. "Now get the hell out of here, asswipe."

Jeremy bent over with his hands on his knees, sucking in deep breaths. He stood and loosened his tie as sweat poured down his now crimson face. Jeremy had never been the brightest, just the meanest.

"Fuck, it was just a few pics for fun. It wasn't like she was a damn virgin; ask anyone on the football—" He crumpled to the floor, his eye swelling immediately.

Mark had moved so fast she hadn't been able to stop him.

"Mark, please, just stop." She blocked him from getting at her tormentor again.

"Where the hell do we go to get a drink around here?" Mark asked, straightening his shirt and tie as if nothing had happened.

Jinx watched dumbfounded as the boy who had made her teen years miserable slunk out of the room like a whipped dog. He slammed the door behind him. No man had ever defended her the way Mark just had. In one leap, she was in his arms and had her legs wrapped around his waist. He staggered, falling against the wall to catch his balance. His hands cupped her bottom under her short skirt, and he grinned into her exuberant kiss.

"Fuck, Lovey. Funeral home sex might just be the kinkiest shit ever. Did you seriously not wear underwear? God, I love your ass."

"I wasn't thinking about sex, and I have on underwear, thank you very much. It's a thong. You, Mark MacGregor are my hero. Would you really find him and hurt him for me?"

"I'd beat the shit out of him if needed, but I'm more bark than bite. I do badass pretty well, though, don't you think?"

Jinx laughed. "Perfectly. Let's go find Leroy."

"Who?"

"Matt's father. He and Gig Johnson make the best moonshine around, and I'll bet my last dollar he has some on him."

Thank God her parents were already asleep. Still, it was going to be a miracle if they didn't wake up as she pushed and pulled an extremely drunk Mark up the stairs. He mumbled incoherently, but at least he wasn't singing about some dumb bullfrog named Jeremiah like he had been earlier. Huffing with exertion, she'd get him up two steps and he'd stumble back one. If she ever got him into bed, she vowed to never let him live it down that she could drink him under the proverbial table.

When they finally reached her room, he collapsed like a giant oak. She yanked his shoes and socks off his feet, panting to catch her breath.

"Fu-uck, Lovey. That was some awesome shit. Leroy is my hero. I *loooooove* himmm," he slurred, flashing a silly, lopsided grin just before passing out cold.

Jinx shook her head and signaled for Winston to follow her out. She took the last bit of moonshine with her. Mark might not love Leroy so much tomorrow.

Stepping outside, she shivered in the still, crisp night air. Millions of stars splayed across the sky like diamonds on black velvet. It was the only thing she missed after she moved to the city: the beauty of the night sky unhindered by city lights. She lit a cigarette and collapsed in a chair by the covered pool as Winston dashed off to play in the yard. The backyard held echoes of the past, and she could almost hear Karen's laughter as they played hide and go seek.

Memories raced through her grief-stricken mind: Karen's joy-filled face as she walked down the aisle to get married, despite having just thrown up from morning sickness. Matt kissing Karen's sweat-drenched face and telling her how beautiful his girls were after Elizabeth was born. Elizabeth's wide smile when she took her first step. Luke's silly, drooly face when he showed off his first tooth. It wasn't fair. Her sister and niece were gone; they were too young and had too much life ahead of them. And Luke…Would he be able to get over this? Her chest hurt at the thought of losing him, too.

At the end of the yard was her favorite place, the wooden fort her father had built for her sixth birthday. She smiled, remembering Karen, who would have been fifteen then, rolling her eyes and saying she was "too big for a fort." But her sister *had* played with her up there, and they'd often hidden there from the upheaval at home—or from Mae when they were supposed to be doing chores. And her moody sister had also come out there alone. Or with Matt…

Jinx wandered toward the abandoned sanctuary and carefully climbed the rickety steps to crawl inside. Sitting with her back against the wall, she wrapped her arms around her knees. Her emotions imploded, her grief escaping in a choked sob. The emptiness of the dilapidated structure mirrored the void left in her heart. Sorrow was a poor substitute for the sister she'd loved.

The last time she'd been up here was after her horrible fifteenth birthday. She'd gone with supposed friends to the Bluff to celebrate and had drunk too much and passed out. Angry because she'd re-buffed his advances, Jeremy Turner had posted nude pictures of her passed out all over social media. She never really knew if he and his dumb friends had tried anything. But it didn't matter. The blistering lecture from her father as he'd driven her all the way to Birmingham to buy a pregnancy test was engraved in her memory. That night, she'd come here to be alone, with her hatred and a bottle of liquor she'd stolen from her father. She'd vowed to become the whore everyone thought she was. After that, she'd been indiscriminate with her body—until the freak-out spells started.

There's something wrong with me. Why is sex with strangers easier than with guys who want an actual relationship? She downed the last of the moonshine.

Silently she beat her fist on the rough-hewn floor, ignoring the splinters that embedded in her hand. When her anger was spent, she collapsed into a fetal position and prayed for Luke. *He's all I have left of Karen…* She pondered how fleeting life was and how meaningless hers had been thus far. *If it had been me who died, would anyone care?* Would anyone miss her as much as she'd miss her sister?

After about an hour of ranting her frustration and pain, the cold night air seeped into her bones, matching the chill in her heart. Her teeth chattered as she rubbed her cramping arms and legs. Crawling back to the opening, she stopped, remembering the secret hiding place where she and Karen had stored their treasures. The board lifted easily over the cubbyhole, and she smiled when she looked inside, running a finger over the items: costume jewelry her mother had given them, feathers, one of her early sketchbooks, a bedraggled Barbie doll she'd given marker tattoos, and a spiral-bound notebook that must've been Karen's. She grabbed the notebook to look at later, when her pain wasn't so fresh. It might be something Matt or Luke would want. Resealing the cubbyhole with the empty jar inside, she climbed down and dropped to the ground.

Winston padded over to nuzzle her neck. His dark eyes peered at her with the understanding only a four-footed friend could offer. But as comforting as Winston was, she longed for connection with another human being. No, not just any human being, *Mark.* For the first time in a very long time, she *needed* someone else.

She was tired of being alone—tired of wearing her mask of indifferent self-assurance, and she was worn out from pretending to be okay. She was far from okay. She was mentally ill like her mother and grandmother. The black holes that marred her memory were terrifying testaments to it.

Mark was different from any man she'd ever known. No one had ever taken the time to try to peel back the layers and find the real her. Could she let him in? Probably not. Two-Time MacGregor would move on quickly once they returned to New Orleans.

Hugging Winston's massive neck, she allowed herself one last minute to give in to the tears slipping down her cheeks. She cried because she missed her sister, mourned the loss of her niece, and because she was terribly afraid she was bound for heartbreak when Mark moved on to another girl.

Tomorrow she'd be strong.

Mark stumbled back from the bathroom, looking for Jinx. Her side of the bed remained untouched. He grabbed a cigarette and cracked open the window, knowing he was too damn drunk to make it downstairs to smoke. By the light on the back porch, he could see Winston running around, sniffing and occasionally hiking his leg on a tree. Jinx must be close by. He looked around until he saw her climbing down from an old fort. She collapsed to the ground, and Winston lumbered over to her. She wrapped her arms around her dog's neck, and his heart ached for her.

Shit, this girl had gotten under his skin. He'd already spent more time with her than any woman since Harley.

Because she's in mourning, his brain rationalized.

Bullshit, his heart answered.

Before he got in too deep, maybe he should just catch a bus and go home.

Jinx wiped her eyes and hugged her dog again, as if Winston were the only friend she had in the world.

Fuck.

Spiraling fast in the emotions surrounding this girl, Mark knew he wanted more, even though he knew it shouldn't happen. He wasn't the type of guy a girl should settle down with, not with his track record. Further complicating things were her issues with sex and his with his ex.

He needed to get out while he could. But he didn't want to. Was she crazy as bat shit? Hell, yeah. But he didn't get the vibe she was any more fucked up than he was. Crazy is as crazy does.

If he left now, he could avoid the funeral tomorrow. Funerals forced memories best left buried. He'd attended a handful in his lifetime. He'd felt lost at his mother's and never knew his father. But another had damn near broken him, leaving him an empty shell of a man. Since then he'd attempted to fill the hole with school, work, and meaningless relationships. But emblazoned in his memory remained the intricate design of Harley's blond braid that day, though he couldn't for the life of him remember one goddamned word the minister had said.

Mark shoved aside the thoughts of Harley. She'd been one of the few constants in his life, and a mistake from the get-go. He looked again out the window at the heartbroken girl. And here was another one. Jinx fascinated him. Her bright smile and swagger were intoxicating, yet she harbored the fragility of a wounded bird. It brought out a fierce protectiveness in him, a desire to fix what was wrong. It wasn't hard for one broken soul to recognize and identify with another.

Fate had thrown them together in the present. What the hell did the future hold for two fucked-up people?

Heartbreak—no doubt about it.

Chapter Eight

The rain began in earnest as they stood in the cemetery, but Jinx ignored it. The dark, dismal day mirrored the emptiness within her. Despite the minister's assurance that God had a plan, the funeral service had been heartbreaking. In his words, the Kingdom of Heaven had welcomed two more angels and everyone would be reunited in the end. If that was God's plan, Jinx wanted no part of it.

Her parents had left before the coffins were lowered into the ground. She had no doubt Daddy would have Mother sedated before they were back at the house. Matt stood motionless at the graveside, looking lost. Luke remained hospitalized, and Mrs. Jordan, his Sunday school teacher, had stayed with him during the funeral.

When the service ended, the crowd began to disperse, though the majority of the funeral attendees would reappear shortly at her parents' home under the pretext of offering comfort to the family. But Jinx knew they would be there, in fact, to partake of the food, for some to see inside a home they would never be invited to socially, and to gossip. She hated this stupid funeral custom. Time might very well ease her pain, but everything hurt like hell right now. The vodka she'd snuck from her father's liquor cabinet had taken the edge off but hadn't been enough to numb her entirely.

Travis Carlton and his younger sister, Lissy, approached. His eyes were red.

"Eugenia." His voice was raw, and he looked ready to cry.

He'd dated Karen years ago; his parents were her mother and father's best friends.

Lissy patted her brother's arm. "We're really sorry. I still can't believe it."

"Hi, Travis. Thank you, Lissy."

"I can't believe Karen's gone…" Travis broke down.

"Me either." Jinx endured Travis's hug and caught Matt watching them. He looked ready to kill before he shifted his gaze back to someone speaking to him.

"Let's go, Trav." Lissy guided her brother away.

Jinx wanted out of here. This was too much to handle.

With a sick heart she looked for Mark and spotted him leaning against her car, smoking, in spite of the rain. Walking toward him felt right on so many levels, like seeking shelter during a storm. Worry creased his face as she approached. He'd loosened his tie and unbuttoned the top two buttons of his shirt, leaving him handsomely rumpled.

Then his face swam in front of her, and her feet felt weighted in place. Her mind shut down, and she couldn't remember how to put one foot in front of the other. She wasn't even sure how to breathe anymore.

Tossing the cigarette to the ground, Mark sprinted toward her, catching her before she crumpled.

"Chin up, Lovey. This horrible day is almost over," he said, wrapping his solid arms around her. He kissed her lips and rested his chin on top of her head, his hand running up and down her back.

He'd become her sanctuary.

Her peace.

Her life.

She couldn't imagine being able to breathe without him. She wouldn't want to.

Jinx clung to his shirt and stepped away, locking her gaze on his face. "I want to go home. Please take me home."

"Of course. We'll go right now."

"*No.* I mean I want to go *home*. We can get Winston, throw our stuff together, and leave. I don't care if we sleep in the car on the side of the road—I have to get out of here."

Mark pressed his lips to her forehead. "Okay, love. What about your parents?"

"I want to go home," she repeated. "Please, take me home."

"All right, Mistress Jinx. Your wish is my command," he teased with a small smile.

"And I want you to stay when we get there. I know you have your two-time rule, but please, may I have one more night?" She swallowed and whispered, "Please?"

Mark's gaze shifted from hers, but after a pause, he nodded. Jinx sagged against him, finally able to breathe again.

Jinx yawned and stretched when the car stopped some seven hours later, opening her eyes to gaze at the man beside her. He stared out the window, tapping the steering wheel with his thumbs. She'd been nothing but an emotional mess since they'd hooked up, yet he'd been tolerant and patient. But she knew his reputation, and by asking him to stay, she'd crossed his line. He wanted out; she could sense it in his brooding gaze and the firm set of his jaw.

"Thank you for everything. You don't have to stay," she told him. "It was just the emotions of the day that made me ask. I'm fine now that I'm home. I'll call you a ride."

He turned to face her, the relieved look on his face answering what she already knew. He wanted to leave.

Reaching out, he cupped her cheek, and without thinking, she turned into it, closing her eyes, drawing one last bit of comfort from him. Physiology forced her to breathe, but she wasn't living.

"You're not fine. I'm staying." Tension surrounded him, coiled like a spring.

"I don't need your charity, sympathy, or whatever else has compelled your offer." She pulled away and threw open the door. What had she been thinking? Two-Time MacGregor would rather poke his eye out than deal with a needy leech. He shot out of the car and was by her side before she could slam the door.

"You can drive my car to the bar. I'll pick it up later. Come on, Winston." Whistling for her dog, she turned, running into an unmovable mountain of man.

"What part of I'm not fucking leaving don't you understand?" he bit out, stepping around her to grab their suitcases from the trunk. "We're both exhausted, and I'm not arguing about this. Get your little ass in the house, *now*." He motioned toward the front door with his stubborn, scruffy chin — the chin she wanted to feel nuzzling her neck.

He stomped to the front door and dropped the suitcases. She knew he was waiting for her to unlock the door and deactivate the alarm.

Spinning on her heels, she marched in the opposite direction, toward the park. *Why is he doing this?*

After being cooped up in the car for hours, Winston bounded after her, sniffing and exploring every tree he came to. Jinx walked through the park, brooding. She didn't want Mark to leave, but she didn't want him staying out of a sense of obligation. She needed…

No! Need has nothing to do with it. I want him, that's it. This is purely physical.

She didn't need anyone. Now that the funerals were over and she was home, she could get her life back. She'd never allow herself to be that vulnerable. Look where being weak had landed her mother. Nervous energy and emotions from the past few days bubbled within her, threatening to erupt. If she didn't let them out soon, she knew she'd combust.

Why Mark? Why did she want a man who wasn't able to commit?

Because he's like me.

And he wasn't afraid of her issues. In the past, her hang-ups had run men off in either disgust or fear. She knew she needed therapy; obviously there was something wrong with her. Who didn't want to be touched? Who freaked for no reason during sex? She was a grown woman afraid of the dark with no idea why…

Now finding it arduous to put one foot in front of the other, she whistled for Winston and trudged back across the street. Her car remained where Mark had parked it, but Mark wasn't there. *I must've been too busy wallowing to see him leave…* She shook her head. He'd left his suitcase in his hurry to get away. *Jerk.*

Disappointment settled around her like a comfortable blanket. He was gone. Unlocking the front door, she punched in the alarm code. She hefted her suitcase and the dog bed.

Before she could flip on the lights, someone grabbed her, and a warm mouth covered hers, taking what he wanted, what she wanted to give. He slammed the door shut, pinning her against the door, and dropped his suitcase. Her suitcase clattered to its side, and she flung the dog bed across the room. Winston growled, and she snapped her fingers. With a snort, he left them to find his bed.

"Listen to me," Mark growled, yanking her arms above her head and holding them with one hand.

"W-What?" She couldn't think. Her heart pounded, and there was no way her erratic breathing could oxygenate her brain. "Where were you?"

"Behind you, keeping an eye on you. You should be more aware of your surroundings. We're going to lay down some ground rules. I'll start: don't get attached. I'm not wired for meaningful relationships."

"Don't call me baby."

He chuckled. "Yeah, I think that one's finally sunk in." He blew in her ear, sending a shiver down her spine. "Don't expect me to call every day. Don't expect me to call, ever."

"Don't tell me how good you can make me feel," she countered, biting his lower lip.

"Don't send mixed signals. I'm not a fucking mind reader."

"Don't overanalyze me, just frog me."

"Know this can be over at any time."

She nodded. "Friends with frogging benefits, only."

"Exactly." He smiled. "I do have one request though…"

She raised an eyebrow, wondering if she could agree to his rules. "Okay, but then I get one."

"At some point I want you in those fantastic fuck-me boots, sans the switchblade."

"My turn." Wiggling her wrists in his ironclad grasp, she found she couldn't move. Blood rushed from her brain to between her legs as her desire skyrocketed.

"Shoot, but not literally," he said, smiling into her neck as he kissed along it.

"I'm not a sugar-sweet kind of girl. I don't want you to whisper sweet nothings to me. They're meaningless. I don't want you to tell me how great everything will be, or how wonderful you can make me feel. I prefer you not speak at all. I like it rough. Don't go easy on me. I want to experience the dark side of you, and in return, you can experience mine, if you're up to it. No matter what you may think, I don't want you to make *love* to me. I want you to, you know…" She swallowed. "Just…"

"Say it," he commanded. The hand not pinning her wrists circled her throat, his thumb rubbing tantalizing circles on her heated skin. "Say it and mean it. The actual word." He bit her neck hard enough to make her gasp, and she threw her head back, offering her throat to him, showing her willingness to be vulnerable.

"F-Fuck me. Hard. Make me feel," she whispered, holding her breath.

In the dim light from outside, his eyes seemed to ignite, and his nostrils flared. "Atta girl. Now breathe, Lovey." He picked her up and carried her to the bedroom.

After they kicked off their shoes and socks, he pushed her onto the bed and was on top of her before she could move.

"One more thing," he rasped, holding her face so she had to look into his eyes. "If you say *eggplant*, I stop. Immediately. Understand?"

A nervous giggle escaped before she could stop it. *Is he joking?* "Eggplant? Why *eggplant* and not *stop?*"

"Because *stop* doesn't always mean *stop*. And I fuckin' hate eggplant. Now say it," he encouraged with a smile and a kiss on the tip of her nose.

When she frowned, he raised an eyebrow and pinched her nipple. Hard.

She rolled her eyes and sighed. "Fine, eggplant."

He let go and sat up, his hands raised. "See?"

"What vegetable means go?"

His eyes twinkled, and he smiled. "Green bean."

"Green bean, Mark. Green bean!" She bolted upright and tore off his coat. He shrugged his shirt over his head without unbuttoning it before throwing it to the floor. She ran her hands up his chest and down his biceps and wrapped her arms around his neck. She tugged on his hair and murmured, "Green bean."

"I fuckin' love green beans." He yanked her coat off and tossed it. Winston snorted and sighed when it landed on top of him. As Mark's mouth ravaged hers, she hummed with the building sexual energy.

His body pinned her down, and he held her wrists next to her head. Not being able to move suddenly scared her and she stilled. *Nooooo, I want this.* She closed her eyes and took a deep breath.

"Where are we?" he whispered.

His voice brought her out of her momentary panic. She felt the bulge in his pants and struggled to get closer, grinding against him, frustrated by the clothes separating them. "G-Green bean."

"Sure?"

She nodded.

He opened his mouth to say something, but stopped when she hissed a warning. To her delight, he winked before returning his mouth to hers. Their tongues danced, exploring, and a growl of need in the back of his throat signaled his impatience for more. His hand moved under her blouse, but pulled back out, frustrating her and leaving her bereft until he ripped her shirt down the middle. He cursed, staring down at her, his brows pulled together.

"What's wrong?" she asked, grabbing him by the waistband. She undid his belt and started working on the button, applying pressure to the tempting bulge straining to be free.

"Damn back-hook bras. Where's that switchblade when I need it?"

Laughing, she stopped unzipping his pants and with a flick of her hand had her bra undone. She flung it and her ripped blouse across the room.

In his hurry, he tripped, falling on top of her.

"Well, hello there, miss. Come here often?" he asked with a wicked grin.

"Hiya, handsome," she replied with a giggle. "I hope to come very often. You?"

"Ditto." He shucked off his remaining clothes, and as she unzipped her skirt, he scooted it and her panties down her legs to the floor.

"Turn over," he growled. When she hesitated, he flipped her over and slapped her bare bottom. "On your knees."

"So help me, if you say *bitch,* I'll find my switchblade…" she replied through clenched teeth.

He smacked her ass again. "You know me better than that, Lovey." His hand rubbed where he'd smacked her, easing the sting. "*Fu-uck.*" He gave the word two syllables.

"Now what?" She gasped, surprised when a finger entered her slickness, followed by another, pumping in and out of her in a steady rhythm. When he crooked his fingers, hitting a spot rarely found, she jolted and whimpered with pleasure. *He's touching me, and I'm okay!*

"Condom."

"Bedside drawer. I can't believe Two-Time doesn't have one in his back pocket."

"Should I be offended that you don't realize I'm not wearing anything, let alone anything with pockets?"

She giggled as he ripped the foil packet open.

Grabbing her hips, he eased into her, allowing her time to adjust to his size. Impatient, she closed her eyes and rocked back. Mark moved slowly, his hands running up and down her back. It frustrated her.

Men. They never listen. What part of rough and hard didn't he understand?

"Harder," she ground out.

A resounding sting on her butt caused her to gasp and moan. He pulled out almost to the tip and slammed into her so hard she nearly collapsed. He kept a firm hand on her back as he pounded into her. The sound of their slick bodies bumping together heightened her need. An orgasmic pressure started low, escalating with his continued onslaught. In a burst of bright, hot light, it erupted, sending her over the edge. She screamed her release, and immediately Winston stood by the bed, growling.

Her limbs trembled, and she panted, coming down from the precipice. Mark released his hold on her neck and she collapsed, resting her face against the sheet. In this position he hit her cervix repeatedly. She winced and gripped the bed, embracing the pain. In a moment, he stiffened and groaned as he followed her into oblivion, falling on top of her. His breathing wheezed in torturous breaths.

Winston continued to growl, and Jinx summoned the energy to snap her fingers. With an indignant snort, the dog returned to his bed. Mark lay heavily on top of her for another moment before he kissed her shoulder and rolled off to dispose of the condom. Immediately the chill of post-coital awkwardness threatened.

Crawling back into bed, he pulled her into his arms.

"Cuddling isn't necessary," she whispered, praying he wouldn't leave. Her body tensed, ready for the rejection.

"I know."

She heard the smile in his words and relaxed.

"That was incredible," she admitted with a happy sigh.

It had been more than incredible; she'd been touched and hadn't freaked. And she was stone-cold sober. To top it off, she'd also had the orgasm to end all orgasms. She grabbed the cigarettes and lighter from her bedside table, handed Mark one, and lit them.

"My favorite cigarette," he replied with a grin.

She lay on her back, staring at the ceiling, and nodded as a single tear trickled down her cheek. Embarrassed, she rolled over, her back to Mark, and put out the cigarette. He reached over her and did the same, spooning her back.

"You don't have to stay," she choked out.

Why was she crying? Disgusted, she dashed the tears off her cheeks. She hated criers. *What's wrong with me?* He'd just given her the best orgasm of her life. She bit her lip, trying to stop the tears through self-inflicted pain.

"May I stay?" He pulled her closer and kissed her shoulder.

"Yes, of course."

His warm hand cupped her breast as he snuggled in closer. "It's normal."

"W-What?"

"Tears and orgasms, sometimes laughter—they're great tension relievers. You've been through hell the past few days. You're okay. Trust me." He kissed the back of her neck.

"Thank you." She closed her eyes, the pull of sleep too great to resist.

"And someday, I'm going to make love to you and whisper meaningless sweet nothings in your ear. And you'll like it," he murmured into her hair.

He's planning on a next time? She drifted off to sleep, a smile on her lips as a welcome peace enveloped her.

Chapter
Nine

*H*e reached out and caught hold of a long, blond braid. Pulling at it, he attempted to disentangle himself. The harder he tugged, the tighter it wrapped around his neck, choking off his air. Stars danced in front of his eyes, and his vision tunneled into darkness. Panic engulfed him as he struggled to break free, but the noose of hair tightened around his neck.

Mark bolted awake, blinking. A hand crept up his arm.

"About time you woke up." Soft lips kissed his neck; short blond hair tickled his nose.

Jinx. Not Harley. Your friend with frogging benefits.

The nightmare must have been triggered by that stupid text Harley had sent toward the end of his shift at the bar last night. He'd deleted it, but it remained inscribed in his memory.

It's time. See ya soon. Love you, H

It was past time he ended things with Harley. She'd also sent a text a couple of weeks ago, but he'd ignored it. In truth, a part of him didn't want to let go. His time with her had provided meaning for his life…though much of that he'd ultimately lost. He shoved her memory away, ignoring the heaviness in his heart.

He rolled over on top of Jinx, resting his head on one soft breast while he tweaked and kneaded her other nipple. She continued to caress his back while the steady thumping of her heart soothed his frazzled nerves. He didn't want to move. He was exactly where he wanted to be, and not just for the moment.

He'd had that thought more than once over the past two weeks, and it terrified him more than any damn dream, or nightmare, or whatever the hell it was.

"What time is it?" he croaked. He nuzzled into her neck, loving the smell of her citrus skin.

"Not early, not late. I don't have to be at work for a few hours. What time is your shift at the library?"

"Starts at nine. C'mere."

Jinx chuckled in his ear. "That gives us just over an hour. I've become a bad habit for you, Two-Time MacGregor."

Shit. She's right.

Since returning from Pine Bluff, he'd been with Jinx several times. Last night they'd ended up at his place, and the settling routine had seemed almost normal. She no longer pulled a switchblade on him during sex. Well, except three nights ago—but she'd worn her fuck-me boots and had simply twirled it in her hand before tossing it on the dresser. It had been hot as hell.

She liked it rough, and he liked being rough.

Sometimes.

It served their purpose—stress relief without intimacy. But the walls they'd built between them to separate feelings from physical needs were bothering him on some level he didn't really want to explore. He'd even found himself daydreaming yesterday about making love to her all night, slowly and tenderly. Of her allowing him to touch her gently and whisper love nonsense in her ear. Geezus, was he turning into some pussy-whipped fool? Maybe he was just rundown and tired. That had to be the answer. Working two jobs and taking classes was kicking his ass.

"At this rate, you'll be stuck buying me a Christmas present," she continued, reaching into the bedside drawer to pull out a condom.

Fuck. "I don't believe in Christmas," he replied tersely, panic settling in around his bachelorhood.

Her face fell for a shadow of a second. She shrugged and lowered her lashes. "Good, because I'm broke anyway."

Her voice had hitched, and unreasonably, it pissed him off that he'd probably just hurt her feelings. Avoiding hurt feelings was the mainstay behind his two-time rule, which he'd shoved out the window with this girl.

He'd rationalized their relationship as feeling sorry for her, knowing in his heart it wasn't true. He wanted her, in a real relationship. Period.

What a dumbass you are.

He did not, however, want the role of Prince Fuckin' Charming again. Been there, done that, and lost his heart to Harley. Nor did he want to be one of the king's men, because he knew Jinx's tough-girl persona was bullshit. Like Humpty Dumpty, she was just a whisper away from shattering.

Or maybe *he* was the damn egg? Because somehow, she'd managed to crawl into his goddamned life and glue the broken pieces of his heart back together. *And who asked her to do that?* He didn't even want a heart. It hurt too damn much when ripped open time after time by those who left him.

He scowled and scratched his scruffy morning beard, reaching for a cigarette. He lit one, offering the pack to Jinx, but she declined with a shake of her head.

"I didn't mean to imply we mean more to each other than friends with benefits." Jinx sat up, her voice cool. "Of course you don't have to buy me a present; it was a joke. As a matter of fact, I, uh, have plans for Christmas."

Mark tugged her onto her back. She closed her eyes, and he sighed as the chasm between them widened. What a goddamned mess. He didn't want to get emotionally involved, but he didn't want to hurt her, either. And he definitely didn't want to lose her.

I'm fucked.

"I didn't mean that the way it sounded," he offered.

She shrugged. "It's fine—actually, more than fine. I know I've overstayed my welcome. I appreciate your kindness to me over the past couple of weeks. You made things bearable." She kissed his lips and attempted to roll out from underneath him.

"Hey, don't go. Look, just because I fuckin' hate Christmas doesn't mean I want you to leave. Not yet."

"'Not yet,'" she parroted with a smile that didn't reach her sad eyes. "I get it." Her brow furrowed. "I think I'll leave now while I still have a shred of my dignity left intact."

"Jinx, you knew—"

Her laugh had a hollow ring to it. "Yes, I knew. It's fine. Really, I'm good. It's been great." She flipped him over and trailed kisses down his chest, working her way lower and lower. When she took him in her mouth, he moaned and watched her. He'd always found it sexy as hell and quite intimate to watch her go down on him. She would meet his gaze and hold it as she worked her magic, but not today. She kept her eyes downcast and continued her rhythmic, almost clinical onslaught until he knew he couldn't last much longer.

"Jinx." His balls tightened as he gave the man-code warning, knowing she'd swallow regardless. He stroked the top of her head, wishing she'd look at him.

She kept a firm hand on his chest, holding him down as she licked and sucked, ignoring his effort to have her look him in the face. He could easily have stopped her, but he didn't. The tension grew until he exploded deep in her throat, moaning her name as a well-satisfied euphoria settled over him. Spent and gasping for breath, he tousled her short hair fondly.

In that moment Christmas didn't seem so bad, after all. Come to think of it, spending it with Jinx would sure beat being alone. Derrick and Ava were headed to see her parents. His family would be in Colorado.

She placed a kiss on his lower abdomen and rolled off the bed, still not looking him in the face.

"Hey, where're you going? I owe you."

She slipped on her jeans and paused before zipping them, her back to him. "You don't owe me a thing, Mark."

No tears, no fits. The perfect girl, except for the flat, resigned voice. The sound of the zipper closing sounded uncomfortably final. She slipped into her bra and sweatshirt, keeping her back to him. Sitting on the side of the bed, she rammed her feet into her socks and shoes.

Mark rolled to his side and grabbed her around the waist, pulling her back to him. "Lovey, don't leave. Not like this. I didn't mean to hurt your feelings."

"Don't be ridiculous. I'm fine. I've got to let Winston out and do some stuff before I get ready for work. We're fine, Mark, really." She gave him a resigned smile.

She's not *fine. We're* not *fine.* "I'll see you later?" His heart hammered in his chest. *What the hell is wrong with me? Why am I pressing her? This is what I want, isn't it?*

"Sure. I'm performing with the band tonight at your bar." She gave him a kiss on the cheek, running the backs of her fingers over his beard stubble. She put her glasses on, and they might as well have been sunglasses, as shuttered as her eyes looked. An unfinished scotch sat on the bedside table. Jinx picked it up and finished it off.

"Hey, you shouldn't be drinking and driving," he cautioned.

She ignored him as she dug for her keys in her jeans pocket. "See ya."

"Okay." He captured her lips for a last quick kiss and watched her grab her jacket and purse. She gave him a little wave and walked out the door. And she was gone.

Jinx hurried down the steps from Mark's apartment, angry with herself. "Stupid, stupid, stupid."

He'd warned her.

Ava had warned her.

Even Derrick had pulled her aside earlier in the week to warn her.

Mark MacGregor was incapable of commitment. Sadly, that was exactly what she'd thought she wanted—until she got to know him.

She took out her phone to call Ava, but shoved it back in her purse after a moment, not wanting to hear the *I told you so.* Instead she grabbed a cigarette, but her hands were shaking too hard to get it lit.

"Need help with that?"

Jinx spun around, her heart pounding. The guy didn't make a move toward her and didn't appear to be threatening. She took a deep breath and relaxed a bit. A respirator rested on top of long, tangled blond hair. His hoodie and torn jeans were stained with paint. In his gloved hand, he held a spray can, which he shook in an almost hypnotizing manner. Tall and slender, he had striking blue eyes.

"What are you doing?" She pointed at the fresh graffiti on the side of the bar.

"Like it?" he asked, not looking the least bit remorseful. His eyes danced with devilment as his smile widened. Despite his unconventional look, he was one of the most beautiful men she'd ever seen.

"Well…" She surveyed the wall and had to admit, he had talent. "Yeah, it's great. But this is private property."

"Really? You own it?" His lips curved into a smile.

"No, but one of the owners lives up there." She pointed toward the top of the stairs. "And he might just beat the heck out of you when he sees this. If I were you, I'd leave."

"I'll take my chances. Now, did you need help with that cigarette?"

"No. I'm fine. I have to go." Worried, she glanced up the staircase. Mark could easily take this guy down. She'd seen sparks of his anger, and he outweighed him by at least thirty pounds of muscle.

"Why were you calling yourself stupid? Did the owner who's gonna whip my ass upset you?"

"None of your business. Look, I won't tell him I saw you, but you need to get out of here. He has to be at work at nine. He'll be down any minute."

"What's your name? Did you say nine? Is it really close to nine? Shit, time escapes me." He tossed the spray can in the air and caught it, his mesmerizing eyes never leaving hers. The sun burst from behind a cloud and cast a halo of light behind him.

"Jinx." *What's wrong with me? What possessed me to tell my name to some stranger throwing up illegal graffiti?* "It's almost eight thirty. Now go on, get out of here."

"How about I stick around and beat *his* ass for upsetting you? I can do it. And maybe you could buy me a beer afterward?"

Jinx rolled her eyes. "It's a little early to be drinking." Her conscience reminded her of the scotch she'd just downed. "Look, it's your funeral. Personally, I don't want to be around to see him. I mean…I don't want to see him beat your butt. Consider yourself warned." She turned and headed toward her car.

"Hey, Jinx!"

She unlocked her car and looked back at him.

"No man is worth it. Trust me on this one," he called out to her. "We're all dogs." He replaced the respirator over his face and went back to work.

All the way home, she berated herself for not sticking to the plan. This was her own fault; she'd pushed Mark further than he was willing to go. She needed to put her feelings aside and move on. Just because he'd put up with her didn't mean he cared. The past two weeks had probably been nothing more than sympathy fucks. *There.* She'd said it.

Mark would've been proud of her if she'd actually said it aloud and to him.

She'd miss him: his sense of humor, his innate sense of right and wrong, his patience with her hang ups. No ifs, ands, or buts. She was falling for him, but he wouldn't have it.

Pulling up to her home, she swallowed her disappointment and threw back her shoulders. It was fine. She'd get through this. She didn't need anybody.

Unlocking her door and punching in the code, she fell to her knees and wrapped her arms around the only male who loved her unconditionally.

Winston licked her face.

Chapter Ten

Four nights later, Jinx paced in front of the bar, her heels clicking with each step. Wanting to avoid Mark for as long as possible, she'd arrived at The Highland Hangout a mere fifteen minutes before she was scheduled to appear on stage. Muttering her new mantra, she exhaled the smoke from her third cigarette.

"I don't need anybody. I can do this."

It was her first night back with the band since the funerals. Like a chicken, she'd called off playing with them every time until now, citing various reasons from being sick to having to study. That was a joke, since she'd managed to bomb all of her finals over the past few days. Her heart just wasn't in school. Last night, she'd drowned her sorrows in a pity party and managed to subdue all feelings, thanks to her new BFF, vodka. She'd ignored Mark's voicemails, texts, and even the pounding on her front door. She'd been polite to Ava and the band members when they called to check on her, but didn't go into detail about what was really wrong. Pathetic as it was, her sister's and niece's deaths were turning out to be great excuses.

Judging by the parking lot, the place was packed—not surprising because this was the last Friday night before Christmas break. Stubbing out her cigarette, she took in the now-complete graffiti on the side of the building and wondered what Mark's reaction had been. The colorful, well-executed piece added to the ambience of the edgy bar.

Shoulders squared with false confidence, she walked in wearing low-riding black leather pants and a black cropped top. She'd painted her lips the same shade of red as her heels and wore her black wig.

"Hey, kid. You look hot as usual." Derrick's eyes scanned the crowd—he was the bouncer tonight. He looked handsome in his kilt, and a tight T-shirt emphasized his massive biceps. "I hear you're making your debut. No artwork, just singing?"

"Thanks, and yes. I'm nervous as heck."

"Want some liquid fortification? Mark will set ya up with anything you need."

"No, thanks." She'd already drunk half a pint sitting in her car. She refused to acknowledge Mark's presence but could feel him staring at her.

"Okay, well, shake a leg, or break a leg, whatever singers do."

Jinx laughed. "Unfortunately, that's likely in these shoes."

"Damn, girl, your outfit is bangin' tonight. I nearly didn't recognize you." The blond graffiti artist from the other day appeared next to her with a beer in his hand and a wide, easy grin on his face. Wearing the same torn jeans, but with a long-sleeved gray thermal shirt, he already had glassy eyes. His pupils were pinpoints, making the blue of his irises even more striking.

"My offer to beat the hell out of Mark's ass still stands. Not that I'd accomplish much more than getting my own ass beat, but hey, anything for a beautiful girl." He ran a thumb down her arm, flashing a seductive smile.

"You know Mark?"

"Well, yeah. He's older, closer to my brother's age than me, but I've known him for years. I'm Angel." He held out his hand and she shook it, smiling, sensing another lost soul.

"He knew you were painting his building?" She raised an eyebrow. "Wait, did you just say you're an angel?"

"Yeah, kinda," he replied with a shrug. "My *name* is Angel. I'm anything but one." He winked. "I slid into town and offered the artwork in exchange for a few meals and brewskis."

Jinx frowned over his shoulder, wondering why Derrick's eyes had narrowed. She raised her eyebrows, and Derrick shook his head.

Angel turned, saw him, and flipped him off. At the same time, Ava threw her arms around her neck, diverting her attention.

"Oh my God, girl! I'm so excited about tonight! You will rock it," she screamed in her ear.

Jinx smiled and ruffled her blue hair. It changed color at least twice a month. A stunning girl with beautiful skin the color of dark chocolate, Ava had an hourglass figure that turned more than a few heads. Jinx chuckled when Derrick's eyes zeroed in on Ava's generous breasts encased in a strategically torn, very tight Highland Hangout T-shirt. Jinx knew he'd make sure the guys kept their hands off his girl. God help anyone who didn't give Ava the respect Derrick deemed appropriate. He'd have his work cut out for him tonight.

Jinx took a deep breath and made her way on stage with the rest of the band. Will offered her a bottle of vodka they'd been passing around, and she downed a healthy swallow. Picking up the tambourine, she scooted toward the back next to Colin, who tapped out the start of the song with his drumsticks. She wasn't ready to be front and center yet, especially with Mark watching her.

For the first few numbers of the set, she sang backup and played the tambourine. As the vodka kicked in, she added some dance moves. Unable to see the intense eyes staring at her due to the stage lights, she still sensed Mark watching. The bitch in her wanted to make him miserable and jealous. The energy between the enthusiastic patrons and the band grew until it was as intoxicating as the alcohol.

In the zone, she didn't see Angel hop onto the stage until suddenly he was in front of her with his hands on her hips. Though his eyes were glassy, his lopsided smile was wide, and his moves bordered on raunchy. The crowd erupted. *Perfect.*

She matched him move for move, their dance seductive and fun. They danced so close only the fabric of their clothes separated them, yet his hands weren't grabby or touchy-feely. When the song ended, he gave her a high-five and a resounding kiss before stage diving into the cheering crowd. She giggled.

Will again handed her the bottle of vodka. Colin offered her water. She downed both.

The lights dimmed, giving her a moment to adjust her eyes. She glanced over at the bar, but Mark was nowhere to be found.

"Okay, Jinx, you ready?" Will asked.

Mark's absence gave her the courage to continue with her first solo song. It wasn't what the band had wanted to play, but they were humoring her and taking a break from the frenzied pace they'd been pounding out all night. She stepped to the mic and closed her eyes. She poured her misery and despair into the song about saying goodbye to an almost-lover. It was cathartic.

The song ended, and there was momentary silence. Nervously, she wondered if her rendition had been that bad. And then the place broke out in cheers and applause. Everyone stood, clapping and calling out for more…for *her*. She'd done it. Her first solo singing performance, and she hadn't bombed. Standing next to Angel, Ava was right in front, jumping up and down screaming her name.

Still in shock, she covered her mouth and stood there until Will hugged her tight. Self-consciously, she gave a little wave before exiting the stage. The rest of the band high-fived her, shouting their praises. Stealing a glance at the bar, she realized Mark had missed her performance. She didn't know whether to be relieved or sad.

Jinx grabbed her jacket and headed toward the door to catch a smoke. Worming her way through friends offering congratulations, drinks, and other less-desirable options, she kept moving, needing air and time to catch her breath.

The relative stillness outside was a balm to her battered nerves. She hurried through the patrons smoking in front of the bar to the back of the building, determined to enjoy a moment of solitude in the alley. She hadn't been back here since the night she'd met Mark. Since then they'd been going upstairs to his place for a quick smoke, hot sex, or a sweet make-out session during their breaks.

The light in the alley flickered on and off, and the moon disappeared behind the clouds. She lit her cigarette and glanced around, her senses heightened to the point of paranoia. Feeling uncomfortable, she decided to play it smart and head back toward the front of the building. At the sound of Mark's voice, she ducked into a shadow and stamped out her cigarette. The moon reappeared, giving the area an eerie, ghostlike appearance.

"I've missed you so damn much, Harley."

She flinched at the tenderness in his voice and bit her lip to keep from crying out. A blond woman, whose hair was so pale in the moonlight it appeared white, had her arms around his neck. Mark hugged her waist.

"You'll be there?" Her voice was soft and breathless.

"Of course. Always. Did you really ask that? You know I'd do anything for you, Harley. Any time, any place."

"I do know that. It's one of the many reasons I love you. I've missed you. It'll be good to spend some time together and settle everything."

"Love you, too."

The girl stood on her tiptoes and kissed Mark on the lips.

The words pierced Jinx's heart with a vicious intensity. And she only had herself to blame. Mark had never lied to her. He'd been honest and admitted he was a man-whore. Heck, that's why she'd sought him out. So where did this woman fit it? *She loved him? He loved her?* That didn't even make sense — but no matter. This was just the sad shot of reality she needed. She was merely another notch in Two-Time MacGregor's bedpost. She'd been nothing to him but a good time, and with her hang ups, maybe not even that.

The frosty air around her had nothing on the ice-cold blood running through her veins. She reviewed her options. She could rant, rave, and kick her way through the pieces of her battered heart, or she could quietly slip away and hold on to the bleeding remnants left in her aching chest. Hopefully the heart was an organ that would regenerate.

She decided to leave. Causing a scene would only lead to trouble. Turning, she frowned as Angel staggered around the corner and ran into her.

"Whoa, Jinx. Fuck girl, whatcha doin' out here? You score some shit? If so, hit me up. I'm crashin' fast."

"Angel? Jinx?" Mark's voice ricocheted down the alley.

Unable to respond, she found herself paralyzed by the numbing cold. She couldn't feel her heart beating. There simply wasn't enough of it left to pump the blood through her body.

"Jinx, what are you doing out here?" Mark asked from behind her.

She turned to face him and, with great reluctance, raised her eyes. The light in the alley flickered on, revealing the blond beauty beside him.

Her tight throat made it difficult to speak. "Who is she?"

"Jinx —"

Fire roared within her and enflamed her chilled body as she stepped forward. Mark frowned. She shoved as hard as she could against his chest, but he didn't budge. The man was like a boulder.

"*Who. Is. She?*" she ground out, hating the note of hysteria echoing in the alleyway.

"This is Harley. She's my—"

Debilitated by fury, Jinx's sole focus turned to getting as far away as possible before she exploded into nothingness. But her escape was sidetracked when her heel caught on a crack in the pavement. A wrenching throb seared through her ankle. Tottering, she fell, and a resounding *thwack* roared in her ears as white light exploded. The shadows in the alley loomed large and monstrous, overtaking her consciousness.

As the darkness surrounded her, the last thing she heard was the word *wife*. The final piece of her heart detonated.

"Jinx? Can you hear me? Wake up, Lovey."

"Holy fuck, Mark. Get out of the way and let the guys work."

"Shut up, Angel."

"How long has she been out?" an unknown male voice asked.

"Are either of you her emergency contact? No? Well, contact her family; we're taking her to the ER."

Hands ran up and down her body. She struggled to make them stop.

"Quit," she murmured, slapping the hands away.

Another stranger's voice, a woman's. "That's a nasty bump on the back of her head, and she may have broken her ankle."

Drifting through a tunnel of throbbing pain, Jinx felt herself being lifted. She was strapped down and couldn't move her neck or her arms. The sudden, jarring movements made her want to vomit as terror infused every muscle and nerve ending in her body. Desperate to be free, she fought, attempting to get away from the restraints that held her. *Please let me go, please stop!*

"Eugenia? Can you hear me? Open your eyes," the unfamiliar male voice called to her from the top of the tunnel she found herself trapped in.

The use of her name made her heart pound like a jackhammer. She stilled, terrified. *Please don't hurt me…*Sometimes if she pretended to be asleep, the darkness wasn't as scary.

"I've got a line," said the female voice.

A roaring sound whooshed in her ears, and fire seared through her arm as the darkness encroached once more. Despite her fear, she didn't move, or make a sound.

This was the only way to survive.

Three hours later, Mark held her hand with both of his, leaning his chin against it. "Come on, Lovey. Show me those whiskey eyes. Cuss me out, hit me, tell me to get lost, whatever. Just open your eyes…Please?"

No response.

Jinx had just been admitted to a room from the ER for observation. She'd drifted in and out of consciousness since arriving at the hospital. After a battery of tests, the doctors had assured Mark she was okay, but they refused to release specific information to him because he wasn't family. Her continued lethargy worried him, but the nurse assured him it was more medication-induced than anything.

Mark stood and paced back and forth, rolling and shrugging his shoulders to ease the tension. The door to the room swung open, revealing Jinx's parents. He'd called them when the ambulance had arrived to take Jinx to the hospital.

"Hi. How did you get here so fast? I mean, I'm glad…" He held out his hand, only to have it ignored.

Mrs. Howell moved like a wraith to the side of the bed, fear and pain shadowing her pale, drawn face. Mark knew it couldn't be easy having a daughter in the hospital again. Her father, on the other hand, looked perturbed at being inconvenienced. He stood with his arms crossed in front of his chest.

"We flew down in a private plane. Thank you for calling. Now that we're here, you can go. As soon as Eugenia's released, we'll take her home to Pine Bluff."

His dismissive manner pissed Mark off to no end, but he remained silent, knowing he had no right to be here, other than the fact that he cared.

A lot more than I realized.

He glanced at Jinx, who remained motionless, the color of the hospital sheets. He hated feeling this helpless, and his anger simmered just below the surface.

"I'd like to stay." He shoved his hands in his pockets, prepared to face off with Mr. Howell.

"I'm sure you would, but I think it best you go home to your *wife*." Mr. Howell smiled smugly as he played his trump card.

Mark's mouth dropped open. *How the hell?*

"Did you really think I'd let someone get involved with my daughter and not run a background check? You're also in debt for student loans and the bar you co-own." James examined his cuticles.

Mark flexed his hands in his pockets with an urge to punch the smirk off his face.

"Married?" Mrs. Howell gasped. The shocked look on her face stabbed his guilty heart.

"I, well…" Mark attempted to explain. "I—"

"I don't want to hear your excuses. Now get out before I call security." Mr. Howell gripped his arm, tugging him into the hall.

Mark could've easily pulled away, but he didn't want to cause a scene. He closed the door behind them.

"Get your goddamned hand off of me." He glared, wrenching his arm free.

"Go. Your presence upsets my wife, and my daughter doesn't need to be involved with a married man." Cold blue eyes bore into him, and Mark shivered. A frosty pall hung in the air, giving him a vague feeling of uneasiness.

"I need to talk to Jinx, to explain—" He stopped and glanced behind him when the man made a motion with his head. A serious-looking hospital security guard walked toward him.

Mark threw up his hands in surrender. "I'll leave. But it isn't what you think, and I *will* explain everything to Jinx—"

Before he could finish, Jinx's father spun around and entered her room, shutting the door.

Mark huffed with frustration and motioned the guard away. "I'm leaving. I'm leaving, goddammit." He marched to the stairway exit. The slamming of the metal door echoed behind him in the stairwell.

Jinx opened her eyes and smiled, feeling safe. "Mother," she whispered, squeezing the thin hand holding hers.

As her eyes focused, her mom's appearance startled her. Although still stylishly dressed, her mother's clothes hung loose on her bony frame. Her light brown eyes were lost and troubled, making her seem distant and unreachable, just like that time before she'd gone away when Jinx was seven.

Jinx had often wondered what had drawn her parents together; they were so opposite. Always subservient to her father, her mother never voiced her own opinion. She was like a beautiful, colorful parrot. The summer after Jinx's seventh birthday, something had changed, dramatically. Mother had stayed in bed in a dark room, almost catatonic. When Jinx asked her father what was wrong, he'd blamed Jinx's misbehavior for her mother "not feeling well."

One night, like a ghost, Mother had leaned over and kissed her good night, whispering *I love you*. The next morning, she was gone. And after a huge fight with Daddy, Karen left for boarding school. Only Mae provided the security and comfort Jinx had needed, feeling lost and abandoned during the six months her mother was institutionalized for a nervous breakdown.

But now her mother was here, and her presence brought Jinx reassurance. When Mother was here, the darkness stayed away. Jinx squeezed her hand, hoping she'd stay, not wanting to be alone.

"You're going to be fine, Eugenia. It was just a bump on your head." Mother removed her hand and glanced toward the door with a weak smile. "Your father's here. He's in the hall."

Jinx forced a harsh, wheezing breath through her clenched teeth. The door creaked open.

"Eugenia." Daddy leaned in and kissed her cheek, and the cloying smell of his aftershave made her nauseous.

The room started spinning like a merry-go-round, and she closed her eyes.

"Lila, why don't you go get me a cup of coffee, my dear?"

The solicitous tone he used when speaking to her mother never failed to rile Jinx. Just once, she wished her mother would tell him to go frog himself. But did she really have any room to criticize? Her father still intimidated the heck out of her.

Jinx opened her eyes and watched her mother nod in her robotic manner before leaving to do her father's bidding. When the door closed behind her, Jinx sucked in a shallow breath and tightened her grip on the sheet. An overwhelming dread crept from her stomach to her tight throat, and the pounding in her head intensified. He was likely mad at having had to come down here.

"Baby girl, as soon as the doctor says you can go home, I think it best you come back to Pine Bluff with us to recuperate." His steely eyes locked on hers. He sat on the side of the bed and brushed a lock of her hair off her face. She vaguely wondered what had happened to her wig.

"I-I've got to work."

"Just for Christmas. Your mother needs you." He cupped her cheek with his hand. "I need you, baby girl."

Green bile spewed from her mouth down her gown and onto her father's pressed navy trousers. It happened so fast it caught them both unaware.

"I'm sorry," she stuttered, her heart slamming in her chest. Raising a shaky hand, she wiped her mouth as her father stood.

A feeling of helplessness overcame her, and her limbs felt like lead. Without a word, her father went to the sink and sponged off his pants with a damp paper towel. If he was angry, for once he didn't show it. When he'd finished, he ran a washcloth under the water, rung it out, and came back to her bedside.

"It's all right," he murmured as he washed her face and dried her tears. "I just thought it would help your mother if you were home for Christmas. It won't be easy this year with Luke still in Birmingham for rehab. The house will be too quiet, too sad without Karen and Elizabeth. Your mother and I have felt lost…" His voice trailed off as he walked toward the door. "I'll get a nurse to help you change your gown and sheets." He stopped at the door and turned to look back at her. "We won't mention *anything*, will we? I wouldn't want to disappoint your mother or upset her unnecessarily. She's once again fragile and may need to go somewhere to rest."

Jinx swallowed and shook her head, not daring to look away. For some reason she felt like he was talking about something more than not coming home for Christmas.

Mark pounded on the door and blew on his hands for warmth. He should've worn a coat, not just a Highland Hangout sweatshirt and jeans. It was colder than usual, but appropriate weather for Christmas Eve. Once he got things straightened out with Jinx, he'd love to take her someplace where it snowed. Snow was such a rare occurrence in the South. Or maybe he'd fly her to the Caribbean. Jinx in a bikini would be nice. *Like I have the money to do either.*

He'd stalled for six days, unsure how to clear up the misunderstanding with her about his relationship with Harley. He'd used work as his excuse for not coming over sooner or calling to check on her, but truth was, it was a douchebag, cowardly-as-fuck move. Even Derrick had told him so. She was injured, not just mad at him.

The door cracked open, and amber eyes circled by deep purple smudges peered at him from behind the flimsy chain on the door.

Sighing, she lowered her eyes to his chest. "What do you want?"

"That chain is pitiful and wouldn't provide any protection against an intruder. You need a peephole. It's dangerous to open your door like this."

He'd kick the door in himself, if needed, to get to her. The door closed and then opened. He was nearly knocked to the ground when Winston stood and put his paws on his shoulders, panting happily.

"Okay, so maybe you have adequate protection. Hey, ol' buddy, you glad your mama's home?" He ruffled the dog's fur.

"Some guard dog, you are," Jinx muttered. "And I have an alarm. Thanks for *caring*." Her sarcasm was as thick as molasses.

Winston panted with excitement and licked Mark's face. Jinx stood with her hands on her hips, which only enhanced the view. Hard, pink nipples underneath her almost sheer white tank top made it virtually impossible to pull his eyes away. Mark wanted to think they'd hardened in response to seeing him, but the goose bumps dotting her skin made it difficult to say. She crossed her arms, clearly annoyed.

"It's cold as fuck out here," he noted. "May I come in?"

She paused for a few seconds, as if thinking, then stepped aside. He lowered Winston to the ground and followed her, closing the door and leaning on it. Shoving his hands in his pockets, he paused, nervous now that he faced her.

She wandered over to the mantle, picked up an almost empty bottle of vodka, and finished it off with a swallow.

"Are you supposed to be drinking with a head injury?"

She didn't reply, her face blank.

"I, uh, wanted to check on you. I didn't want to bother you while your mother was here. I know your parents don't care for me. Your dad told me he was taking you to Pine Bluff to recuperate."

She didn't say anything, so he continued.

"But Ava told me you were, uh, still here with your mom. I, um… Fuck…I have no excuse except cowardice." He patted Winston's head as he gazed at her.

The dark circles surrounding her bloodshot eyes and obvious weight loss concerned him. The hipbones he loved nibbling and licking were even more prominent in her black yoga pants, as were the ribs beneath her collarbone.

"How's your hard head?" he asked, hoping to get a smile from her.

Jinx turned away and shrugged into a yellow sweater. Her silence unnerved and infuriated him at the same time. Lifting canvases and drop cloths around her studio, she searched until she found her cigarettes. She held the pack out to him, but he declined with a shake of his head. Her hands shook like an alcoholic in DTs as she lit one. She inhaled deeply and let it out slowly, as if buying time before responding.

"I'm fine. The headaches are better, ankle just has a bad sprain. I'm supposed to wear a boot…" She shrugged and, folding her legs underneath her, sank to the floor. "How's your wife?" Her eyes blazed.

Mark paced with a restlessness he couldn't contain. Now that he'd seen her, he wasn't sure this was the right time to discuss Harley. "Look, Jinx. It's complicated—"

She sprang back to her feet and winced. "Yes, I know. I know. She doesn't understand you. She's lousy in bed, she nags, whatever. Just save it, Mark. It doesn't really matter because, quite frankly, I don't care." She limped toward the window, not making eye contact with him.

Mark grabbed her wrist. "That's not true, Lovey, and you know it. You *do* care! And you're not fine, you're in pain, and I've royally fucked shit up by not telling you—"

"Jinx? Where'd ya go? This bed is freezing-ass cold, come back."

Mark's nostrils flared, and his eyes narrowed. He dropped her arm as if burned.

"I'll be there in a sec, Angel," Jinx called.

Her eyes swept to the floor before she raised them to meet his with a defiant look.

"What the hell is Angel Sinclair doing here?" he demanded.

Jinx shrugged. "It isn't any of your business, but at least he isn't *married.*"

Hanging his head in defeat, Mark blew out an exasperated sigh. "I told you, I can explain everything."

"I don't want, nor need, an explanation. You and I were friends who occasionally fooled around, although it would've been nice to know your marital status. I don't do married men. Anyway, I've moved on, and you can go back to your wife—unless you have anything else to say?" She aimed a pointed look at the door.

Goddammit. He liked Angel, he really did. But the thought of him with Jinx angered and worried him. Angel had some serious issues. Derrick had caught him shooting heroin four days ago and given him a choice: rehab or leave.

Angel had left.

And Jinx is mine.

"You don't need to get involved with—"

She interrupted him, fire flashing in the depths of her eyes. "Who I'm involved with isn't your concern. Now, is there anything else? Angel needs me."

Her face settled back into a carefully composed look of disdain as she stared at his chest. His emotions jumped the track from wanting to grab that stubborn chin and kiss her senseless to wanting to ram his fist through the door. *Goddammit.*

"Nope. It was great while it lasted." He paused and added with a sneer, "Make sure you get tested. Angel's a fuckin' junkie. See ya around."

Mark squelched the urge to storm to the back room and tear Angel apart with his bare hands. *What is it with these goddammed Sinclair brothers and my girls?* Instead he left, slamming the door behind him with enough force to shake the windows and bring her neighbor outside.

It was best things ended like this. Maybe not neat and clean, but at least it was over, not a prolonged goodbye. He already had too much shit going on in his life. He didn't need to add a troubled pixie to the mix.

Pulling the jewelry box out of his jeans pocket, he tossed it in the air a few times. With every ounce of his anger and frustration, he threw it at her front door.

Merry Fuckin' Christmas, Jinx.

Jinx locked the door and sank to the floor, her weak legs unable to hold her up another moment. Covering her face with her hands, she sucked in a ragged breath. Winston whimpered, nudging her shoulder with his massive head. She scratched him behind the ears, feeling his despondence.

"I know. I liked him, too," she whispered.

The sound of something hitting her door made her jump. Her sprained ankle protested as she stood and hobbled to the window. Mark sped off, nearly hitting another car in his haste. She opened the front door and stared at the small wrapped Christmas present lying battered on her doorstep.

Her hands trembled as she opened it. Inside she found a silver heart locket engraved with the word *Jinxed*. Inside was a tiny selfie of her with Mark and on the other side a picture of Winston. It was the most thoughtful gift she'd ever received.

He's married. It doesn't mean anything.

Behind her, Angel staggered to the bathroom; the sound of vomiting soon followed. Jinx sighed and reluctantly limped back to help. She found him curled in the fetal position by the toilet. Stepping over him, she wet a washcloth and mopped his face, rubbing his back. His T-shirt and jeans were drenched with sweat, and he shook uncontrollably.

Tears streamed down his face, and his teeth chattered so hard, she was afraid they might crack.

"I changed my mind. I can't do this. Please, just give me something, anything. It doesn't have to be heroin; any kind of pain pill will help." He pulled himself up and once again heaved into the toilet.

"Let me take you to the hospital. I'm not a nurse. I don't know what to do." She tried to keep the panic out of her voice, but Angel's withdrawals scared her. His pupils were so large it was hard to see his blue irises, and he had to be dehydrated. He'd been going through this for three days.

"No," he choked out and closed his eyes. "Just get out. If you can't help me, get the fuck out." Tears streamed down his haggard face.

"Why don't you try to sleep this off?" She should've asked Mark to help her. He was Angel's friend.

"Goddammit, don't be stupid. This isn't a hangover. I'm in fuckin' withdrawals. I haven't slept or eaten anything in days. Everything hurts—even my eyelids hurt. I'm fucking dying…Just a little something, any kind of pain pill," he begged between dry heaves.

Overwhelmed by her scattered emotions, she didn't move or say anything else, not knowing what to do. This was the topper to her crappy week, and it was too much. Dealing with Mark, exams, her parents, and now an addict in active withdrawal wanting her to score drugs was too much to handle. And she was out of vodka. She'd bought two bottles after putting her mom on a flight home.

She hadn't shared with Angel.

The need to get away grew. Racing to the bedroom, she found her phone and scrolled through her contacts. It was Christmas Eve.

Her parents had gone to Key West after she told them she wasn't coming home. Matt would still be at the rehab place with Luke. Ava and Derrick were out of town for the holiday. Even the guys with the band had gone home. Like Angel, she had no one.

Returning to the bathroom, she found him weakly attempting to clean up his mess. She leaned against the doorjamb, watching. "I'll do it; just go back to bed."

He shook his head and dashed away his tears. "I'm sorry, Jinx. I shouldn't be here. I shouldn't have yelled at you. You're a nice girl, and I'm a sorry-ass junkie and a terrible person. You're not the only friend I've let down." He tossed the soiled towels in the hamper and rinsed his vomit-soaked T-shirt under the faucet. "I'll leave."

"No. Don't go. I can't have you on the street; I'll help you get through this."

Swaying on his feet, Angel sank to the floor in the bathroom, his back against the wall. He looked at her with watery eyes and whispered, "Why are you being so nice to me? I got nothing to give in return. I *am* nothing."

"I'm not that nice," she blurted. "I had vodka, but it's gone. I drank it all. I'm so sorry."

He gave a bitter laugh. "All's fair in love and addiction. I probably wouldn't have been able to hold it down, and I would've done the same damn thing."

"I guess we all have problems, and right this second, all we have is each other." She paused. "It's Christmas, Angel. Neither one of us needs to be alone."

He nodded and sighed. "Is this our fuckin' Christmas past, present, or future?"

"If you don't get clean, there won't be a future."

"Sometimes I wonder if that would be so bad. What have I contributed to this world?"

"Your story isn't over. You have to fight this."

He looked at her sadly. "Remember those words, Jinx. We can't keep running from our demons."

"I know. But for today, let's just ignore them."

"Minute by minute, hour by hour, day by day. All we have is each other. It's a tenet of recovery." He reached out and took her hand. "Thank you for reminding me. Someday, this shit might stick…"

Chapter
Twelve

Mark wiped down the bar in preparation for ringing in the new year, glad the damn holidays were almost over. After the fight with Jinx on Christmas Eve, everything had gone downhill. Christmas had been lonely and hard; it always was. He mourned the loss of loved ones more keenly in this season. And this year, it had been more difficult than ever, compounded by the two women no longer in his life: Jinx, who'd hooked up with Angel, of all people, and Harley, who'd gone back home, leaving him with nothing but his memories and regrets. If he'd asked, his parents would've welcomed him, or his sister, Claire, but he didn't want to impose his depression on them. Only Harley knew all his secrets—from his fear of abandonment to the greatest loss in his life—and now it was official; they were over, getting a divorce.

Harley Taylor. He'd fallen hopelessly in love with her when they were teenagers. They'd married for all the right reasons and stayed married for the wrong ones. He'd always love her. And in his heart, he knew she still loved him. But they'd grown up and apart. As much as he hated to admit it, she was right. They were better as friends.

This past week, he'd come to the painful realization that he'd failed at every relationship in his miserable life: his mother, his adoptive family, Harley, and now Jinx. For five days he'd drowned his self-pity in expensive scotch and cheap beer. When Derrick and Ava had showed up the day after Christmas and found him passed out, they'd threatened to ship him off to a damn rehab.

Maybe he should've gone and dragged Angel with him. God knows he'd failed Angel, too. Angel had looked up to him when they were kids. Together, they'd pulled pranks, skidded on the wrong side of the law, and enjoyed plenty of drugs and alcohol. But Angel hadn't let go. Now he was so far immersed in his addiction, Mark feared he was lost forever.

This morning, after two pots of coffee, a handful of ibuprofen, a pack of cigarettes, and some serious soul-searching, Mark had circled back to the conclusion that he was never meant to be involved in a meaningful relationship. Just ask Harley. Or any of the women he'd been with over the years. He'd learned long ago not to get attached to people, not to risk the heartache; the end result was always the same.

Sure, I cared about Jinx, but it was just about the sex. The girl had a wicked mouth and serious talent…

He threw the rag down. *Who the fuck am I kidding?* There was something about her that made him want to hold on, a haunting vulnerability encased in barbed wire.

During his week-long bender, despite all the warnings to stop, his mind had kept straying back to the girl with whiskey-colored eyes and a shitload of issues. He'd never met anyone as fucked up as she was, and for some damn reason, he was drawn to her, even now that he was clearheaded.

He busied himself filling popcorn bowls and setting up the bar for the busiest night of the year. Thinking about work was better than thinking about feelings. *And pixies.* Work made sense. Feelings and pixies were a mystery.

Will and the band entered the bar with shouts and laughter. Casually, he looked for Jinx. Pride had kept him from asking Ava about her. He hadn't seen her since Christmas Eve when he'd found her with Angel. His eyes narrowed when she strutted in a few minutes later. Not once did she glance toward the bar as she embraced Ava and then Derrick—or rather, they embraced her. She stood ramrod straight, giving Ava an awkward pat on the back. Hell, no wonder he was attracted to her. She was as ill at ease with relationships as he was. It was pure physics. Like attracts like.

Ava jumped up and down, smoothing a hand over her non-existent baby bump. Jinx's heavily rimmed eyes widened, and a genuine smile cracked her restrained exterior. Mark chuckled. Ava was only a few weeks along. Poor Derrick was still getting used to the idea of being a father, and Ava had the kid's future all mapped out, complete with an anticipated Ivy League college education. *As if.* Derrick was a diehard LSU alum.

Mark was happy for them. Maybe even jealous. It seemed like only yesterday since he'd anticipated the same…

Gripping the bar, he reached for a shot glass, but stopped. This maudlin trip down memory lane had to end or he'd lose his shit, and alcohol wasn't the answer. He took a deep breath. Looking up, he found Jinx staring at him. For one second, her eyes appeared unguarded and filled with an overwhelming sadness. She looked away and turned her attention to Will.

Mark scowled, hating the spiky black wig and the heavy makeup of her stage persona. Tonight she wore jeans with strategically torn rips that revealed a hint of her delightful ass cheek and knees. A ripped band T-shirt barely covered her perky breasts and left her stomach bare, making her just covered up enough to provide a fantasy. Her famous stiletto boots only added to the picture.

Mark didn't need the fantasy. Instead he found himself longing for the real Jinx—naked, with tousled blond hair and her face free of makeup. He wanted her body beneath him, her warm breath fanning his skin…

"Yo. Earth to Mark." Fingers snapped in front of him.

He blinked and glared at Derrick's smug smile.

"You'll have plenty of time to moon over Jinx after your shift. I need you to make sure the bartenders and waitstaff stay on top of it tonight. Stay focused, lover boy."

"Shut the fuck up, asshole," Mark snapped.

Derrick threw his head back and laughed.

Drink orders piled up as fast as the bar filled, leaving no time to stay angry. It would be a profitable night. Mark hustled to pour the drinks, barked at two waitresses arguing over a tip, and roared at Billy to move his ass and work, not flirt with the patrons. Then the Spellcast Socialists started playing, and the place erupted.

Out of the corner of his eye, he watched Jinx moving her hips as she painted. The band was playing a new piece, not a cover. Will wailed about slamming doors on unspoken feelings, and Jinx joined him on the chorus, her eyes closed as her voice harmonized about lost opportunities.

It pricked his conscience almost as much as the song about almost-lovers she'd sung the night of her accident. He'd been talking to Harley in the office and had stopped to open the door and listen.

This time it was Billy yelling at *him* to get his ass in gear and back to work. For the remainder of the evening, Mark hustled orders out and didn't have time to pay attention to the music from the stage, but he remained cognizant of *her* presence.

Ten, nine, eight… The entire bar chanted the New Year's countdown and toasted one another with drinks, hugs, and kisses. Will played a raucous, heavy-metal version of "Auld Lang Syne," and Mark noticed he wasn't the only one not participating. Jinx had quietly put her paintbrush down and now wiped her hands with a cloth, looking detached and uninterested in her surroundings.

Ava bounced into Derrick's arms, and Mark watched with a growing emptiness as people paired up, immersed in the joy permeating the air. It was basic human nature to long for hope and new beginnings. He motioned to Billy that he was taking a break and stepped outside for a smoke. Forgoing the alley, he took the stairs toward his apartment but halted midway there, eyelevel with his favorite boots. His gaze ran up the torn jeans. He fought the urge to lick the kneecap taunting him.

Her gaze met his, but her face was void of expression. Only the pounding pulse at her throat gave her away. She exhaled a stream of cigarette smoke mixed with chilled night air.

"Care if I join you?" he asked.

Jinx shrugged. "They're your steps." Her hands trembled as she zipped up her leather jacket.

Mark lit his smoke and collapsed onto the step next to her dangerous-looking shoes. "How's Angel?" he asked, proud that his voice sounded calm—polite, even.

"Okay. He's at an NA meeting tonight."

Mark raised his eyebrows. "Really? That's great." He meant it.

"It's been a rough week," Jinx admitted softly. She stamped out her cigarette. "So what's your New Year's resolution?" Elbows on her knees, she rested her chin on her fists, staring at him with an unnerving intensity.

"Not to make a resolution I know will be broken."

A smirk lingered at the corner of her lips, but pain flickered across her face. "Sounds perfect for you—no commitment." She glanced away, settling her features until they were once again a mask of apathy.

Unreasonably, it pissed him off.

"And yours?" He stamped out his cigarette.

"I don't believe in looking to the future. Day to day is hard enough." She crossed her arms in front of her chest and pulled her feet closer, withdrawing into herself.

"Well, that's depressing; surely you have some goal in mind."

"Nope. I believe in living in the moment." She rose to leave, and he leaped to his feet, blocking her descent. Standing a step below her, he almost met her eye to eye.

"Don't leave." The words tumbled from his mouth before he could stop them.

"I have to go back to work. Don't you?"

"Look, we need to talk. I don't like the way things ended. Let me explain—"

Cold fingers pressed against his lips. "There's no need to explain anything." She leaned forward, her warm breath on his face as she kissed his cheek. "Friends with benefits. That's all we were. I appreciate all you've done for me, but due to our convoluted meeting, things were getting too personal…"

"That's bullshit, and you know it." He drew her into his arms, holding her close. "I'm not asking for anything but a conversation later," he whispered. When she shook her head no, he added, "Please? I'm begging, Mistress Jinx."

Begging? *Am I drunk?* No. *Just stupid.*

Pissed off at himself, he turned to leave.

Jinx gave a small laugh. "Okay, since you begged. I'll call Angel and tell him I'll be late. He can take Winston for his walk."

Mark looked back at her and nodded. *Dumbass. She's with Angel now.*

Stepping aside, he watched her walk down the steps. When she reached the bottom, she spun around to face him. "Complete honesty, or I'm out of here."

"As long as it's a two-way street, Lovey."

Jinx rapped on the door and shivered. Her breath swirled in front of her face. She had no idea why she'd agreed to this. Honesty wasn't even in her vocabulary. Earlier, she'd lied about her plans for the future, maybe because she wasn't sure. Will had asked her to go on the road with the band. It would mean ditching school.

But it would also provide a way to get away from Mark.

Shaking in the cold night air, she turned to leave. Then the door opened, and she almost licked her lips at the sight of Mark clad only in his kilt. She warmed as she stared at his bare chest. She wanted to pull him to her and rake her nails down his back.

"Hey, come on in. I just got here and was about to change clothes." Mark smiled, motioning her to enter with his glass of scotch.

"No need to get dressed on my account," she quipped as he closed the door behind her.

He chuckled. "I see. Is this your opener to honest conversation? If so, I like it."

Shrugging out of her jacket, she let it drop on the arm of the couch. "Whatever."

She accepted the glass of scotch and took a gulp, loving the burn in the back of her throat. Handing it back to him, he polished it off. With a sweep of his arm, he indicated for her to sit. She slipped off her boots and tucked her feet under her as she curled into the couch.

When he sat next to her, the smell of his aftershave and the sight of his carved chest and abs made her stomach clench with need. They sat in an awkward silence for a few moments, not meeting each other's gaze.

Mark let out a huff of breath. "Okay, so I'll start. I'm sorry about the way you found out about Harley."

Jinx folded her arms in front of her chest. "I don't like men who cheat on their wives," she spat, before reeling in her anger.

"Look, it's not like that." He clasped his hands together and looked at the floor before speaking further. "Well, technically, I guess it is. I mean we're married, but not together. We haven't been for years."

"Isn't that what all cheaters say? Don't forget to add the '*she doesn't understand me*' line."

"I'm being honest. She and I parted ways years ago. We just never made the parting legit…" He shook his head and paused, as if reflecting on what to say. "We married too young. The marriage was doomed from the beginning."

Perfect. He wants to speak in riddles. She stood. "I'm tired and don't feel like playing games." He yanked her back onto the couch and pinned her beneath him. Glacier blue eyes glared at her.

"Get up one more time and I'll tie you down. Understand?" He raised one eyebrow and his gaze lowered to her now-hardened nipples. His smirk widened into a megawatt smile.

Hot, shameful need pooled between her legs as embarrassment flooded her cheeks.

"Get off me," she hissed between clenched teeth.

"Harley and I are getting divorced. It's over. She came down a few weeks ago to discuss it and get the ball rolling. I'm sorry you found out that way. That's it."

She no more believed that was "it," than she believed in Santa Claus or happily-ever-afters. She wiggled her wrists, unable to break free of his hold, and truthfully, not really wanting to. Her chest heaved with her sharp inhalation. Her mind turned to mush, and every nerve in her body sped to high alert as she lay trapped underneath him.

She shouldn't be enjoying this. Had he turned the heat up? She could feel a trickle of sweat inching down her back. *This is wrong.* Spots danced before her eyes, and she closed them.

"Why don't you like to be touched?" he asked softly. "Or is it just me?"

Her eyes flew open and she struggled to get loose, but again her effort proved futile.

"Answer me," he commanded.

She turned her face from him; irrationally afraid his penetrating stare had some sort of superpower.

"Goddammit, you wanted the honesty. Now answer me." He let one of her wrists loose, and it was all the leverage she needed. She had her switchblade out of her pocket and snapped open before he could react.

She held it to his throat and ground out, "Because. I. Don't. Like. It." *I don't know!*

"Liar." He climbed off her and stormed to the kitchen, returning with the bottle of scotch. Not bothering with a glass this time, he turned it up and drank, wiping his mouth with the back of his arm as he glared at her.

"I'm not lying. If you're not man enough to get a girl off without—"

"Shut the fuck up, Jinx. If you can't be honest, at least be honest about not being honest."

His eyes softened as he moved back toward her. She watched him, leery of what he might do, but refusing to cower. Raising her chin, she glared up at him, still holding the blade. He took his thumb and pulled it across her bottom lip, loosening it from her teeth. The metallic taste of blood filled her mouth.

"You're bleeding." He pulled her off the couch and toward the bathroom. Wetting a washcloth, he held it to her lip. "You weren't even aware you'd bitten your lip, were you?"

Flicking the blade shut, she kept it in her hand, not looking at him. The unspoken words formed a lump in her throat. Physical pain meant nothing to her. At times, she even needed it to remind herself she wasn't completely dead, just emotionally so.

"Why won't you let me in, my sweet pixie? I don't want to hurt you," he murmured as he washed the heavy makeup off her face. He took off her wig and tossed it to the counter, tousling her short blond hair.

"I'm not a math problem to be figured out."

"No, you're so much more. A complex, sexy, funny, but troubled woman." He placed her on the counter and stood between her legs. "And cute as hell when you wear your glasses, but scary as fuck with that damn switchblade."

She flicked it open and ran the blade from his kilt to his neck, pressing hard enough to mark the skin but not break it. His nostrils flared and pupils dilated, but he didn't move.

"I think you like scary," she purred.

A slow smile spread across his face. "Honestly? I think you're right." With his forehead to hers, he rested his fists on either side of her thighs. "Now answer my question."

"Do you love Harley?"

"Yes, but it's complicated. We aren't together anymore; the marriage is over. Your turn. Answer my question, Jinx. Why are you afraid of being touched, letting loose?" He backed up a step, crossing his arms in front of his chest. "Or you can leave."

"I don't know." Tucking her fingers in the waistband of his kilt, she pulled him back toward her and licked his chest, her fingers fumbling with the buckle on his kilt. "You don't want me to leave," she whispered, determined to use sex to get out of the question.

That's what she did: use sex to avoid intimacy.

"No, I don't." He stilled her hands. "But you're going to be honest and answer me, or leave."

But I can't. Because I don't know.

How could she explain that some unknown fear made her anxious all the time? The only thing that helped anymore was alcohol.

Jinx hopped off the counter, but he didn't budge, and the impressive bulge under his kilt pressed into her stomach. He reached around her, placing his fists on the counter, caging her against his immovable body. Pressing her face to his chest, she closed her eyes and inhaled, taking comfort in his presence. He always made her feel safe.

"I can't talk about it. That's as honest as I can get."

"That's not good enough. Did someone hurt you?"

She held her breath, not moving, and kept her eyes closed. *I don't know.* The crux of her biggest fears were these black holes in her memory. She was crazy like her grandmother. Her knees sagged, and strong arms wrapped around her, holding her. He kissed the top of her head. Pulling herself together, she did what she always did. She lied.

"N-No."

"Sure?"

"No, no one hurt me," she replied, more firmly.

"Okay. Breathe, Lovey. I've got you."

She drew in a deep breath, willing her hammering heart to slow down. "I'm fine. Quit trying to be a psychiatrist, Mark. I just need to eat."

He sighed. "So much for honesty." Pulling away, he ran a hand through his hair. "Look, I don't know what I was thinking. You're right: I can't commit, and you can't be honest. Can we at least be friends?"

"With benefits?" she asked, looking at the wall behind him. *Friends? Could I ever be friends with him and not want more?*

No. And that was her problem.

He shrugged. "I'm not sure that's going to work for us right now, but we can leave our options open. As long as you know it isn't anything permanent. What about Angel? Where does he fit in to this?"

She tucked away her disappointment. What had she expected? She wasn't loveable. She was useable. Like a throwaway container. And crazy. Her own father didn't even like her.

Strike first, strike hard, before being struck. That was her father's motto. A shiver ran up her spine. A small part of her wanted to assure Mark she wasn't interested in Angel like that. But her wounded pride kept her mouth shut.

She gave a noncommittal shrug and the loosest honest answer she could. "We're still exploring our relationship. I need to go home. I'm hungry and really tired." She ran a finger along the grout of the tiled counter.

When she'd told him she wanted total honesty, she'd been lying. She wanted honesty from *him*, even knowing she could never reveal her own darkness. If people knew she had memory lapses, they'd send her away like her grandmother, or overmedicate her like her mother. Plus, words could haunt you, even if your memory was blank. Her parents were pros at throwing stuff back in her face and hanging on to past mistakes. In her experience, love was a weapon.

"I'll make you a sandwich."

"No, thanks. Really, I need to check on Angel and make sure he took Winston for a walk."

His face fell, and he looked at the ceiling for a moment. "Jinx? If I asked you to stay, would you?"

Oh how she wanted to say yes, to have him hold her and tell her everything would be all right. That she was all right.

But nothing was right and never would be. She couldn't do it; she'd end up hurting him in the end. Better to make a clean break of it now.

"Nope, 'fraid not. Like you said, it probably wouldn't work out."

Chapter Thirteen

Nine months later

September in New Orleans was really no different than August, except for football fans wandering the streets. In this part of the country, the air remained heavy with humidity. Nevertheless, this was a special night at The Highland Hangout: a private, invitation-only party to celebrate Ava and Derrick's wedding and the birth of their daughter, Lena. The happy noise from inside reminded Jinx of Mardi Gras — festive chaos. Too bad she felt more like Ash Wednesday.

Shaking out her apprehension, she paced in front of the building, unable to enter. *Why am I so nervous? I'm over him. It's been nine months.* She and the band had rolled in today for a quick stop as a gift to Derrick to thank him for giving them their first break. Their following was slowly growing as they now toured and played festivals and bars. In a few months they were cutting their first single.

During her time away, she'd analyzed and compartmentalized her feelings for Mark, rationalizing that it had been her grief that had made her so needy and ridiculous around him. There was no other explanation for the way she'd let her guard down and fallen for Two-Time MacGregor.

Back on a track and keeping themselves in the friends-with-benefits zone, they'd even exchanged a couple of friendly calls and texts…

And then there was that night of drunken phone sex a couple months ago. The next day's text from Mark had been full of awkwardness and excuses, and she hadn't replied.

Jinx inhaled a deep breath, squared her shoulders, and stepped into the dimly lit, crowded bar.

Despite the number of people inside, she found Mark immediately. He stood behind the bar, his bicep flexing as he drew a beer. Shaking his head, he laughed loud and long at something the brunette sitting at the bar said to him. The girl played with her hair, giggling. Unexpected jealousy flowed through Jinx's body like water through a sieve.

Two arms wrapped around her waist, and an ear-splitting squeal drew her attention from the flirt at the bar. Smiling, she hugged Ava tight, happy to see her.

"Oh my God, you're really here," Ava screamed with a bright smile. "Will told me you were coming, but I didn't believe him." She stepped back to look at her, keeping her arms in her vice-like grip, as if afraid she'd slip away. "You look exhausted."

Jinx didn't deny it, just peeled Ava's fingers off her arms. "I've missed you, too, even if you are an old married woman. Good gosh, girl. Look at you."

Giggling, Ava slapped her arm. "I'm not that much older than you, bitch." She jiggled her breasts. "The girls are gonna be at my waist by the time I quit breastfeeding."

"Is Lena here?" Jinx glanced around the raucous bar.

"Lord, no. Both grandmas are babysitting." She rolled her eyes. "Derrick swears he hasn't been allowed to hold her for the past week with both of our moms here. You have to come by tomorrow and see her. And you have to fill me in on everything. I can't believe your brother-in-law remarried already."

"It was a bit of a shock. He introduced Sammie to us on the Fourth of July when I went home for Mother's birthday. Well, reintroduced, actually—she grew up in Pine Bluff. She's nice, but still…"

She shrugged, her feelings convoluted. It hurt that Matt had married so soon after Karen's death. But the way it had pissed her father off was almost worth it.

"I can't wait to meet Lena. I have a painting for her nursery in the car." Jinx hugged her friend again. Before she could take a step, massive hands lifted her in the air.

"Jinx! We're glad you and the band made it. It means a lot to have all of our friends here."

Derrick must've started celebrating early, judging by the silly grin on his face. He swayed and handed her a cigar, which she tucked in her purse for later.

"Look, you left in such a hurry, we just threw your shit in a huge-ass box. It's still in the office, and I need the space to put a cage or something for the kid back there."

"Cage?" Ava smacked her husband on the back. "You're not putting our baby in a stinkin' cage, you drunk asshole. It's a *crib*."

Jinxed laughed. "Before I leave, I'll put it in my car. I can't imagine there's much in there I want."

"Thanks, hun." Derrick gave her a kiss on the cheek.

Turning, he threw an arm around the still-fussing Ava as they accepted congratulations from another couple. Jinx made her way to the stage.

The band played two sets, and then a DJ took over so they could enjoy the rest of the party. Without looking at the bar, she felt Mark's gaze on her as she left the stage. Ducking through the crowd, she worked her way through the throng to the other bar. After four shots, she felt much better and convinced Billy to give her the almost-empty bottle of vodka.

Drinking was now her nightly routine. Feeling numb made life bearable. She weaved through the crowd toward the office, not seeing Mark. He must be on break out back or upstairs. This might be her only chance to retrieve her box. She darted into the office and damn near tripped over it. No wonder Derrick wanted it gone; it was huge and in the way.

Crouching next to it, she lifted the lid. Inside were some dried tubes of paint, paintbrushes, some sketch books, and schoolbooks. She couldn't even remember where she'd left all this stuff—probably here, Mark's, and at Ava's. Winston's squeaky toy squawked as she sifted through the contents. She pulled it out and placed it in her purse. A spiral notebook she didn't recognize caught her attention. Glancing at the first page, she realized it was the notebook she'd retrieved from the fort when she'd been home for the funerals. She stuffed it in her purse as well. Would Matt want it now that he was remarried? *I'll save it for Luke…* Downing another swig of the liquor, she jumped and hid the vodka in the box as the office door swung open.

Mark opened the door to the office, planning on slipping out back for a much-needed cigarette. He stopped short when he came across Jinx sitting on the floor next to her damn box of shit.

If he were being totally honest, he'd admit he'd never moved the junk because its presence gave him hope she'd return someday.

"What are you doing?" *Brilliant opener, dumbass.*

She struggled to pick up her stuff. "Casing the place. What's it look like I'm doing?"

"Ah, well, if you're looking for the family jewels…" He gave her his best leer as he moved to help her lift the box.

Though she got to her feet, she dropped the box before he could reach her. A bottle of vodka rolled out but didn't break. Eyes unfocused, movements slow and deliberate, she fumbled in her purse for her keys.

"I got what I wanted," she told him. "Thanks for storing it. Winston's missed his toy…" She swayed and giggled. "I'm just gonna throw this other stuff in the dumpster and be gone."

The girl was shitfaced. "No way am I allowing you to drive off the premises. You're a lawsuit waiting to happen." He placed a steadying hand on her arm. "If you have everything you want from the box, I'll trash it later."

"'Kay. I'm going home. Sleep this off. G'night, Thurston." Only it sounded like *Thurshston.*

She reached over and picked up the bottle, uncapped it, and took another deep gulp, draining it. His cock twitched at the sight of her mouth around the bottle. Damn, she turned him on even when sloppy-ass drunk.

"You're too drunk to drive. You can stay with me," he offered.

She laughed. "Oh no, I've had my two times *and* phone sex. I wouldn't want to ruin your repu…reputate, whatever. Just point me toward my car." Tears welled in her red eyes.

Mark took the bottle from her. She was well on her way to an ugly crying jag at this rate. "You're right. I'm just a frog. But you're no princess. At this moment, you're more like a tavern wench. Where's Winston?"

"In my motel room," she slurred, swaying. "I have to let him out. He's gotta *go*." She blew dark bangs out of her eyes.

He hated that damn wig.

"Fine. I'll get my car keys and take you."

"My Prince Rescue. When are you going to learn you can't save me?" Her face fell as she whispered, "Nobody can…"

He placed his hand on the small of her back and steered her toward the bar. The party was winding down, so his leaving wouldn't be a problem. Seeing Derrick, he motioned he was out of there. His partner's brow lifted, but he gave a thumbs up when he saw Jinx. Mark grabbed her hand and groaned when she molded into his body, rubbing against him. *Shit.*

"You come here often?" she asked, grabbing his ass under his kilt.

He removed her hand, wondering how many he'd just flashed. He worked his way through the crowd and outside, dragging her behind him to his place upstairs. She tripped and they both nearly fell. With a sigh, he picked her up and carried her, a little concerned by how light she felt. She licked the shell of his ear, which in turn flipped the switch on his dick, and he damn near dropped her.

"Mish me?" she asked with a smile. As she slid down his body, she pushed aside his sporran and fondled his now-hard cock. "Nice sword."

"Like a hemorrhoid, you little pain in the ass," he grunted. He went in search of his car keys. Distance between them would be best.

His dick strongly disagreed.

Locating them, he returned to find her wiggling her bare toes and stretching. With her arms above her head, her shirt rose, exposing her ribcage, which was more pronounced than he remembered.

"Let's go." He motioned with his head toward the door, not trusting himself to touch her again.

"Bossy." It took her three tries to actually stand.

"Me? I'm not the one who pulls a switchblade every time we have sex."

"Not every time. Just sometimes." She paused, still swaying. "Are we having sex?" The hopeful glint in her eyes nearly undid him.

"Did you bring your switchblade?"

She frowned, patted her jeans pocket, and pulled it out. "Yep."

"Probably not. Come on, Lovey."

"Pity."

He took her hand in his, positive she'd break her neck going down the stairs, even if her shoes were tucked under his arm. In one hand she clutched a purse the size of a small suitcase, and the other held the now-empty bottle of vodka. He took it and tossed it in the garbage. Barefoot, she followed him down the stairs and tripped into him. He picked her up in his arms.

"Sexy skirt-wearing man," she whispered, kissing him drunkenly, sucking on his lip. "Mmm, I could so sex you up. But I've had my two times, plus some. Your loss. Hey, wait a minute, does phone sex count? Maybe we could negotiate an out-of-town clause, since I don't live here anymore. Claus…" She chortled. "I want my big package, Santa." She fell into a giggling fit.

"We'll discuss this later, okay?"

"Call me!" she sang, channeling Blondie, but her hiccups interfered.

Mark shook his head and chuckled. She was bound to have one helluva hangover in the morning.

Once settled and buckled into her seat, he asked, "Where are you staying?"

"Thatta way." She motioned expansively.

Realizing this was going to be the extent of her directions, Mark searched through her purse, pulling out four pairs of sunglasses, a notebook, and six tubes of lipstick before finding a receipt for the motel.

"You okay?" he asked, stuffing the crap back in her purse.

"Feelin' no pain," she mumbled, closing her eyes.

While the motel wasn't a five-star hotel, it was on the highway and had a good reputation. He wouldn't have to worry about her. But when he glanced over, she'd passed out with her mouth open. Scratch that. No way she'd be able to take care of Winston and get back to her room safely. He sighed. This had the potential of turning into a long, frustrating night.

Pulling in, he found her room and parked. "Jinx?" She was out cold. He walked around and opened her door and tried to rouse her, this time by shaking her. "Jinx, wake up." Still no response. *Eugenia.*

Her nostrils flared as she flailed against the seatbelt. "No," she whimpered with her eyes squeezed shut.

"Hush now. Let's get you inside and tucked into bed."

Her nails found his face, and he was pretty damn sure she drew blood. She fought him kicking and screaming. "No, no, don't touch me. Stop, please, stop!"

"Hey, hey, hey…It's me. Jinx! Stop it." He could smell her fear as he managed to unbuckle her seatbelt while she beat against him with her fists.

Lights flipped on in three of the rooms, and eyes peered through the windows. Odds were high the law had been called. Maybe he should just dump her drunk ass in the parking lot and leave. Let the cops deal with her. But no, he couldn't do that. Goddamn his conscience. He shook her again.

"Open your eyes. It's me, Mark."

An elderly man in a robe approached. "S-Son, you need to leave her alone."

The old man's voice wobbled, and his eyes were wide, but Mark silently applauded his bravery. He knew the situation looked bad.

"I promise, everything's okay. She's just a little drunk. I'm trying to get her into her room, so she can sleep it off. I'm her friend, and her designated driver. Here's my driver's license." He offered it to the man, who looked a little less skeptical by the time he handed it back.

"Well, I let the front office know, and I'm still going to stay right here to make sure she's okay," the old man reaffirmed, crossing his arms.

"I appreciate that, sir." *Now mind your own damn business.*

A siren wail approached. *Fuck.* Jinx stopped fighting him and started crying. *Great.* He prayed it would be an officer he knew. He and Derrick often hired off-duty cops as bouncers at the bar.

He hauled Jinx out of the car. "Come on, Lovey. Everything's okay." She quieted from sobbing to sniffling and stared at him with a wild-eyed look. Her pulse pounded at the base of her throat. Collapsing against him, her fingers gripped his shirt. He wrapped his arms around her, kissing the top of her head and stroking her back.

"Mark. I'm sorry." She clung to his neck, still shaking. "I think I might be a little drunk."

"It's okay. You're safe with me."

"Don't leave me."

Her whispered plea, coupled with her warm body pressed against his, let him know he was in trouble. She might as well have his balls in her hands, ready to twist.

"I won't leave you." *Dammit, what's wrong with me? Obviously, you can't fix stupid. First Harley, now Jinx.*

First thing tomorrow, he was signing up for a damn 12-step group for co-dependent dumbfucks. And for sure he was keeping her in the friend zone, no benefits involved.

The old man offered a wary smile as the police car pulled to a stop behind them. "I guess everything's okay. Sorry about reporting you. I just don't cotton to anyone hurtin' a woman."

"You did the right thing. She's just had too much to drink and needs to sleep it off. Sorry for the disturbance."

"I'm okay. He's my *friend*," Jinx slurred in agreement. "You're my friend, too."

"Good luck." The old man chuckled and disappeared into his room.

The cops and night manager gave them two options: leave, or be arrested for disorderly conduct and disturbing the peace.

Jinx clutched his shirt. "Don't leave me," she whispered.

It was a no-brainer. "We'll get out of here. I just need to get her things."

Winston jumped out of the room, and the cops looked like they damn near wanted to piss themselves. Mark chuckled.

Jinx knelt and hugged her dog's neck. "I want to go home."

"That's where I'm taking you."

The cops stayed until he'd collected her suitcase and passed the Breathalyzer and sobriety tests. He slipped the manager a hundred bucks when he started complaining that pets weren't allowed.

He packed Jinx and Winston into his car and began the drive back to his place. Unsure what he had at home, he stopped at a convenience store and bought Jinx some ibuprofen, a box of crackers, and bottle of water. "Here. Drink every last drop. I don't feel like cleaning up puke tonight." He scrubbed a hand down his face, watching her down the pills and water. She nibbled on a cracker.

"I'm sorry," she mumbled, staring at her lap. She appeared almost sober after the run in with the cops.

"You're gonna feel like shit tomorrow."

"It's my new norm."

The tinny laugh that followed unnerved him.

"What's going on, Lovey? Is this the alcohol talking? Has it become a problem?"

"Honestly?"

"Honestly."

"I'm drowning, and I can't keep my head above water much longer."

Chapter
Fourteen

A loud snore startled Jinx awake. She lay still with her eyes closed, wanting to cry, knowing she wouldn't. *Not again! Where am I? Whose bed am I in?* The last thing she remembered was Mark carrying her…

Mark. She relaxed, knowing she was safe, and opened her eyes. But Mark would ask questions. Maybe if she was quiet she could leave before he woke up. Gently, she eased herself to sitting, her pounding head protesting all the way. Before she could get her feet on the floor, an arm snaked across her, trapping her on the bed.

"Going somewhere?"

"I've got to let Winston out."

"He's fine. I took him out a couple of hours ago when I smoked. How are you feeling after last night?"

"I'm fine." She froze, wondering if they'd had sex.

It wasn't that she was worried about Mark. She knew him well enough to know he'd cover up. But the hole in her memory was concerning. She needed to quit drinking; it was making the blackouts worse and more frequent.

"You're not fine. You were drunk off your sweet little ass."

"You're not my parent," she snapped. "Or my *husband*."

"No, I'm not. And in case you're interested, I'm not *anyone's husband* anymore. I'm your friend. If you'd let me be one."

The tightening in her chest eased a bit. But she was still wary, trusting no one. If anyone found out how truly sick she was, it would be all over. Being around the mentally ill was tiring. That's why her father shipped her mother off on a routine basis.

Mental illness was the secret her father forbade anyone from talking about. Even her sister had suffered bouts of depression, but silence prevailed. That Christmas she'd spent with Angel was the closest she'd ever come to telling someone about her blackout spells. But she hadn't. He'd had enough problems of his own.

"Well, friend. Thanks for whatever happened last night. I guess I need to go check out of my room." *Please say I didn't make a fool of myself…*

Mark yawned. "Nothing happened between us last night — if that's what you're wondering. And you checked out of the motel last night. Rather, you were thrown out for public intoxication. Luckily, the cops didn't haul both of our asses in. Your suitcase is in the other room."

She hid her face in her hands. *Why? Why am I always at my worst with this man?*

Mark sat up and kissed the top of her head. "Don't worry about it. Let's shower and go down to the Quarter and get some coffee and beignets. Your treat. It can be my payment for keeping you outta jail."

She relaxed and gave him a genuine smile. He truly was a good guy. "Sounds fair enough. No lecture?"

"Not before coffee. Do you want first shower or second?"

"You go ahead. I'm going to drink some water and check in with Will."

She watched as he climbed out of bed, stretching. Was he doing it on purpose? Looking so sexy with his low-riding pajama pants? When he caught her staring, he adjusted himself, winked and headed toward the bathroom.

Was that an invitation to join him? She decided not to press her luck. He was being exceptionally nice, considering he'd had to put up with her drunk and passed out. At least she hadn't puked.

An hour later, they hopped off the streetcar and meandered through the French Quarter. Jinx grinned. She loved this place. It had an old world feel to it. People didn't hurry here because of the heat. The streets were being hosed off as they walked past the Cathedral toward Café du Monde. Street artists, fortune tellers, and performers hawked their wares and services in Jackson Square. Jinx smiled at all of it. She'd missed it.

"Whoa!" Beside her Mark stopped, shielding his eyes.

She peered up at him. "What's wrong? Are you okay?"

"I don't know…It's like the sun just came out and blinded me. Was that an actual smile on your face?"

She wrinkled her nose and punched his arm. "Very funny."

He laughed. "It's so rare; I was shocked. Sort of like the Saints winning a Super Bowl."

"True dat…Ugh. Don't make me laugh until I've had caffeine. But you're right. I do tend to be a little too serious. It's my tortured artist persona."

"I would've said narcissistic, but to avoid an argument, I'll go with your definition. So now that you're relatively sober, tell me how you've been. I know we've had a rocky past full of miscommunication. But being your savior last night entitles me to some non-deep answers to polite questions. Even Ava said you haven't been in touch much, and she's your best friend."

They passed a guy painted silver, standing on a box like a statue. Beside him a mime pretended to take his photo. She wondered if they found it as tiring as she did to always wear a mask, hiding in plain sight.

"I can handle polite conversation. Thanks for keeping me out of jail. That's not a phone call I would've wanted to make to my parents. I stay busy, and you seemed like you regretted the phone sex. It was awkward afterward…I'm touring with the Spellcast Socialists. I sing more now."

"I didn't regret it. I was drunk and afraid I'd overstepped by initiating it. What about school?"

"I was drunk, too. It was kind of fun…" Heat filled her cheeks.

He grinned. "Hell yeah, it was."

"Does it count, Two-Time?"

He chuckled. "Truthfully? That was a first for me. I'm thinking not. What do you think?"

She bit her lip. "I may have done it a time or two. I, um, actually did phone sex for money to help pay for school."

He laughed outright. "Damn, so were you faking it?"

· She shook her head.

"Okay, back to school—phone sex still paying for it?"

"I ditched school. It's too hard being on the road, and if that's your polite way of asking, no, I don't do phone sex for money anymore."

"Don't give up on getting your degree, Jinx." Mark pulled out her chair for her. The waitress brought them some water, and they ordered *café au lait* and beignets.

"And your artwork?" he asked.

She shrugged. "Not inspired these days. What about you?" Opening her purse, she found a bottle of ibuprofen and downed two with her glass of water. "Thank God. I didn't remember having these."

"I bought 'em last night. I stay busy with school and work. At some point, the plan is for Derrick to buy me out, and I'll get a real job in accounting. Have you been home to Pine Bluff?" He smiled at the waitress as she delivered their order. "Thanks, Sophie."

"My pleasure, Mark," she replied.

Jinx tried not to glower at the exotic-looking girl, wondering why and how Mark knew her name. *What all has this girl done for his pleasure?* The waitress left to wait on the next table.

"Once. It was a disaster. I met Matt's new wife. That's it? Just school and work? No one special?" Jinx asked, staring at the powdered sugar spilled on the table.

"Nope. You know the rule."

She sipped her coffee to hide her pleased reaction. "I'd think you'd be running out of girls." She stared at the tattoo that read *Analiese*, but didn't ask. That would delve deeper than polite conversation.

"Not in this city of tourists and college kids," he said after a moment. "So Matt remarried? You okay with that?"

"Yes…I don't know. I mean, she's nice, but so different from Karen." She shrugged. "It's hard."

His answer about the girls made her strangely sad. Not only for herself, but also for him. It really was a shame they couldn't overcome their personal demons and be together. She dabbed the sugar with her finger, not wanting him to see her disappointment.

Mark watched Jinx lick confectioner's sugar off her finger and shifted in his chair. The memory of that mouth wrapped around his dick was one of his favorites when alone and taking things into his own hand. *Friends. No benefits, remember?*

"The bar seems to be doing well," Jinx commented.

"It is. We're actually making a profit. Nothing to retire on, but better than I'd hoped."

"That's good."

An awkward silence ensued as they finished their coffee and doughnuts. Eight months of limited communication had only served to shore up her walls. She was so closed off he'd never be able to chip through. Even Ava had admitted she didn't feel like she really knew her friend.

Jinx seemed to relax as the caffeine kicked in, and some color returned to her wan face. She was much too thin for his liking, but having a sister, he knew better than to comment.

Instead he offered, "Want another round?"

"No, thanks. I probably should head back, pick up Winston, and get on the road. I want to stop by and see Ava and Derrick's baby, too."

"She's a cutie—already has me wrapped around her finger. Derrick, too. I don't envy him when she's a teen." He chuckled. "Where is home these days?"

"Usually wherever my head hits a pillow. We stay on the road. But I have a small apartment in Nashville."

"Do you travel in a bus? Who takes care of Winston?"

"The guys have a van, but being the only girl…" She wrinkled her nose. "It gets gross, so if it isn't too far, I usually drive. Sometimes one of the guys will ride with me to give me a break. I take Winston when I can. Sometimes we stay at a campsite, sometimes a motel. If necessary, I have my neighbor take care of him, but I don't like leaving him…"

"Because he's the only constant male in your life?" He leaned his cheek on his fist. "Do you like being on the road? It sounds lonely to me. I like having roots, a home. Don't you want a place to call your own?"

For one brief instant, she looked wistful. "I don't know. Maybe. Someday. And you're right, Winston loves me unconditionally..."

"The right man could do that, too. Do you ever think about settling down—a family, kids?" he pressed.

She laughed outright. "Yeah, sure. You applying for the job?"

Looking out toward the street, he didn't answer. Why had he gone down this path?

Being around Derrick and Ava with Lena. The happiness on his friends' faces as they cared for that little girl, witnessing their loving banter, it highlighted his loneliness every damn day.

"Can you really see me as a mother? What about you?" she asked. "Is Two-Time getting the urge to settle down?" She laughed like it was a joke.

He didn't.

Running a hand back and forth across the table, he answered honestly. "I don't know. Maybe?"

Leaning forward, Jinx motioned him closer and whispered, "I'll let you in on a secret. You'd have to do a lot more than frog a girl twice to form a real relationship."

"Ah, well, there is that..." He sighed. "You ready to go?"

She nodded and stood. "You know...people like us aren't meant to be monogamous, much less family oriented."

"People like us? What do you mean by that?"

"Mardi Gras people."

"Are you still drunk?"

She gave him a look. "We're Mardi Gras people. We act like everything's just hunky-dory; life's a great big party. But the truth is hidden behind our masks."

He tousled her short hair. "And wigs. Sadly, you may be right."

Walking through Jackson Square, he stuffed his hands in his pockets, resisting the urge to hold hers. *Friends don't hold hands...*

They stopped and listened to a jazz band. Closing her eyes, Jinx swayed to the music.

When they finished playing, she threw a ten-dollar bill in the hat. "Gosh, how I love this city."

Like a child at a carnival, she wandered around, taking in all the vendors. Seeing an artist she recognized, she hugged his neck, and they talked about his work and their mutual friends. Mark hid his jealousy. As they were leaving the square, a tarot reader motioned them over. The elderly woman was a regular and had been here as long as Mark had lived in the area.

"Come here," she said with a wave, her bracelets clinking down her thin arm. As they approached, her wizened face creased with her toothless smile. She'd dressed the part that tourists expected with her long skirt, faded blouse topped by shiny plastic beads, and a raveling cardigan. Mark wondered how she could stand wearing a sweater in this heat; sweat already dotted his forehead. Her gnarled fingers held multiple rings that flashed in the sun, and her dark, shrewd eyes crinkled as they approached.

"I want to talk to you." She motioned to the chair in front of her table. "Sit."

"I don't believe in this stuff," Jinx told her. "And I just gave my last ten to the band over there."

"Aw, go ahead. Get the full French Quarter experience before you head back home." Mark threw a twenty on the table.

"Did I ask for your money?" the old woman snapped, shoving the bill aside.

"No, ma'am. Sorry." He pocketed the bill, surprised. *What's this woman's game?*

Taking a worn deck of playing cards, the woman shuffled them and placed them on her table. "Put your hand on the deck."

Instead, Jinx sat on her hands. "This is stupid—"

Her statement was interrupted by Mother Bettie Ruth slamming her fist on the table, making the crystals and cards jump.

The old woman picked up the cards and spit on them before throwing three down. She worked her mouth, muttering under her breath. When she looked up from the cards, her brow was furrowed, and she shook her head.

"You need to take care," she warned.

Jinx crossed her arms.

"No attitude!" Mother Bettie Ruth shook her crooked finger. "You listen. See this card?" She pointed at the first of the three cards she'd turned over. "Secrets. Dark secrets, missy."

Jinx shifted back in her seat and narrowed her eyes.

"What kind of secrets?" Mark asked.

"This is ridiculous. Let's go, Mark."

"You heed my warning, little girl. No secrets! Secrets kill…"

Mark snorted, now convinced she was just a crazy old bat. But Jinx sat still, barely breathing.

Mother Bettie Ruth moved on to the center card. "Drowning. Going under."

His gaze whipped back to the old woman, and his mouth dropped open. Jinx had said something similar last night…

"Don't be ridiculous," Jinx retorted. She moved to get up and leave, placing both hands on the rickety table. Crystals slid to the ground.

The fortuneteller gripped Jinx's wrist. "I'm here to help you! Sit. This last card?" She tapped it with her crooked, bejeweled finger. "Death."

The color drained from Jinx's face, and her throat bobbled. "W-What?"

"Death?" Mark barked. "Okay, lady. Now you're crossing the line. What's your angle?"

"No angle. Not all death is bad. Think of it as a time for rebirth." Her voice softened. "Girl, listen to me. Your life is not cursed. You determine your future. Just make thoughtful choices."

"Let go of me," Jinx hissed, jerking her arm away.

She turned and practically ran toward the streetcar. Mark glared at the old woman and hurried after her.

"Hey, slow down, Jinx. You know that's all bullshit, right?"

Jinx didn't speak the entire ride home on the streetcar, appearing lost in her thoughts. As she marched upstairs to get her dog, he grabbed her hand.

"Lovey, it meant nothing. She's just really good at reading people and then preys on the human psyche and fear." He ignored the weird thought that some of her observations seemed uncannily accurate. It was all bullshit. *Wasn't it?*

Jinx turned so fast they both nearly tumbled backward down the stairs.

"Then why didn't she take the money?"

He shrugged. "No clue." Reaching around her, he unlocked the door and opened it.

Winston barked and wagged his tail. Jinx's phone buzzed. She pulled it out and read.

"Will's heading out in an hour if I want to drive in tandem."

"I think that's a good idea."

"I guess so," she replied distractedly. "Look, will you take Winston down to let him do his thing while I get my stuff together? I need to call Ava…I don't think I'll make it to see Lena. And will you grab the painting in the backseat? It's for Lena's nursery." She handed him her keys.

"Sure. Come on, old boy. Want to meet us at your car?"

"Huh? Um, no, back up here. The boys are always late except to a show. They'll text me when they're in the parking lot…" She looked lost in thought.

"Okay." He took Winston and walked him around the block. Maybe she just needed a few girl minutes. Her stuff was pretty much packed. Or she was going to rob him blind? In that case, she'd be disappointed. Everything he had went back into the bar and school loans.

As soon as Mark's footsteps disappeared, Jinx went into his kitchen and found his scotch. Vodka was her liquor of choice, but right now anything would do. She took a long swig, welcoming the burn, needing the oblivion it offered. The old woman had unnerved her; her observations seemed so accurate. She did have secrets, and alcohol was her way of muting the voices that told her she was losing her mind.

Taking another huge gulp, she replaced the scotch, brushed her teeth, packed up her stuff, and texted Ava. Ava responded that the baby was sleeping anyway. Relieved, she assured her friend she'd be back soon. She really didn't want to explain how she'd ended up here last night.

Mark returned and patted the grateful Winston on the head, scratching behind his ears. "He should be good to go. I'll make sure Ava gets the painting. I like the carousel horse." The dog appeared to be grinning, his tail wagging as he lapped up the attention. "I could run you by Derrick's to see the kid if you want. They don't live that far from here."

She stared at the gentle hands petting her dog, and a part of her was jealous, wanting those hands on her. The man had strong hands with long fingers. Someday she'd sketch them. Looking up at his handsome face, desire flickered in his eyes. *Did he read my mind?*

Feeling vulnerable, she looked away. "I texted Ava and the baby's sleeping, worn out from the grandparents."

He was in front of her before she knew it and grasped her face, kissing her hungrily. Wrapping her arms around his neck, she returned the kiss, wanting more, so much more.

"No drinking and driving," he whispered, picking her up and carrying her to the bedroom. "The toothpaste didn't work."

She giggled. "Busted. I'll get Will to drive."

He threw her on the bed and was on top of her before she could move.

"W-What about your rule?" she gasped as his hand kneaded her breast.

"You had a good idea even though you were drunk off your ass. We're instituting an out-of-town clause," he replied, peeling her shirt off and biting her nipple.

She moaned and helped him out of his shirt, running her hands over his firm torso. "What clause?" She undid his belt buckle as he unbuttoned her jeans.

They both laughed as they tried to kick off their shoes and socks. In their haste, they fell off the bed. Winston grunted his disapproval and padded back to the living area. Jinx moved to climb back on the bed, but Mark pinned her to the floor, reaching into his bedside table for a condom. They were naked in seconds.

"The out-of-town clause is the license to have more than two times, because we both know this is just a hit and run," he explained.

"How many have taken advantage of this clause?" she asked, helping him with the condom, stroking his length.

He opened his mouth to answer, but she covered his with her soft, warm lips.

"Don't say her name…"

"*She* doesn't count. You're the first…" A look of longing crossed his face before he flipped her onto her knees and swatted her ass.

Teasing her entrance, he leaned in and whispered, "We good?"

"Green bean," she panted, moving against him.

He nipped her shoulder with his teeth and entered her swiftly, one arm on the floor, the other wrapped around her waist. Being held this way made her feel strangely secure and unafraid. He paused, kissing her back. She wiggled her butt, wanting him to move, and laughed when he smacked it again.

Setting the pace, he started slowly, teasing. His hands moved up and down her back but never crossed to the front of her.

"Mmm…" He licked her shoulder blade, making her giggle.

"Will," she ground out.

"Will what?" he asked, taking his time, pulling almost completely out before swiftly re-entering.

"He'll be here…"

"Mood killer," he retorted with a hard smack to her other cheek.

She gasped with pleasure, not shock. Her ass now burned, but he eased the sting with feather soft strokes. Thankfully, he took heed of her warning and picked up his tempo until his grunts mingled with her moans. As usual, it felt good, but it wasn't enough, and she wanted to cry with frustration. Sensing her dissatisfaction, none too gently he pushed her shoulders down and angled her differently. In so doing, he hit her sweet spot.

"Oh God, yes," she hissed.

He pounded into her until she cried out with a mind-numbing orgasm that seemed to go on forever. A minute later, he followed, collapsing on top of her, his breath sawing, his body shaking. He bit the back of her neck like a male lion claiming his lioness, and she purred in response.

He pulled out, kissed her shoulder, and excused himself to the bathroom.

Jinx dressed quickly, ready to get out of there before the shouldn't-have-had-sex awkwardness set in. For some reason, emotions ran deeper with Mark than any other man she'd been with. And it was disturbing—like free-falling, or her blackouts.

She grabbed her things and herded Winston out the door as Mark came out of the bathroom.

"Gotta run. Will's here. See ya."

"Jinx! Where are you going? When will you be back?"

Is that disappointment?

"Halloween!" She slammed the door behind her.

Fuck. Did I do something wrong?

Grabbing the afghan from the couch, he wrapped it around his waist as he chased after her and threw open the door. He watched as she let Winston in the backseat. Will got out of the van and walked over to the driver's seat of her car. When he saw Mark, he threw an arm up in a wave. Jinx blew him a kiss.

Guess not.

He closed his door and leaned against it. Now that his orgasm-induced brain fog had cleared, he sighed, kind of relieved. *Why do you always break the rule with Jinx?* Collapsing on the sofa, he lit a cigarette and stared at the ceiling.

After he'd nipped her shoulder, she'd turned and looked back at him with a sweet smile. And for one brief, shining second, he'd felt something he hadn't felt in a long damn time. He'd not tapped this emotion since Harley.

Fuck me. I'm falling in love. He groaned.

Chapter Fifteen

"You're gonna leave me, aren't you, Two-Time?" Derrick batted his eyelashes.

Mark shook his head. "You've had more than your two times. Way more. And yeah, in a little over a year, ya drunken sot. But you know I won't leave you hangin'. Does Ava know you started partying early?"

Derrick grinned and put a finger to his lips, glancing around for his wife. "I'm proud of you, man. You've been working hard getting your masters. But even after I buy you out, you're doin' my books for the bar—at a discount, right?"

"Of course. God, you sound like my father, except drunk."

"I'm *not* your father. I would *never* have allowed you to go to Tulane. Geaux Tigers!" Derrick raised his arms in sloppy salute. "Who ya bringin' to the party tonight?"

"No one special. There should be plenty here to choose from."

"Such a man-whore. I'll want all the details later so I can live vicariously through you. Sometimes I miss those days…"

"Derrick!"

He rolled his eyes at the sound of his wife's voice walking in the door.

Derrick stood with his hands in his pockets, listening to Ava fuss. He nodded and gave his patented, "Yes, dear," response.

Mark bit back his laughter. It was funnier than usual since Derrick and Ava were dressed as Marge and Homer Simpson.

Halloween meant a huge costume party at the bar. Orange and black decorations filled the room, and the entire staff was supposed to be in costume.

Finished with Derrick, Ava whipped around and headed toward him with Lena bouncing on her hip. The baby was dressed as Maggie Simpson in a blue onesie with a pacifier stuck in her mouth.

"And as for you—"

"What did I do?" Mark grinned at the baby and tickled her chin.

The passy dropped out, but was attached by a ribbon to her outfit. Taking Lena in his arms, he enjoyed her soft baby smell and the way her wispy hair tickled his nose. He felt a pang of longing.

"Jinx will be here, and I don't want drama. Understand?" Ava frowned, giving him the onceover. "A kilt? How original."

"Jinx and I are fine."

And they were, he guessed. Since last month, they'd texted once a week or so, nothing ever personal or too deep. The one time they'd tried again for phone sex, Jinx had passed out on him.

"Mama's a little testy, isn't she, sweetheart?"

The little girl's eyes looked heavy and drool trickled down her chin. Ava went back to bitching at Derrick. She'd hired a babysitter to keep Lena in the office during the party.

"Another female drooling all over Two-Time MacGregor. Just another typical day at The Highland Hangout." Dressed as a rag doll, Eunice, his favorite waitress, walked over and smiled.

"What can I say? I'm a chick magnet." He tried to pawn Lena off on her.

"No way. I've got two of my own at home. You need a couple of kids, Mark. You're a natural."

"Nah, I like to think of them like library books. Check 'em out and return 'em." He managed a grin despite the heaviness in his heart. This time of year was full of painful memories. Harley had left this morning after her annual visit, further darkening his mood.

Eunice laughed and went to help Ava.

The door opened and slammed, startling the sleepy baby.

He patted her on the back and took in the beauty walking toward him. Wearing a saloon girl outfit, she looked pretty fuckin' hot. He wondered where the switchblade was hidden.

"Hello, Jinx," he called.

Jinx smiled and endured a hug from an excited Ava. The rest of the Spellcast Socialists entered, carrying equipment. He winced as Lena's crying intensified to the point of breaking the sound barrier.

Ava took the little girl into her arms. "She's ready for a nap. I'll be right back. You two play nice."

"Yes, ma'am," Mark answered. He turned his attention to the girl who haunted his thoughts. "You look great." Now that she'd come closer, he realized he was lying.

Her color was sallow, and despite her attempt to hide the circles under her eyes with makeup, she had the look of someone who partied too much and too hard. She wasn't wearing the wig, but her makeup was still applied with a heavy hand. He didn't like it; she looked harsh and older.

"Not very original with the costume, there, Two-Time."

"Walk with me to my car?" he asked.

"Why?"

"I have something for you. I found it a couple of weeks ago when I was cleaning the empty fast food bags from the floorboard."

"Okay. Is this some cheesy pick-up line? I've already seen your big sword," she teased.

He laughed and opened the door, motioning her through first.

"Are you being a gentleman or looking at my butt?"

"Both. I like the way the ruffle on your ass moves when you walk."

"Oh, brother." She stopped at his car. "If you want sex, just say so." She shrugged. "Or not. I don't care."

Mark grabbed the spiral notebook from the trunk. "Liar. You do care. And let's play it by ear. I think this was in your box of shit and got left in my car. It says Karen Howell on it." He handed it to her.

She stared at the notebook, running a reverent finger over her sister's writing. "I forgot about it. It's hard to believe it's almost been a year. It's weird; I think about Karen every day, I've even picked up the phone to call, and then remembered she won't answer."

She looked down at the notebook and then clutched it to her chest. "Thank you for not throwing it out." Her voice broke off, full of emotion. "I don't know if Matt will want it now. But Luke might, when he's older. I dunno…"

"Hey. It's all understandable. You loved your sister. But look at it this way: Matt remarrying is testimony that maybe marriage can be good, like ice cream. I mean, he went for seconds."

"Perhaps." She pulled away and looked up at him. "I guess not everyone enjoys solitude like you and I do. Thank you."

On impulse he kissed her forehead. *Like solitude?* He was a man-whore precisely because he didn't like being alone.

Her eyes were shiny, and when she smiled, his heart did a funny flip-flop. *Not again. Raise the pixie shield, dumbass…*

"I'm going to put this in my car. Thanks again."

"No problem. Where are you staying? Is Winston with you?"

"I left him at home. My neighbor's son is taking care of him to earn some money. I'm bunking down on Ava and Derrick's couch."

"I'm all for activating the out-of-town clause," he offered.

"Maybe…" Her eyebrows rose as she stared past him.

"Jinx! Mark!" Angel Sinclair approached with a wave. His blond hair was in a messy man bun, and a backpack bounced on his back as he jogged toward them holding a duffel bag. "Hell yeah! I'm crazy glad to see y'all. I wasn't expecting to luck up and find Jinx here, too."

She tossed the notebook in her driver's seat and lit a cigarette. From under her skirt she pulled out a flask and turned it up, guzzling it faster than a college freshman at a frat party.

Mark frowned. It was a bit early for that.

Angel's clear blue eyes zeroed in on the flask in her hand.

Jinx studiously ignored him. Seeing Karen's notebook and talking about her sister had made her sad. She needed to numb those feelings.

"Angel. This is a surprise. You look good, man." Mark and Angel pounded each other on the back.

"I'm great! Just got out of a halfway house. I'm six months clean." He pulled an NA coin out of his pocket.

Mark looked puzzled.

Jinx decided to state the obvious. "So, you left a halfway house to come to a bar?"

Angel was worse at communication that she was, but lately, when he'd bothered to text, it had been all about recovery this and recovery that. It was boring and repetitive.

"I'm here for a purpose." The light of fanaticism lit his eyes. "I've come to apologize to Derrick, Mark, and you, Jinx. For what I put y'all through the last time I was here. I'm working through the steps, slowly. Although I gotta say, number four is kicking my ass…This searching and making a moral inventory of yourself sucks big time." He glanced back at the bar. "I texted Derrick. I'm not going in…"

Derrick walked out, and Angel waved.

Mark slapped him on the back. "About damn time. I'm proud of you, Angel. That's great!" They tussled a bit like kids, laughing. Derrick joined in when he heard the news and then listened to Angel's apology.

Strangely, although Angel's newfound sobriety was great, seeing him with Mark and Derrick only highlighted her loneliness. Her relationships were superficial by choice, even with the band and Ava.

"Congrats, Angel. I'm going in—" Jinx paused when he grabbed her hand.

"No, wait! Gimme a moment, please?"

Nodding, Mark and Derrick said their goodbyes and left as Angel pulled her to the steps to Mark's apartment. She lit a cigarette as they sat.

"I wanted to thank you for what you did for me last year. I was a fuckin' mess and put you through a lot of crap. I'm sorry. And if you ever need me, I'll do my best to help you."

She grinned. "It's okay. No need to apologize. I'm happy for you, Angel. You do look good. And we'd both need to learn to communicate better—like actually answer a text—to be there for each other."

Angel laughed. "That's true. My friend Emma fusses about that, too. I never remember to get minutes. It's hard, this recovery shit. I'm not gonna lie to you. God knows how many times I've tried it. And it sucks knowing any minute I could lose everything if I get complacent. But right this minute, I choose to be clean."

He turned and looked at her. Concern flickered in his eyes. "You're not alone. Just know that."

Jinx looked away, afraid he'd see the empty shell where her soul should be. "I'm not you. Don't project. I don't have a problem. I just drink on the weekends, and I don't get drunk that often. Just, you know, sometimes. But thanks for your concern."

Angel sighed. "Since I've been going to 12-step meetings, I've noticed something weird. And this is a total generalization…To me, it seems like addicts tend to exaggerate their use, and alcoholics tend to minimalize how much they drink."

Sucking in a sharp breath, she glared at him and snapped, "I'm not an alcoholic."

"I didn't say you were." He patted her leg, right where the half-empty flask was hidden in her garter belt.

She huffed and crossed her arms.

"I'll never bullshit you or sugarcoat anything. When you're ready, I'll be here for you." He stood. "I'm gonna go find a meeting, and then I'm outta here. This is, like, the worst place in the world for someone like me."

He stood and pulled her to her feet, giving her a bear hug. "Take care, Jinx."

"I will. I'm fine, really," she mumbled into his jacket.

He squeezed her a little tighter and repeated, "You're not alone."

Leaving the party, Jinx went to her car to wait on Ava and Derrick to follow them home. She found her sister's notebook and pulled it out to read just as her phone buzzed with a cryptic text from her brother-in-law.

Sammie's in the hospital.

She called, and he picked up on the first ring.

"Hey, Matt. What's going on? Why is Sammie in the hospital?"

Her brother-in-law sighed. "It's a long story. But your father and I are going to have a 'come to Jesus' meeting, as Sammie would say. I may need bail money. I've had it with his shit. There was an accident at the bank, and witnesses said he was involved. Look, the doc is coming in, and I need to go." He hung up.

Jinx wondered what her father's involvement could be and hoped Sammie would be okay. Despite growing up in the same town, Jinx didn't know her very well. She was closer to Karen's age, but she and Sammie had a lot in common, being tomboys. When she was ten, her family had served a Thanksgiving dinner at church for those less fortunate. After seeing Sammie and her mother in the line, she'd asked if Sammie could come over. Her mother had looked ready to cry, and her father had immediately shut down any conversation on the subject. She hadn't pushed it, knowing to do so was pointless. Her parents were snobs, and the Morgans had lived in a rundown rental house on the edge of town. Sue Ellen, Sammie's mother, was known for her religious fervor. Sometimes she'd wander the streets talking to herself. In comparison, Mother seemed sane.

Jinx sat on the hood of her car, lit a cigarette, and began to read her sister's journal under the dim parking lot lights. Karen's teenaged warning of epic consequences for anyone who dared to read the contents made her smile. In the diary she'd written about falling hard for Matt, the son of the local bootlegger, and how handsome he was.

Jinx understood Karen's attraction. As a little girl, she herself had developed a huge crush on her future brother-in-law. Matt had that bad-boy attitude, a killer body, warm brown eyes, and unruly black hair…He was the stuff of fantasies. Jinx grinned as she read about how Karen and Matt snuck around until they finally did "it" in the backseat of Matt's car in her parents' driveway. She skimmed the details of their hormone-fueled sexcapades until she reached the part where Karen had told her parents she was pregnant.

The aftermath of that revelation had been a difficult time at home. Jinx well remembered the shouting matches, slamming doors, and then the silence…Afterward, her father hadn't spoken to Karen except in the company of others to maintain the lie that all was well in his household. The only reason he showed up at the wedding was to avoid a scene. Image meant more to Daddy than grudges. Karen had suffered serious morning sickness to the point that everyone, except Daddy, had been worried about her health. Quiet and withdrawn, Karen didn't seem to come alive until after she'd moved out.

Jinx kept reading, until she couldn't. Karen's memories became more personal and horrifying. The words swam before her eyes, and bile burned the back of her throat.

Everything became eerily still, until all she heard was the pounding in her ears.

It was as if someone had removed the blinders from her memory, and images flashed before her in rapid succession until everything became crystal clear for the first time.

And she absolutely could not breathe.

"Mark?" Ava's blue Marge wig bobbled precariously.

"What's up?"

"Is Jinx at your place?"

"Not that I'm aware of. Why?" He pulled out the last garbage sack and glanced around the now-empty bar. Eunice had been the last of the staff to leave. Derrick was in the back doing inventory.

"I can't find her. She's not answering my texts." Ava chewed on her lip. "I even texted Angel and all the guys in the band, but she isn't with any of them."

"Maybe she hooked up with someone?" The thought was up-setting, but he was too tired to mull it over. "Let me throw this in the dumpster, and we'll set up a search-and-rescue party. I'm sure she's fine."

He headed through the office to the alley and found Jinx on the back step, head on her knees, arms wrapped around her legs. She didn't bother to look up as he walked passed her to toss the bag of garbage. Bottles clanked as it hit the side of the dumpster.

"Ava's looking for you."

She didn't move.

He stomped back up the steps and toed her leg. "Jinx. Did you hear me?"

Not so much as a swat for him to stop. Had she passed out? Annoyed, he stooped next to her. Tending to a drunk wasn't how he wanted to end his night. He took her hand in his. It was ice cold. A shudder shook her body as she slumped over.

"Go away," she croaked.

"Are you hurt?"

She didn't answer, but something was off. When he picked her up, she didn't protest or pull the switchblade. He hurried back inside.

"Ava, Derrick!"

Gently, he sat her down and began examining her for injuries. In her hand was the spiral notebook he'd given her earlier. Blood seeped between her fingers from the wire binding. She began to shake more violently.

Mark grabbed his coat and covered her. "You're okay, Lovey."

Jinx's eyes were huge in her pale face. "I feel sick…"

"Throw-up sick?" He looked to Ava for help. Moms had instincts about shit like this.

"Are you hurt, honey, or need to throw up?" Ava asked in a soft, low voice, wiping the blood off her hand.

Jinx panted, her eyes darting around the room until they fixed on him.

"I need to go home."

"Nashville's a long drive, honey. Come home with Derrick and me."

"No! I have to go home! To Pine Bluff! I need to talk to Matt. His wife's in the hospital…I need to talk to my father."

She continued to shake uncontrollably, panting like an injured animal.

"Is this life or death?" Mark asked.

She looked up at him, and her eyes flickered. "Y-Yes."

"Yes?"

Her head dropped. "No. I g-guess not, technically."

"Then not tonight. We've all been drinking. We'll discuss this in the morning, okay? A few hours won't make any difference. You're staying with me. No arguments."

"Or you can stay with us. The ride share is on the way." Ava rubbed Jinx's arms, peering into her face.

"I don't know."

"I'm taking you upstairs. Come on." Mark held out his hand.

Jinx looked at him and nodded. The pain on her face took him back to a year ago and the wreck that had taken her sister's and niece's lives. Would this girl ever know happiness?

Guiding her, they walked upstairs. He waved at Ava and Derrick as they left.

"I have to get home…"

"Tomorrow."

"Will you go with me?" she asked, clutching the bloody notebook.

He nodded and propelled her to the bathroom. *Here we go, again.* "Sure, yeah. But I have to be back by Thursday, latest."

Taking her purse and the notebook, he handed her a new toothbrush and a washcloth and towel.

"Thank you."

She stood there looking lost, and he gave her a gentle push toward the bathroom, but left her alone, unsure what she was going through.

The answer was in that notebook, but it wasn't his place to pry. Having his own secrets, he wasn't going to breach her privacy. When she was ready, she'd tell him. *Maybe.*

As usual, she emerged from the bathroom in a billow of steam, her skin bright red, hair wet. She clutched the towel closed and moved toward him in an almost trance-like state. He grabbed one of his clean T-shirts and helped her in to it. Pulling back the covers, he eased her into bed and for some reason felt compelled to kiss her forehead before taking his own shower.

Fifteen minutes later he joined her, leaving the bathroom light on and the door cracked. To his surprise, she rolled over and curled into him. Her damp hair ticked his nose.

He kissed the top of her head. "I already know the answer, but I'll ask anyway. Want to talk about it?"

"I think I'd just like to cuddle, if that's okay."

He opened his arms to her, surprised.

She nestled into chest with her arm and leg pinning him to the bed. He rubbed her back and remained silent. Even though he had no clue what was going on, he could no more leave her than he could leave a wounded bird.

"Why are you so good to me?" she whispered.

"I think you've cast a pixie spell on me. And I think we're cut from the same cloth and hide behind the same masks. Someday maybe we'll trust each other enough to remove them…"

A soft snore was her answer.

Would he ever see the real Jinx instead of the damsel in distress? She wasn't the first he'd tried to save. And he failed every damn time. But it was his nature to be needed, to care for those unable to look after themselves. It had started with his birth mother. How many nights had he listened to her crying because nothing he did could make her stop? Then there was Harley, although she really hadn't needed saving, just a safety net. He glanced down at the tattoo on his wrist and sighed.

Analiese had been the one he'd failed most.

Chapter Sixteen

Mark lay awake as Jinx tossed and turned for two hours. "This is ridiculous. Get up."

As she dressed, he sent a text to Derrick saying he was taking a couple of days off. Derrick would understand. He'd listened to enough of his drunken ramblings about Jinx and had commented many times that Mark needed to shit or get off the pot where this girl was concerned. He didn't have class until Thursday afternoon.

They were on the road by five in the morning. He drank a cup of coffee and wolfed down a biscuit, but Jinx refused to eat, although she did drink some water when he prompted her. She stared out the window, clutching that damn notebook to her chest and giving robotic yes and no answers when she bothered to answer his questions at all.

As they pulled in to the Howells' white mausoleum-style house just after noon, Mark glanced over at Jinx. She sat ramrod straight, her lips pressed into a thin line. A niggling aura of fear permeated the air. If asked, he wouldn't be able to say if it was hers or his. Probably a combination of both.

He rubbed his burning eyes. *Why am I getting involved?* The question had nagged him for the entire silent trip.

Because you love her, dumbass.

He let out a slow hiss between his teeth.

And there it was.

The answer to whose fear he felt? *It's mine.*

Jinx looked at him and bit her lip.

"You don't have to stay. I'll get back somehow. I always ask too much of you. And you always deliver…You're a very nice man. One of the few…" Her hands shook. He wondered if it was because she hadn't had a drink this morning or the stress of being back home.

"Why are we here? What am I walking in to?" he asked for at least the hundredth time.

The front door opened, and Lila Howell walked toward the car, a pale imitation of the woman he'd met twice before. Her hair looked as if she'd run her fingers through it, and mascara smudged her swollen eyes.

Jinx stepped from the car and endured her mother's hug without hugging her back.

"I was shocked when you called to say you were coming home. Did your father call you?" Mrs. Howell asked, stepping back, smoothing her hair.

"No." Jinx's cold, flat tone sent a chill up his spine. "Matt did. What happened to Sammie? What did Daddy do?" Her voice sounded shrill.

"Calm down, dear. We don't air dirty laundry…Hello, Mark." Mrs. Howell's voice wasn't friendly by any means, but not hostile either.

"Ma'am."

"Anything you say can be said in front of Mark. As a matter of fact, I insist on it."

Her mother's eyes widened as she brought her hands, prayer-like, to her mouth. "I…well, I'm sure this is just a misunderstanding. Your father would never intentionally hurt anyone—"

Jinx raised an eyebrow. "Are you really that clueless, Mother?"

"What's going on?" Mark asked.

"Matt's *new* wife argued with James and tripped. She's in the hospital, but she'll be okay. It's all just a misunderstanding…" Mrs. Howell repeated. Her voice trailed off, and tears streamed down her face.

Jinx looked ready to combust. She hesitated at the front door, as if steeling herself to walk in.

Her mother's tears were coming nonstop now. "George and Travis Carlton are here. Matt just can't press charges. What would it do to us? He needs to think about Luke. This family's been through enough this year."

"God forbid anything tarnishes the Howell name," Jinx replied, sarcastically. "Mark and I need to get settled."

"Yes, of course, dear. Your room is always ready. I'll tell Mae you're here." Mrs. Howell floated past them toward the kitchen.

Mark followed Jinx up the stairs. Her back was stiff, her motions stilted. As they passed the Howells' master suite, he heard muffled male voices. When they reached Jinx's room, he closed the door behind them.

She pulled out her phone and dialed. "Matt? It's Jinx. How's Sammie?" She paused to listen, her face expressionless. "You may want to bring a lawyer. Travis and his father are here." Listening, she clenched and unclenched her hand against the notebook.

"See you soon. And Matt?" Her body shook as if feverish, but it was the feral look in her eyes that unnerved him most. "Everything will be okay. He won't go unpunished. I *promise*." Hanging up the phone, she collapsed on the bed and covered her face with her hands.

"Why are we here?" Mark asked. "I don't like being blindsided, and I'm getting a little tired of my role as Prince Fucking Rescue. And who are the Carltons?"

"Travis is vice president at Daddy's bank. Mr. Carlton is his father and owns the paper. He's also a lawyer and Daddy's best friend." She paused for a moment. "Hold me?" she added in a small voice.

Well, shit. Call me Prince Fucking Rescue.

Mark sighed and kicked off his shoes. Crawling beside her, he hauled her into his arms. Her head rested over the heart that beat for her. No matter how hard she pushed him away, it was like this girl was seared into his soul, a part of him.

Her hand gripped and released his T-shirt over and over, like a cat kneading. He kept his mouth shut, too tired to deal with a switchblade to the throat. He knew from experience not to press her.

"Do you know what today is?" she asked almost in a whisper.

"The first. Yesterday was Halloween."

"*Dia de los Muertos.*"

"Day of the Dead. Yeah, the Quarter is full of *calaveras.*"

"Part of the celebration is to remember children and babies who have died."

Mark held his breath for a second, not liking where the conversation was headed.

She laughed, and it sounded tinny and harsh. "Or in my case, the death of innocence. The irony will be lost on the bastard."

The doorbell rang. She sat up and sighed, still gripping the notebook like a shield in front of her. Lifeless eyes stared at him from her pinched, pale face. "I'm sorry for dragging you into this. Please don't hate me."

"I could never hate you." A knot the size of a boulder was now lodged in his stomach, and his heart slammed into his throat. "Tell me what the hell is going on."

"Daddy…" she whispered.

Angry, muffled voices came from downstairs. Her nostrils flared, and goose bumps rose on her arms. Standing up, she trembled all over, looking like someone about to receive a death sentence.

"It's Matt. He needs me. Please, I'm going to ask one more thing."

He nodded and sat up on the side of the bed.

"Don't follow me. I'll explain everything later. Absolute, total honesty. I promise. And it's ugly." She ran from the room.

Beyond exhausted, he covered his face to collect his scattered thoughts.

There was a reason he'd avoided commitment since Harley. Love hurt like fucking hell.

Jinx slipped into the living room. Tension filled the air like smoke, and she found it difficult to breathe. Matt stood with his hands fisted, the tic in his cheek jumping. He looked as if he hadn't slept in days. George Carlton sat with her mother. No surprise, as the Carltons had been friends with her parents forever. Their son, Travis, stood with his hands in his pockets, shifting back and forth and looking like he wanted to be anywhere but here.

Mr. Carlton cleared his throat. "Matt, calm down and hear us out. We asked you here to discuss the incident that happened at the bank yesterday—"

Matt whipped around to face George. "I'll tell you exactly what happened. James hurt my wife, sending her to the hospital. So don't you dare fucking tell me to calm down. I've had it with him. I'm encouraging Sammie to press charges, and I hope he rots in jail. Do you hear me?"

Silence filled the room, except for the soft crying from her mother. On impulse, Jinx applauded. She hoped her father rotted jail, too.

Mr. Carlton glared at her like she was a four-year-old acting out in public before returning his attention to Matt. "I understand your anger. Your, er, wife has been hurt. But James is not himself. He's not well," Mr. Carlton offered.

The excuses for her father's behavior expanded the bubble of fury inside of her to the point of being physically painful. She paced back and forth, unable to keep still.

"Eugenia, sit down, dear. You're making me nervous." Mother's rings spun on her thin fingers as she wiped her eyes.

"I think we can work this out quietly without any further publicity. As it is, James's actions at the bank have seriously damaged his reputation." George Carlton held up his hand as Matt started to interrupt. "Just hear me out. James is sorry for what he did. He lost control. As a matter of fact, he's had a complete nervous breakdown."

Her mother's sobbing intensified.

"Bullshit!" Matt closed his eyes, pinching the bridge of his nose. "You know, Mr. Carlton, I may be many things, but I'm not stupid. That man has been trying to ruin me ever since Karen and I got together. I have a whole laundry list of crap he's tried to pull. This is the last straw."

"Matt—" Travis said.

"Don't you say one goddamned word to me, motherfucker!" Matt looked ready to take a swing.

Travis's face turned red, but he kept his mouth shut.

Her mother's soft tears intensified to outright sobbing, and the men shifted and looked around at one another. Matt found a box of tissues and handed them to her.

"Thank you, Matt," her mother said. "Please, just listen. What George is telling you is true. My husband isn't well. What he did was wrong. But think of the publicity. Let him retire, quietly. He's not a bad person. It's just been so hard on us, losing Karen and Elizabeth. And Eugenia hasn't been around." Her voice trailed off for a moment as she looked pointedly at Jinx, who wanted to slap her for her ignorance. "I didn't realize just how hard this has been on James. He loves his family; his girls meant everything to him."

Jinx's stomach twisted in protest.

"I'm done listening. It's time for action. I'm going to get a lawyer." Matt stormed out of the room.

Shaking, Jinx fled behind him.

But instead of leaving, Matt marched upstairs.

She wanted to go after him, to tell him what she knew, but bile choked her throat, and she raced out the front door, barely making it to the edge of the porch before vomiting.

Her father cared for his girls? Another spasm hit her stomach. No more. One way or another, her father's reign of terror would end today. It just remained to be seen who would be left standing. Using the hose, she rinsed her mouth and splashed water on her heated face. As she stood she saw Mark walking down the drive, smoking. *Is he leaving?* It might be for the best.

Shoulders squared, she crept back inside. Quiet murmuring drifted from the living area.

Upstairs, from behind the closed door to the master suite, she heard Matt's agitated voice.

Jinx took the stairs two at a time and burst through the door. "I want to talk to my father." Her voice squeaked, and she forced herself to take a deep breath.

Her father stared at her with his typical look of annoyance.

"Jinx, your father and I have a long history of animosity. This doesn't involve you, and I don't want you caught in the middle. Please, go back downstairs. Your mother needs you." Matt spoke gently and reached for her, but she shrugged away.

She glared at her father but spoke to Matt. "Stop it. I'm not a little girl anymore. Give me five minutes alone with *him*. I think I can solve this problem once and for all," she replied, ignoring the icy fear coursing through her veins.

"Eugenia, baby girl—"

"Don't! Don't you ever call me that! Get out, Matt," she said through gritted teeth, motioning with a jerk of her head toward the door. "Now!" Her eyes remained pinned on her father.

"But—" Matt protested.

With a scream, she shoved him out the door and locked it behind him, leaning against it for support. She squeezed her eyes shut, and her lungs burned as if she'd been held under water for too long. When she opened her eyes, she found her father leaned back in his chair, drumming his fingers and staring at her as if assessing an opponent in a boardroom.

"You. Y-You're despicable," she croaked. "Why? Why are you doing this to Matt?"

"He wasn't good enough for your sister."

She reached his desk in three angry strides, clutching her sister's diary to her chest. "And you were?" she hissed.

The bastard didn't even so much as blink.

"Answer me!" She slammed her fist on his desk. "You did things to *her*, just like you did to *me!*"

"W-What? Karen loved me." His voice hitched before he collected himself. "She betrayed me." He glared at her. "You were *never* your sister." Her world turned topsy-turvy. Rage blinded her for a moment.

"We were just kids," she gasped in horror. "You did unspeakable things…"

He stood and faced her across the desk. "You have no proof and a very overactive imagination. Baby girl, let's talk…"

Looking at him, she didn't see her father. She saw unadulterated evil.

"You drugged us! It's in Karen's diary. That's why I can't remember," she screamed. "You're our father. You're supposed to protect us, not hurt us! I'm going to the police. I do have proof—right here, in writing. For years, I've had these gaps in my memory, unexplained anxiety, and what I thought were unfounded fears, but now I remember some of it—why I hate chocolate, why I'm scared of the dark. I read Karen's diary. You will not hurt me or anyone else ever again. Did you do this to Elizabeth before she died? Have you ever hurt Luke?" She pounded his desk so hard all the pictures toppled. "Tell me!"

"No." His shoulders hunched over, and he suddenly appeared old and almost feeble. "Karen never left the children alone with me..." His voice trailed off.

The breath she'd been holding hissed through her clenched teeth. *Thank God.* Karen had protected her kids.

"I'm going to ruin you if it's the last thing I do. I hope they lock you away forever..."

His hand clamped down on her wrist. She froze as black spots dotted her periphery. When she wrenched her hand free, her arms looked like a plucked chicken.

"You won't say a thing. Think about your mother," he hissed.

"Were you thinking about her when you violated your daughters?" She slapped him hard across the face. His head snapped back, and he looked stunned as he sat down. Jinx straightened. "You're done. I refuse to be silent any longer. I refuse to live with the fear and the shame of what you did to me. I'll never forgive you, and Karen and I will bring you down."

Gripping the notebook, she turned and walked toward the door, feeling as if a burden had been lifted.

"I love you, baby girl."

"You don't know the meaning of the word." She spun around to sneer at him, but never had the opportunity.

A gunshot splintered the air, followed by a scream. Without bothering to close the front door behind him, Mark raced up the stairs, reaching the locked door to the master suite before Matt. Heart pounding, he kicked it in and found Jinx next to her father's inert body.

"Daddy! Oh my God, Daddy!"

At first, he couldn't tell whose blood was splattered everywhere, but when he pulled her away, James lay slumped in his chair, unmoving, blood spilling down his temple. Pieces of his skull and gray matter were everywhere. Matt phoned in a frantic 9-1-1 call.

Mark pulled Jinx into his arms, holding her tight, trying to shield her from the gruesome scene. "You're okay, you're okay, you're okay..." Inane as it was, it was all he could think to say.

He watched as Matt checked for a pulse. Ashen faced, he shook his head and closed James's eyes.

Keeping his body between Jinx and her father, Mark walked her toward the door. "Let's get out of here, Lovey."

George and Travis burst in the room. With one look and a gasp, George blocked the door to stop Lila from entering. Mrs. Howell's frantic screams were unnerving, but not nearly as bad as the vacant look in Jinx's eyes. Whimpering, Jinx reached for Karen's notebook on the floor. Mark picked it up for her, and keeping an arm around her, he walked her down the hall to her room. He tossed the journal on the bed.

"Don't lose it!" Jinx shrieked. "That monster will never hurt any-one else. I want everyone to know the truth!"

His stomach twisted as the pieces fell into place. "He's dead, Lovey. He'll never hurt anyone again. Karen's notebook's right here. It's safe." Sitting on the side of the bed, he held her tight as he gently rocked, rubbing her arms.

"He called me *baby girl*," she whispered, staring at the blood on her hands.

Like a ghost, she stood and slowly moved to the bathroom. Mark followed to offer any assistance he could. A siren sounded from the driveway, and he breathed a little easier.

"Let me help you get cleaned up," he offered.

She stared at the mirror and slowly wiped her blood-stained hands across her pale reflection, until she'd obliterated it.

Chapter
Seventeen

Mark trudged through the door of Mae's apartment. It had been one hell of a day. After the police and coroner left, he and Travis Carlton had handled the disgusting job of cleaning up the master suite, removing personal items. A professional cleaning crew would be in tomorrow. Mrs. Howell had been heavily medicated and was staying with the Carltons. Jinx was here, with Mae, in the two-bedroom apartment attached to the pool house.

"Is she asleep?" he whispered, following Mae into her kitchen. Karen's journal lay open on the table, next to a glass of whiskey and box of tissues.

"She's in bed, but I don't know if she's asleep," she whispered in return, taking a glass from the cupboard and pouring him a shot. "I don't generally approve of hard liquor unless it's needed as a toddy, but this…"

He downed it in one gulp and signaled for another. She handed him the bottle.

"She's suffering in silence. She didn't say a word or shed a tear the entire time I helped her with her bath. It's like she died right there beside her daddy." She pointed at the notebook. "How did I not know? I knew Mr. Howell was firm, but I thought he was standoffish and strict. I never dreamed he was hurting them, that he was evil. I tried to be a parent to both girls, what with Mrs. Howell's problems. I'll never forgive myself for letting my babies down…" Mae wiped her eyes. "Eugenia thinks she's strong, but she needs somebody. Please don't leave my girl or give up on her." Mae wept into her soggy tissue.

Mark gave her a hug. "Mae, you can't blame yourself. The only one to blame is dead."

"This has been too much. I'm going to bed and have a good talk with the Lord." Patting his arm, she shuffled past him to retire to her room.

Mark quickly perused the diary and felt sick. He pushed the liquor away and made his way to the guest room. Slipping through the door, he peered at Jinx. As always, the dark room was lit by a sliver of light from the bathroom. No wonder she was scared of the dark. Cleaning the suicide scene had been horrifying, but it paled in comparison to Karen's recounting of her father's abuse.

He had questions, but now wasn't the time to ask. Past ready for a shower, he stopped by the bed and kissed Jinx's forehead, tossing the notebook on top of her overnight bag. He knew from her breathing that she wasn't asleep, but she didn't acknowledge his presence.

Stripping off clothes he'd never wear again, he stepped into the hot shower. The alcohol churned in his empty stomach. He beat his hand against the wall, trying to let loose some of the overwhelming rage within him. He was so goddamned angry that James Howell was dead; he wanted to kill the sonofabitch himself. He wasn't an overly religious man, but there had to be a special place in Hell for anyone who would hurt a child.

Taking a deep breath, he knew he had to get a grip before he spoke to Jinx. After the violence she'd witnessed this morning, anger was the last thing she needed to see. Six times he bathed himself and washed his hair, and still he felt dirty. He didn't think he'd ever get the smell of gunpowder and blood out of his nose or the vision from his nightmares.

Slipping into his sleep pants, he crawled into bed behind Jinx. She stiffened her cold body and inched away from him. With a gentle hand, he turned her over and, by the dim light from the bathroom, searched her eyes. The diamond piercing in her nose glinted like a single star on her gaunt face.

"I'm so sorry. I wish I could've protected you from that monster."

She sighed, and he had to strain to hear her.

"You're not Prince Fucking Rescue, remember? I had memory lapses and terrifying nightmares. I thought I was crazy like my mother and grandmother. They make sense now, and yet they don't. Who does that sort of thing? Did I do something wrong?" Pulling away from him, she sat up and wrapped her arms around her legs, her forehead resting on her knees.

"No. Stop it." He switched on the bedside light and grabbed her by her shoulders. Emotions on edge, without thinking, he shook her and yelled, "Your father was a vile, depraved man. You did *nothing* wrong!"

Frustration made him damn near spit the words out. *Dear God, what's wrong with me? Why am I screaming at her like a madman and manhandling her? Am I no better than that bastard?*

She stared blankly at the wall, not struggling against him, her body like a rag doll in his arms. He almost wished she'd pull her damn switchblade on him. He let go, and she crumpled on the bed and curled into a tight ball. He felt like the biggest dick on the planet.

There was a knock at the door, and he covered his eyes and took a deep breath.

"Everything okay in there?" Mae asked.

Mark opened the door and croaked, "Fine, sorry." Not taking his word for it, Mae shoved past him.

Tucking Jinx in to bed, Mae crooned, "Everything's going to be all right. We're here for you and nobody—" she gave Mark a pointed look "—will hurt you again. You want that medicine the doctor called in for your nerves?"

Jinx nodded, and Mae gave her one of the pills. Giving Jinx a kiss on the forehead, she prayed, "Dear Heavenly Father, look down and watch over my sweet girl. Keep her safe and secure in the knowledge of your love. Amen."

Mae leveled another warning look at Mark before leaving, shutting the door behind her.

Running his hands through his hair, he sat next to Jinx on the bed.

"I'm sorry," he repeated, not knowing what else to say.

He grabbed a cigarette and offered her one, but she ignored him. Her face relaxed, and her eyes became heavy-lidded as the medication took hold.

"Mae hates smoking…"

He put the cigarettes down and stroked her cheek.

"I feel disconnected, shattered. There are too many pieces to ever put back together again…" she whispered as her eyes glazed over and drooped.

"We can fix this. I can fix this," he mumbled. "I promise I'll fix it."

Her lack of response unnerved him. Maybe he should take her to the hospital? Was she still in shock? No, it was that damn pill. Eerily silent, her face expressionless, he might as well be talking to the wall. He brushed her bangs out of her face. Instead of flinching or pulling away, she remained still. Mae was right; it was as if she'd died with her father. Her beautiful soul no longer resided in this fragile, broken body at all.

He watched her until she was sound asleep. Tears slipped down his face as he turned off the light and crawled into bed, wrapping his arms around her unresponsive body. He buried his face in the back of her neck. When he was a small boy, his mother never told him goodbye. She simply walked out and left him in bed—alone and hugging his only toy, a metal dump truck. That same heart-stopping fear filled him now.

Mark snored behind her in slow, easy breaths. The room spun for a moment as she sat up, but she managed to ease out of bed without waking him. Yesterday was a blur. She didn't think she'd be able to breathe until she was out of this godforsaken place. Quickly, she threw her things into her overnight bag and left, closing the door behind her. Mae was in the kitchen, and Jinx cursed her luck. Anxiety, fear, and disgust swirled through her medicated brain, suffocating her.

A hasty text to her brother-in-law and his instantaneous response reassured her she'd be gone soon.

Walking into the kitchen, she found herself enfolded in Mae's arms.

"My sweet girl."

This woman, who was more like a mother than her own, cupped her face in her warm, brown hands—hands that had held her, bathed her, and wiped away her tears many times, including last night. For a few seconds, Jinx closed her eyes and drew comfort from them.

"You get any sleep?" Mae asked.

Jinx nodded. Mae moved to pour her a cup of coffee, but Jinx placed a hand on her arm, stopping her. Finding her voice, she took a deep breath to steady it. "I'm going to go have a cup of coffee with Matt. He's on his way over to get me."

"What about Mark?"

"Let him sleep," she replied, turning away. It was impossible to look Mae in the face and lie. "He needs it."

Luckily, Mae agreed. "Okay, honey."

Her chest felt tight with her rising anxiety. She used to wish she could remember. Now she just wanted to forget. A knock at the door made her scurry so Mae wouldn't see she was leaving for good.

She gave her a final hug. "I'll get the door. I love you."

"Don't be gone too long. At some point you need to go see your mother and help her with the arrangements. Mrs. Carlton called and said she cried all night. She's going to need you."

Not. Going. To. Happen. "Bye." She ran out of the room.

I can't take care of myself, much less her. How much did she know? Jinx refused to stick around and find out.

Matt raised his brows with surprise as she slung her overnight bag on her shoulder, closing the door behind her.

"Jinx?"

She put a finger to her lips and motioned with her head toward the car. Jumping in the passenger seat, she buckled up. As Matt drove away, her knee bounced. Nervously she prayed no one saw her leave with her bag packed. She glanced over her shoulder, but the house remained quiet, and she let out the breath she'd been holding.

"Thank you for coming to get me."

"I take it this isn't just coffee and talking. Want to come back to the house? Luke would love to see you. It's been hard…explaining." Matt's scruffy jaw clenched, and the exhaustion around his dark eyes made him appear older.

"No, thank you. How's Sammie?"

"Coming home today and good as can be expected. Um…matter of fact, she *is* expecting. We just found out. The news may be what set your father off. Now quit stalling and tell me what the hell is going on?"

"I need a ride to the bus station."

The car swerved a bit with his reaction. "What? You can't leave. What about your mother?"

"I can't deal with this right now."

"I know this is overwhelming, but running isn't the answer. Your mother's going to need you. Yesterday was a nightmare—"

She shook her head, motioning with her hand for him to stop talking. She couldn't deal with this. *Get out, get out, get out…* The refrain repeated in sync with her pounding pulse. They rode in silence for a few minutes, the passing scenery a blur as she concentrated on keeping her rising panic at bay.

"Turn here. I need to show you something." She motioned Matt to pull over onto the deserted road that led to the bluff. He sighed, pulled over, and waited.

"I, I know you and Karen had ups and downs, mostly because of my family. And I'm glad you're happy with Sammie. And a new baby…Will I still be Aunt Jinx?"

"Of course." Matt sighed and rubbed his face, his shoulders sagging a bit. "I loved your sister—"

"I know! I know. I'm not blaming you. But we both know she had issues. I have something that might help you understand Karen a little better. I don't know how much she told you, or how much you know after yesterday…" She pulled the spiral notebook from her bag and handed it to him. "The blood stains are mine, not…Please don't hate her," she blurted. Her hand shook when he took it from her.

His brows drew together. "I don't. I was angry at the world after she and Elizabeth died…" His voice trailed off as he thumbed through the pages. "What is this?"

"It was Karen's. I found it in our fort in the backyard." Jinx swallowed the lump in her throat. "Don't read it now. I have to get out of here. The bus leaves soon."

"I thought Mark brought you." He started the car.

"He did, but I'm not going back with him."

Matt shot her a worried frown. "Why? Did he do something to you? Where are you going? I'm sure there'll be a funeral or something. You can't go. Leaving isn't going to solve anything. Tell you what, come stay with us. Luke would love it." He swerved and made a U-turn to go back home.

"Turn the car around." She hadn't raised her voice, but the opened switchblade she held at his throat trembled with her shaking.

"What the hell?" He blanched as he slowed the car to a stop.

"I-I'm sorry, Matt. Just drop me off at the bus station. I can't talk about this."

"Put the knife away. You're not going to use it." Sounding annoyed now that the initial shock had worn off, he easily disarmed her and threw the closed switchblade in her lap. She gripped it like a lifeline.

He was right, of course. She'd never hurt him. *What's wrong with me?* She couldn't seem to gather her scattered thoughts. "I have to go. Please, Matt."

"You're overwrought. How about I take you to the hospital?" he coaxed softly, as if she were Luke's age and having a meltdown over a toy.

He started the car and headed toward the hospital. The only red light in town stopped him, and Jinx took the opportunity to get out. Even if she had to hitchhike, she'd get out of this place. Grabbing her bag and purse, she jettisoned from the car and started to run, not looking back, darting through lawns and backyards to avoid Matt.

It took her fifteen minutes to reach the bus station. When she arrived, she cursed her luck. Matt had beat her there and parked across the street, watching her. Mark paced in front of the bus station, his hair disheveled, still in his sleep pants and an inside-out T-shirt.

Mark trained his eyes on her. She felt like prey in the sight of a wild animal.

She glared and lifted her chin. "I should've known Matt would call you."

"Where the hell do you think you're going? Are you fuckin' crazy?"

She laughed. "With my family history? That's a moot point. I'm leaving."

"You can't leave! What about the funeral—" He paused and gentled his voice. "Your mother needs you."

"So everyone keeps saying. She's never needed me before. She was never there for me when I needed her!" She spun around, digging her nails into her palms. *Not. Going. There.*

"I love you."

She stopped and closed her eyes. "Don't say that. I don't need you to try and fix this with meaningless words."

He stood so close to her she could feel his warm breath on her forehead. "They aren't meaningless. You've been through hell, but you're a survivor. I love you, Jinx. I won't let you be hurt again. I promise."

"Don't be ridiculous. You can't promise that. I don't want your love. I'm broken, and you can't fix me. I'm not the princess in a fairy tale, and you're not froggin' Prince Charming. Like I told you last night, I'm broken. Pieces of me are scattered all over the place like my father's brains," she said, unable to keep the bitterness from her voice. "Leave. I don't want you here." She rubbed her thumb along the switchblade, drawing comfort from it.

Mark held her chin between his thumb and index finger. "You little coward."

Startled, she looked up. Anger flashed in his eyes.

"If I leave now, this is it. Do you fuckin' hear me?"

"Loud and clear." She spun away from him and marched inside to the ticket desk. *Come after me,* the small piece of her fragmented heart screamed silently. She paid for the ticket and turned around. The part of her brain functioning on autopilot replied, *It's for the best.*

The bus pulled up, and she ran to hurry aboard. Through the window she could see Matt and Mark arguing.

She sank into a seat, and thankfully, the bus pulled away. Her grief and pain streaked down her face as all color seemed to fade from her surroundings, turning everything into a grainy old newsreel. The outside world was now only a shade lighter than the darkness within her.

Her phone lit up with texts from Matt and Mark. She turned it off.

Stunned, Mark had stared at her back as she boarded the bus. He'd be damned if he'd beg her to stay. Matt had run toward him.

When the hell am I going to learn my lesson?

Now.

Fuck her. Fuck meaningful relationships. Fuck every goddamned thing about Jinx Howell.

"Are you going to let her leave?" Matt had asked breathlessly. "We have to stop her. She isn't thinking clearly."

"You know that, and I know that. But she's an adult. What the fuck are we supposed to do?"

And she doesn't love me.

He was done. He'd never set foot in this damn hick town again. Still, he'd fired off three texts to Jinx before spinning on his heels and marching to his car.

As expected, she ignored them. He'd watched as the bus pulled away and then returned to his car, oblivious to anything else Matt had to say.

Flooring the gas pedal, he drove until the road blurred and he knew he'd wreck if he continued. With a curse, he pulled over and shut off the engine. Choking on the lump in his throat, he attempted to pull air into his burning lungs.

The refrain from his lonely childhood looped through his brain. *Don't leave me, don't leave me, don't leave me…*

Chapter Eighteen

Ten months later

Holding a squirmy one-year-old Lena on his hip, Mark tickled her wet chin, enjoying her laughter.

"Drop my kid and you'll have to buy me a new one," Derrick joked. He flinched when Ava slapped his arm. "Ow, woman, that hurt."

Mark laughed and pointed at Ava's expanding belly. Junior was due in five months. "How much for that one, Ava? This one's spoiled, rotten. P-U. You got a poopy diaper, Lena?"

"Uh-oh!" Lena giggled and repeated her newest phrase a few more times.

"I ain't sellin' my baby, and you better not break the one I've got," Ava grumbled, rolling her eyes. Her mouth popped open as a delivery guy rolled in a keg of beer.

"Who ordered a keg for a kid's first birthday party?" she fussed, running after the guy as he headed toward the backyard.

"You're taking the hit for me, right?" Derrick asked.

"Will do," Mark answered, laughing.

"So who's the date *du jour* for this shindig? Lemme guess—it's a Christina, a Shannon, or an Ashley."

"Why do you say that?"

Derrick shrugged. "Those are the names you tend to cycle through most, Two-Time." He grinned at Lena. "Remember, sugarplum, never date a man like Uncle Mark. Daddy will have to kill him."

"Uh-oh!" Lena responded.

"Very funny. And none of the above. Maybe I'll pick up someone here."

"Okay, creeper. This is a one-year-old's birthday party."

"Yeah, but you ordered a keg, so surely some of the girls will be legal."

It still amazed him that Derrick was a father, and a good one. Although the second baby had been an unexpected surprise for him and Ava, they were excited about their growing family. A mild twinge of jealousy zipped through him as Lena reached for her father, a bright smile on her face. *Analiese…*He shoved the incomplete thought aside. Now wasn't the time to dwell on the past.

"Oh crap, she's loaded for bear." Derrick wrinkled his nose. "Hey, Mark, I meant to tell you, and I'm sure you won't mind—"

Derrick stopped and turned when someone called his name. He greeted the throng of guests arriving. The noise in the small house escalated.

"Tell me what?" Mark asked.

"I'll text you. I've got to change this stinky diaper," Derrick yelled over the clamor.

Mark rolled his eyes. Turning away, his heart slammed in his chest when he saw her. It had been almost a year since she'd dumped his ass at the bus station. After she'd ignored his texts and phone calls, he'd given up and moved on.

But in truth, he was growing tired of his lifestyle and longed to settle down. Maybe it was because he was close to finishing his degree. Derrick was going to buy him out. Roots. He wanted to belong somewhere…and to someone.

At first glance, Jinx didn't appear to have changed much—except now her bleached blond hair almost brushed her shoulders and had a streak of pink. Her matching neon nails clutched the arm of some guy in a suit. The overdressed couple stood out at the one year old's birthday party. A minuscule black dress clung to her thin frame, barely covering her ass. He didn't like the way the guy patted it with familiarity.

Not one damn bit.

Amber-colored eyes, heavily rimmed in black, met his. They were glazed and lifeless, as if Jinx had given up on living. Only her teeth on her lower lip revealed her knowledge of his presence. She looked away and sidled closer to her date, almost using him as a shield.

Shrugging her fingers off his arm, the jerk said something that made her hang her head and shift on her fuck-me stilettos. When the asshole walked away, she threaded her fingers together and glanced around, as if looking for someplace to hide. She only smiled when she accepted a drink someone offered her, throwing it back.

Mark didn't waste any time easing through the crowd to get to her, even as his mind screamed, *don't do it.* Her gaze fell to the floor. Reaching out, he eased her bottom lip from her teeth with his thumb.

"Don't touch me," she hissed under her breath. Looking up, her wide eyes shifted to her date, her hands twisting together.

"Don't flatter yourself."

Hurt flashed in her eyes. Mark frowned and stared at the fresh bruises on her arms in the shape of fingerprints.

"Who's been mauling you?"

Her gaze darted again to the gray suit. "N-Nobody. I just bruise easy. No kilt today? I bet you still wear a kilt better than anyone I know." Despite her small smile, an aura of profound sadness surrounded her.

"Thank you. You look like shit. Are you okay?"

His questions were interrupted by Lena's happy giggles; she squirmed in Derrick's arms as he approached.

"Hey! Glad you made it." Derrick gave Jinx a quick hug. "Ava will be excited to see you. Here." He pawned the little girl off on her before hurrying to the backyard.

Across the room, Ava shrieked and hurried over. A genuine smile lit Jinx's face as she hugged her. Jealousy crept into Mark's heart, unannounced. He wanted her to smile at *him.* It was disconcerting to realize how much he'd missed her.

She was the reason he was bored with life. And it made him mad at himself to realize he still wanted this fucked-up chick. *I must be more of a masochist than I realized.* The damn woman had kicked him to the curb as easily as putting her garbage out on the street.

The jerk walked back over, grimacing at Lena's laughter as Jinx tickled her. Giving Ava a cursory glance and nod, his eyes narrowed on Mark, and his lips turned up in a sneer. Ava walked away when someone asked where she wanted the birthday cake, leaving Lena with Jinx.

The suit lifted a condescending eyebrow as he held out his hand. "Bob Lalande."

"Mark MacGregor."

"Oh, I know who you are. You're infamous."

Mark reluctantly shook his hand, adding a bit more pressure than necessary to let the fucker know he wasn't intimidated. "I don't know about *infamous*."

"Well, I've heard your name cross her lips more times than I care to remember." He motioned toward Jinx, who blushed and focused her attention on the little girl in her arms. "But we've almost worked that out, haven't we?" He gripped the back of Jinx's neck, and she nodded with a forced smile.

Lena squirmed in her arms, as if sensing the tension. Mark took the child to keep from throwing a fist into the smug bastard's face.

What the hell is wrong with Jinx? Why was she with this guy? Dammit, if he'd ever treated her like that, she would've sliced his balls off and handed them back to him on a platter. Someone walked by with a tray of drinks, and Jinx grabbed one, chugged it, and replaced it on the tray before taking another. She swayed on her heels and reached for Bob to steady her.

Mark winced when Lena pulled on his lip, and he shifted her to his other side where she grabbed his ponytail instead. At least it was a tolerable pain — not like the one squeezing his heart right now.

"Let go," Bob hissed, shaking Jinx off. "Has seeing your old fuck buddy made you forget your place?"

In her inebriated state, Jinx stumbled, and Mark caught her, balancing her while juggling the squealing kid in his other arm. Derrick flew to his side, rescuing his daughter. When Bob started berating Jinx, Mark had had enough.

Fueled by all the feelings he'd buried since Jinx had left him at the bus station, Mark drew back and punched Bob in the face. The asshole's head snapped back as he crumpled to the floor. Several guests held Mark back as Bob struggled to his feet and slunk toward the exit.

Shaking his hand, Mark apologized after a moment and freed himself from the hands that held him. He prepared for the wrath of Ava, knowing he deserved it. He should've hit the prick outside and not disrupted Lena's birthday party.

Not that she seemed to mind. Lena clapped and bounced in her father's arms. He and Derrick kept silent as Ava started her blistering diatribe. It was a matter of self-preservation. Even on a good day, no one wanted to cross the feisty Ava, but these days she had the temperament of a honey badger.

When she'd finished, he nodded contritely and glared at the front door, contemplating going after the stupid piece of shit. "Goddamned motherfucker," he muttered, accepting a plastic bag filled with ice for his swelling hand.

"Thanks, Eunice…" His eyes narrowed as Jinx slipped through the crowd, stumbling several times.

He was at her side in an instant. "Going somewhere?"

Her breath hitched, and he watched her breasts rise and fall with her labored breathing. "He's my ride. I have to go. He's going to be angry."

"All the more reason you're not going home with him." Grabbing her hand, he pulled her down the hall and into the bathroom, locking the door behind them. He tossed the makeshift ice pack in the sink, picked her up, and sat her on the counter. "What the fuck is going on with you, Lovey?"

For a brief second, a flare of the spirited girl he remembered flashed across her face, but it was gone so fast he wondered if he'd imagined it. She opened her mouth to speak but shut it and shrugged, looking away. He wanted to hit something. Why was she so beat down? His breath hissed between his teeth.

"You don't deserve to be treated like this." He cupped her cheeks in his hands and turned her face up to his. "Look at me."

"Don't I?" she whispered so low he had to strain to hear her.

The weary, sad gaze that met his wrenched his heart. This wasn't the girl he'd obsessed about since their meeting in a dark alley when she'd held a switchblade to his throat. This girl was a ghost of herself.

"I need a drink," she said, louder, pushing at him as she wiggled to get down.

"You've shut me out for months. I may not be your lover, but goddammit, I'm your friend. How much have you had to drink already?" He could smell the alcohol on her, and it wasn't just from today. It was the stench of an alcoholic; it seeped from her pores.

"Not nearly enough to deal with all this shitake." Her forced laugh sounded tinny.

"I'm taking you home."

"To Nashville?" she asked.

"To my place. Come on, I'll take you to get your things."

"I c-can't—"

He silenced her protest with his mouth, and a part of him wanted to cheer in triumph when she returned the kiss hungrily. Her fingers wrapped around his ponytail, and he lifted her by her ass and turned, shoving her against the door. She ground against his erection, and a moan escaped her lips. It was like coming home, and he hadn't realized how homesick he'd been.

Someone pounded on the door, bringing him back to the painful present. The harsh sound of their ragged breathing filled the small space.

"Why do I lose all sense of control around you?" he rasped into her ear, still holding her close.

He felt her lips curve into a smile against his neck. "I've wondered the same thing."

"We need to talk."

"I know, but—"

Another pounding on the door, this time followed by a dire warning from Ava. "Whoever is in there, get the hell out. Some of us don't have full control over our bladders. You have until after I kill my husband for having a keg at a kid's party. That gives you about five minutes. If you're not out by the time I return, I'll bust this door down and kick your ass."

"That's scary as fuck," he muttered, allowing Jinx to slide down his body, wanting her as badly as he ever had.

She wobbled on her feet, and he remembered she'd had a lot to drink.

"Come on. I'm taking you to get your things, and you can stay at my place. There's no way in hell I'm letting you go back to that abusive jerk. You have lousy taste in men."

She shrugged. "The good ones tend to be taken."

When the door flung open, she shook her arms, trying to loosen her tight muscles, preparing to take the hit.

"About damn time you got home, you whore."

Bob's anger dissipated, and his one visible eye darkened when he saw Mark standing behind her.

Holding an icepack to his swollen face, he stepped aside and let them enter. Jinx gathered her things, vaguely wondering in her alcohol-induced fog how she'd get back to Nashville. For sure she wouldn't be traveling with Bob. To her surprise, when she walked back into the sitting area of the hotel suite, he held out some money.

She stared at it in a daze, twisting the strap of her purse perched on her rolling suitcase.

"Take it." He shook it at her and she reached for it, a sinking feeling in the pit of her stomach. She wondered how he'd make her pay for it later.

"But what about—"

"I'm leaving tonight," he said, cutting her off. "I don't ever want to see you or hear from you again. I'll have the crap you have at my house sent to your apartment." He lowered the icepack and glanced over at Mark, as if needing approval.

She was pretty sure he'd been coerced into being reasonable, but she wasn't about to argue.

"Thank you."

He grunted in return and slammed the door behind them on their way out.

Jinx bit her lip as she fastened her seatbelt. She'd known since the day she started running that this moment would arrive. Mark deserved an explanation, and she still didn't have one other than she was trash, disposable. *God, I need a drink.* She couldn't pinpoint when it had become as necessary as water to live; it just happened. It numbed the feelings and allowed her to function. Searching through her purse, she pulled out the travel size bottle of mouthwash that held her emergency shot.

Mark grabbed it from her, sniffed it, and poured it out the window, shooting her a look of disgust.

How dare he? Fury coursed through her body. "You had no right to do that. It was mine."

"We're going to talk whether you like it or not. You're in trouble."

She ignored him. He couldn't make her talk.

She wanted to talk.

She needed to talk.

But she couldn't. If she started, she wouldn't be able to stop. And losing control like that was too scary. Her life already felt like that awful ride at the state fair where you went round and round at a breakneck speed until the floor dropped, leaving you clinging to the wall. But her wall was crumbling. And she was barely hanging on.

"I'm fine."

He hit the steering wheel with the hand already bruised from punching Bob and winced. She reached over and pulled it to her lips. His fingers wrapped around hers and gave her a comforting squeeze before letting go.

He pulled into the parking lot of the bar and turned off the ignition. He rolled down the window, pulled two cigarettes from his pack, and lit them, handing one to her. She smiled; the simple act brought back so many memories.

"It wasn't your fault," he said with a tired sigh. "What that sick bastard did to you wasn't your fault. You were just a kid."

She paused with the cigarette in midair. Leave it to Mark to get right to the problem: her messed-up childhood.

"I guess." She really needed a drink.

"Do you drink all the time now?"

Dammit, is he a mind reader?

"No."

Not when I'm sleeping.

He flicked his cigarette out the window and sighed. "Someday, you need to learn what the word *honesty* means." He opened the car door and slammed it.

How the heck could he expect her to be honest with him when she couldn't be honest with herself? Blinded by unshed tears, she opened her door and stood up, tossing the cigarette to the ground, and ran into him. His arms wrapped around her.

Closing her eyes, she stole the moment of comfort and relaxed just a bit. It usually took a fifth to feel this way. The thought crossed her mind that if she had Mark, maybe she could stop drinking—maybe she could come to terms with her life.

"Let's go upstairs and have an honest to God conversation."

"I'm scared…"

"Me, too. I want the switchblade where I can see it," he teased in a strained voice.

His lips brushed her forehead before he pulled away, leaving her feeling empty. Swallowing her disappointment, she watched him get her suitcase from the car and followed him up the stairs to his apartment. It was like walking to her execution.

Dead girl walking. It was a pretty apt description of her life.

He opened the door and motioned for her to enter. Hopefully he'd have something to drink inside; he owned a bar. She needed it. Her buzz from earlier was fading fast. *I need help…*Maybe Mark could get in contact with Angel; last she'd heard he was in Mississippi somewhere.

The bathroom door opened, and a blond woman wrapped in a towel walked out, rubbing lotion on her damp skin. Her long hair hung down her back in a bedraggled braid.

"'Bout time you got home, you wanker." Her large eyes widened. "Oops."

"Harley?" Mark gasped behind her. "What the—"

Yanking her suitcase from Mark's hands, Jinx didn't stay to listen. She ran down the stairs and waved for an approaching cab to stop.

"Wait!" Mark ran after her and grabbed her arm. She hit him as hard as she could with her purse. He staggered backward, and she broke free. The cab screeched to a halt, and she threw her suitcase in the back. But Mark grabbed the door before she could slam it shut.

"Jinx, let me explain—"

"*I hate you.* You're no better than any other man. Your wife, ex-wife, whatever the heck she is, is waiting on you, '*you wanker,*'" she screamed. Turning to the cabdriver she said, "Drive! I don't care if you run over the son of a sea cook. I'll tip you an extra twenty to get me out of here *now.*"

Following her direction, the cab lurched forward, and she yanked the door closed as Mark swore. Her heart hammered in her chest.

"Where to?" the cabbie asked.

"The airport."

She was terrified of flying. But the airport had a bar.

"What the hell are you doing here?" Mark roared, slinging his keys on his coffee table.

Harley's chin rose, and she jabbed her finger into his chest. "Don't yell at me. I left you a text and a voicemail telling you I was coming. When you didn't respond, I told Derrick, and he said he'd let you know. He gave me the key to get in. I have a yoga certification class tomorrow and needed a place to crash—just for one night. I didn't realize you were having spend-the-night company."

Fuck. His phone was on his dresser and had been all day.

"I didn't see your van in the parking lot. And you just found out about this class?" He collapsed on the couch, closing his eyes.

"Uh, well, no. But you know me—I'm spontaneous. I took the train." She snuggled in next to him and wrapped an arm around his waist. "I'm sorry."

He sighed. "It's okay. She probably wouldn't have stayed anyway. Why, dammit? Why does everyone leave me…"

Harley cupped his cheek in her hand and looked straight into his eyes. "Wow. She's the one, huh?"

"No. Yes. Maybe. I don't guess I'll ever have the chance to find out." Mark sighed. "It's a pity we couldn't have found that with each other."

"We were never meant to be. As much as I love you, it wasn't right."

"Jinx is in trouble, and I don't know how to save her," he admitted softly.

"Call her; explain things."

"She probably wouldn't answer, so why bother?" He closed his eyes for a moment. "How goes it with your elusive lawyer? Is he still a dick?"

Harley shrugged. "Hush. You two used to be friends. I haven't been home in ages. Damien Sinclair doesn't even know I exist, but I haven't given up hope…"

"God, we're pathetic."

Harley giggled. "Nah, I like to think we're persistent. You can't save her, Mark. She has to save herself. But don't give up on her. Heard from Angel lately?"

"Rarely, but he's doing good, still clean."

"I'm glad. Do you ever wish we could go back to being kids and carefree?"

"Maybe high school, after I came to live with the Lassiters. Before that was hardly carefree."

"Adulting is hard. I'm not doing a very good job of it."

Mark looked over at her and smiled. "Think it's time for us to grow up?"

She scrunched her nose.

He laughed. "I didn't think so."

They sat in a companionable silence for a few minutes.

Yawning, she gave his leg a pat. "Bed or couch?"

"You take the bed. I'm gonna stay up and mope a bit."

Kissing the top of his head, his ex-wife disappeared into the bedroom, leaving him alone.

Is this my destiny?

A week later, Jinx sat on the side of the hospital bed, exhausted. "I don't know if I can do this." Getting dressed had required Herculean effort.

"You have to," Ava responded.

Angel raised his eyebrows and shrugged. "If you don't do this, is there anything special you want me to say at your funeral?"

Her mother shot him a hurt look.

"Please, Jinx. You have to do this!" Ava dabbed her eyes with a tear-soaked tissue. "You're my best friend; I need you."

Beside her Mark stood silently, arms crossed.

Angel shrugged. "Sorry to be a downer. I'm just keepin' it real. Mrs. Howell, why don't you go get the car?"

Without so much as a *See you in a minute*, her mother left. She'd aged since Daddy's death, and still seemed to need someone to tell her what to say and do. Jinx's worst nightmare was to become like her mother.

"You're stronger than you think." Ava kissed her forehead. "I need to get home. Derrick's probably ready to throttle Lena. You can do this. You ready to go, Mark?"

"In a minute."

Ava waved as she left the room.

Jinx's stared at her hands, not wanting to look at Angel. His sharp blue eyes saw everything. And she didn't have a clue what to say to Mark. "I don't know…"

"You're not doing this alone. You have support and love," Angel said. "Although your mom's not exactly a warm and fuzzy person, she's here. I'm here."

She glanced up and saw him give Mark a pointed look. He remained silent.

Jinx struggled to put her shoes and socks on. "Don't blame my mother. I abandoned her before my father's funeral. Me being in the hospital…I'm sure it's taken a toll on her. She's never been well, emotionally, and our relationship is strained at best. I'm actually surprised she's here. Having an alcoholic daughter isn't exactly something to be proud of."

Angel leaned forward in his chair. "Trust me, I get it. I'm a disappointment to my family, too. But, Jinx, you're not alone. And you nearly died. You had alcohol poisoning. This is some serious shit."

She hung her head, ashamed all over again. From what the shrink had said, she'd been found passed out in the women's room at the airport, lying in her own vomit. Along with the psychiatrist, her mother, Mark, Angel, and Ava had done an intervention this morning. Now she was headed to rehab. And she was terrified.

"I wish you could go with me."

"I know, but only you can do the work, Jinx."

"Am I going to be real sick?"

"You've been through the worst. Give it a chance. If you don't trust me on anything else, trust me on this. Without it, you're going to die. Do this for yourself, my friend. You're worth it."

She wanted desperately to believe him, but deep down, she didn't think she was.

Still, what other option did she have?

Angel stood. "I'll wait on you outside, Mark. The nurse will be here with a wheelchair in a few."

Jinx's heart pounded as he left, closing the door and leaving her alone with Mark.

"You didn't have much to say at my intervention." The words tumbled out layered thick with sarcasm.

"I didn't figure you'd listen. You don't seem to give me or my words much credence."

"I'm sorry." She meant it. "I really don't see how this can work…"

"It's worked for Angel. Hell, he was slammin' heroin. You can do this; just be honest with them. Be real. You've been through shit. Your only job right now is to take care of yourself and get sober."

"Easier said than done," she whispered.

"I brought you a gift. It's one of the few good memories I have from my childhood."

Her head snapped up. He handed her a bag she hadn't even noticed. Inside was a copy of *The Velveteen Rabbit*.

She blinked back her tears. Mae had read this book to her when she was a little girl.

"Th-Thank you, Mark." She added in a whisper, "Where does this leave us?"

"Honestly? I have no fuckin' clue. Friends, maybe? Look, Angel, Ava, even your mother, and I wouldn't have been here if we didn't believe in you. Hold on to that." He slipped out the door.

Friends. She'd take that. It was something. He'd given her this gift, but she still didn't know why his ex-wife had been at his place. They had so much baggage between them.

Despite everyone saying they were here for her, she felt terribly alone.

She tossed the book in her purse as she considered making a run for the nearest bar.

Chapter Nineteen

Three months later

Jinx stood by herself in the cemetery. A cold breeze blew, but the sun was bright and warm on her face. Christmas would be here in a couple of days, but she didn't feel like celebrating. She gazed at Karen's tombstone and settled the poinsettia between her stone and Elizabeth's. Karen had loved Christmas. Jinx looked over at her father's austere, black headstone and swallowed. Her feelings were convoluted as she took in the dates. But at least she wasn't afraid.

Yesterday was the first time she'd seen his final resting place, and it hadn't been by choice. Beside it the ground was covered with flowers, still fresh from her mother's burial. Mother had passed much as she led her life: silently and alone. They said it had probably been a massive heart attack.

She blinked back her tears, wishing things had been better between them. They'd started the slow progress of mending their relationship with family counseling, but now there would never be any resolution. And questions remained unanswered.

She felt very alone, unsettled. Her alcoholic brain whispered an easy fix.

Turning on her heel, she walked away. *I will not drink today.*

Two months later

Mark lay on top of the covers, staring at the ceiling. Beside him, Harley yawned. Why he'd ever agreed to bring her here, of all places, was beyond him. Of course, she had no way of knowing Jinx was from this area. Nor had he revealed the details of his previous painful visits here.

"What's the deal with Damien? I thought you were done with him for good. What gives? You still moving to New Orleans with me?"

He'd been home visiting his parents in Atlanta when things went sour between his ex and his ex-friend, Damien Sinclair, Angel's older brother. He hadn't liked it, but Harley and Damien had hooked back up just after Christmas. And the dumbfuck had already screwed things up between them, *again*. True to his pattern, Mark had offered Harley an out when she came to him and suggested she move to New Orleans and take a job at The Highland Hangout. Their trip had been delayed because she'd wanted to stop in Pine Bluff—of all the damn places—to see Angel and meet his new love interest, Maggie.

Unexpectedly, Damien had been here when they arrived as well, and he and Harley had gone off together last night to talk.

"He says he's falling in love with me," Harley said with a sigh. Doubt laced her voice and she curled into his side with her head on his shoulder.

Mark frowned. "You do know guys will say anything to get into your pants, right? It doesn't sound like much of a commitment to me."

"Spoken from experience?"

He blew out a harsh breath. "C'mon, Harley. That was a low blow, and you know it."

"I know. I'm sorry. It was as much my fault as yours. Maybe more. Forgive me?" She traced their daughter's name where it was tattooed on his wrist. "I don't regret one minute of my life, except I wish I'd never hurt you. But I'll be honest, I'm not a fan of your two-time rule. You need to let someone in, Mark. Don't let our failure in the past color your future."

Mark sighed. "I'm just a little on edge. Being here has brought back some memories best left buried. And I'll always worry about you."

She *had* hurt him. Deeply. But deep down, he'd always known he didn't have one hundred percent of her heart. Damien was her first and true love; he'd been a poor substitute. If she hadn't gotten pregnant, marriage would never have been in the cards for them.

He kissed the top of her head. "That was a long time ago. I just want you happy. I'll kick Damien's ass all the way back to Georgia if he hurts you again."

Harley sat up and smiled down at him. "I know you will." She pushed a wayward strand of hair out of his eyes and gave him a kiss on the cheek. "I have to give this a chance. As we both know, life is too short to hold on to the past. I have to see if Damien and I have a future. If not, I'll move on and try to find happiness elsewhere. You need to do the same, Mark. I want you to find someone who loves you with every fiber of her being. You deserve it. You're a great husband. I'll even write you a recommendation." She patted his chest.

Brushing her hand away, he sat up. Last night, as Harley had reconnected with Damien, he'd sat and smoked on the dock, thinking about the tragic girl he'd fallen for and apparently lost. The last time he'd tried to text her, her phone number had been changed. Ava had accidentally let it slip that Jinx was back living in this area. But when he questioned her further, she'd been tight-lipped. Pride had kept him from asking Angel about Jinx. After all, *his* number was the same. She could've reached him. And it hurt that she hadn't tried.

Was she still clean? Involved with someone? He still hadn't decided if he should stop by to see her.

"Earth to Mark," Harley teased, ruffling his recently trimmed hair. "I like your hair like this. My bad boy looks almost corporate."

"Marriage isn't in my cards; I'm a player, remember? Job hunting has made me grow up. I even wear a suit and tie some days. And I hate it." He laughed and moved toward the door, but turned back to face her. "Be happy, Harley." *Not lonely like me.* "And have a nice Valentine's Day in a couple of weeks. I'll forget to send you a card, as usual."

She laughed. "I know. You, too, Mark. Thank you."

Mark threw his duffel in the car and swore when he realized he'd left a pack of cigarettes on the bedside table. The damn things cost too much to leave behind. He retrieved the smokes and, of course, ran into Damien hauling his suitcase out of his room. They'd been close friends in high school, but things had changed when Mark hooked up with Harley on the rebound.

"Don't hurt her," he growled at Damien's back. The asshole was always impeccably dressed in boring black, without one dark hair out of place.

Damien stopped and turned to face him. His eyes narrowed. "Our relationship is none of your damn business. However, we *are* in a relationship, so stay away from her. She's *mine*."

Mark held up his hands. "Trust me, *I know*. She always has been." He sighed. "But I'll always love her and care for her. Her brothers live too far away to protect her, but I can be on your doorstep in seven hours to kick your ass if I need to." He punctuated his next words by pointing at Damien's chest. "So I'll say it again, *do not hurt her*."

"I don't plan on it, so stay out of it," Damien snapped.

A slow-burning irritation ignited in the pit of his stomach, but he didn't want to cause a ruckus with the audience now forming at the bottom of the stairs. Angel leaned against the wall, gazing up at them and smirking. His fiancée, Maggie, a curvy brunette and the proprietor of the bed and breakfast they'd been staying in, tugged on his arm and whispered in his ear, motioning for him to follow her.

Harley ran out of her room, tying her robe, her hair damp from the shower. "What's going on?"

"Looks like a pissing contest to me," Angel replied.

"Angel, I need *help* in the kitchen." Maggie again pulled on his arm.

"What? And miss this? No way in hell." Angel laughed.

"I'm leaving. Harley, get packed and get moving," Damien instructed.

"Don't talk to her like that," Mark growled.

Damien headed down the stairs with Harley following. Mark went after them.

The doorbell rang, and Angel's dog bounded past them, barking as Maggie answered the door.

"Hello, Jinx! Angel told me your meeting was canceled, but won't you come in? My goodness, he wasn't lying about the size of your dog!" Maggie laughed. "Can I get you some coffee or tea?"

She kept talking, but Mark couldn't hear for the pounding in his chest. He glared at Angel. *Why didn't the asshole say anything? Was he playing matchmaker?* He'd admitted last night to finagling things so Damien and Harley were here at the same time. Had he also invited Jinx over?

"Thank you." Jinx's voice floated in from the front porch. "He did cancel, but I stopped by to firm up our decision on paint colors. The workmen want to get started on the inside later today. Angel said it was okay for Winston to visit…"

Winston trotted into the house with his tail sweeping back and forth like a windshield wiper. He barked once and ran up the stairs, placing his giant paws on Mark's shoulders. Mark staggered backward but managed to remain on his feet.

"Hey, old buddy." He scratched the dog behind the ears as he drank in the sight of the woman walking in the door.

"Jinx?" Harley gasped, giving him a side-eye.

The color blanched from Jinx's face. She stepped back, reaching for the doorknob. "I didn't realize…Uh, hello." She spoke to Harley, but her attention remained on him.

She looked different—curvier and healthier than the last time he'd seen her. Her eyes were clear and her makeup applied with a light touch, enhancing her natural beauty. Her blond hair was now a honey color and worn in a low, messy ponytail.

"Why are you here?" Harley blurted.

Angel grabbed his barking dog and slipped out of the room.

"I'm here to see Angel…I understand now why he called off the meeting. We can discuss our plans for The Phoenix Rising later." Jinx gave a sharp whistle, and Winston scrambled down the stairs to her side.

Looking decidedly uncomfortable, Angel reappeared and took Jinx's hand, pulling her away from the door. "I should've explained why I canceled. I was going to tell you later…This is my brother, Damien. He's on the board and the one who's going to help us understand all the legal stuff. You know Maggie, and, er, of course you know Mark, and I guess you know Harley. Shit. I'm sorry, Jinx."

Damien nodded at Jinx, and she offered a small smile in return. She ran a nervous hand down her paint-splattered sweatshirt, which hung off both shoulders over her dark leggings. She stared at Harley for a moment before looking away. Awkward didn't begin to describe the situation.

She scratched Winston's head, and she appeared to struggle with her words before facing Harley. "I…We've never been formally introduced. I-I'm sorry for any pain I may have unintentionally caused you. I didn't know you and Mark were married…"

Nobody moved or spoke as the words hung suspended in the air like the blade of a guillotine. Before he could react, Mark found himself shoved to a sitting position on the staircase.

"What the hell is she talking about?" Damien asked through clenched teeth.

Mark slowly stood back up and looked at the floor, not saying a word. *Shit, Harley.*

Damien shoved him again. "*Tell me.*"

"I think we all need to sit down and talk." Mark made no move to defend himself. Damien had just been blindsided, just like Jinx had in the alley. *Jesus, maybe Harley and I deserve each other.*

Angel took the stairs two at a time and grabbed his brother's arm, pulling him away. "Calm down, Damien. I'm not having a knock-down-drag-out in here. Somebody's going to get hurt, and you're upsetting Maggie."

Damien shrugged loose from Angel's grasp. Picking up his suitcase, he took Harley's arm, herding her toward the front door.

"Sin?" Harley struggled to pull away. "What are you doing?" Only she still called Damien by his childhood nickname.

"We're going home. Don't say a word. I can't talk about this right now." Damien glanced around the room.

"But I need to get dressed and pack." She shook free of his grip. Mark could tell she was working hard to suppress her nervousness.

Damien's neck flushed red. "Pack and get in the goddamned car," he told her through clenched teeth. "You have ten minutes."

Mark shook his head. This was too much. The man was too angry to drive safely. He raced down the stairs. "Don't get in that car with him. Not if—he's acting irrational." He raised an accusatory finger to Damien. "And *never* talk to her like that again!"

"Irrational? You motherfucking sonofabitch, I'll show you irrational." Damien dropped the suitcase and lunged toward him.

Mark responded with a punch to the gut that brought Damien to his knees. He was bigger and stronger, but Damien was fueled by unadulterated rage. He leaped back up and shot a right upper hook that caught Mark's chin.

Shit, that hurt. Mark gave Damien another punch to the gut that threw him to the floor. Angel jumped between them, but it was Winston's angry growl that diffused the situation.

Sobbing, Harley fell to her knees, covering Damien's body with her own. "Stop. Please, just stop. I'll explain everything, just stop…" She brushed the hair off his face and kissed him over and over.

Her love for the asshole was obvious. If he didn't realize it, he was a dumbfuck.

Damien returned her kiss and calmed down, but Mark barely noticed as he stood staring at Jinx. He rubbed his swelling jaw.

"Okay…Okay. Just pack and let's get out of here," Damien replied as he accepted Angel's help to stand. He gasped, holding his side, and Mark wondered if he'd cracked one of his ribs. *It would serve him right.*

Harley cupped Mark's cheek in her hand. "Are you okay?"

Giving her an imperceptible nod, he kept his eyes on Jinx. He was afraid if he looked away she'd vanish, like a mirage. If Harley and Damien could finally get their chance…

Jinx snapped her fingers, and the dog stopped growling and collapsed to the floor. Her gaze met Damien's for a few seconds. Mark winced at the deep sorrow and pain exchanged between them.

"I'm not coming with you, Mark," Harley announced. "At least not yet…"

"I figured as much. Just remember, I love you and I'm always here for you," he assured her, realizing a moment too late how that would sound to others in the room.

A strangled sound came from Jinx's throat, and red splotches stained her cheeks as she flew out the door with Winston on her heels. She was in her car and speeding out of the driveway before anyone could react.

Mark's shoulders sagged. *Shit. If the girl would ever stick around long enough to listen to the entire story…*

"Please, everyone. Let's have breakfast, calm down, and talk," Maggie offered, twisting the dishtowel in her hand. "Angel, should you go check on Jinx?"

Angel check on Jinx? Why the fuck should Angel check on Jinx? Angel lives with Maggie…

Damien sighed and looked as confused as Mark felt. "I'm sorry, Maggie. I just…I need to go. Your inn is lovely, and I'm very happy for you and Angel. This…" He motioned around the room. "I don't know what the hell this is. I can't think, I can't breathe…I have to go." His gaze locked with Harley's. "Are you coming home with me or staying with your…*husband?*"

"He isn't my husband. He's my *ex*-husband. And yes, I'm going home with you. I need five minutes to pack." Damien watched her run up the stairs to her room.

Mark stood with his hands on his hips, looking at the floor for a moment before raising his gaze toward Damien. "I meant what I said; don't hurt her. If you can't handle what she tells you, let her go. And for what it's worth, I'll repeat it again. It was you she loved, all along."

He turned to Maggie and Angel. "*I'm* going to check on Jinx." With one last warning look, he headed through the kitchen and out the back door.

"Mark, wait."

He heard the crunching of the leaves as Maggie followed him toward his car. With a sigh, he put his unlit cigarette back in the pack and waited for her. She was his hostess; he owed her a thank you. This mess wasn't her fault.

Maggie tucked a strand of her dark hair behind her ear. Compassion lit her green eyes as she stared up at him. "I know Harley's leaving with Damien, but don't feel like you have to go. You're welcome to stay here, rest and regroup."

He smiled in spite of himself. "You make it sound like war. I wish Angel had mentioned Jinx was coming over."

"He canceled the meeting hoping to avoid this. He, uh, told me you two had a history, and he'd planned to talk to you later about Jinx. They're business partners and creating an in-patient facility for kids called The Phoenix Rising. It's really helped Angel focus some of his restless energy. He's hoping it will do the same for Jinx. I'm proud of them."

Mark nodded. "Last time I saw Jinx, she wasn't in a good place. I'm glad her life seems to be back on track…" He sighed tiredly. "I just don't know."

Maggie placed a hand over his heart and looked into his eyes. "Listen to your heart. I saw the way you looked at each other. Don't let the past ruin what the future may hold."

He shook his head. "We're no good together. This is what we do—hurt each other and leave. We've been doing it for years."

"Maybe it's time you tried a different approach?" She smiled and patted his arm.

Do I have it in me to do this again?

Maggie stepped away and headed back toward the house. Easing into the car, he stared out the window. Decision time. Run toward another potential heartache, or go home, and wonder for the rest of his life. He sat for a few minutes with the car running, facing the road, trying to decide what to do.

Slowly, he pulled out and turned toward New Orleans.

Chapter Twenty

Jinx leaned her head against the steering wheel and attempted to control her breathing the way she'd learned in therapy. Five months, four days, and three hours sober, she hadn't been prepared for the overwhelming emotion seeing Mark had invoked. Her hand shook as she started the car.

She wanted a drink.

She needed a drink.

She deserved a drink.

Her mouth watered at just the thought.

No! She hit the steering wheel as she drove away from Maggie's inn, angry that her rollercoaster emotions threatened her sobriety. *One day at a time, one hour at a time, one minute at a time,* looped through her brain like a mantra until she could breathe normally.

What was Mark doing at Angel's? Why hadn't Angel warned her? Did her hurried apology to Harley count as making amends? So much had changed since she last saw Mark. From the hospital, she'd entered rehab. She'd checked herself out after twenty-four hours and gone on a two-day drinking binge. When she woke up, she'd found herself in a motel with no recollection of how she'd gotten there or who she'd been with. That day she'd taken a cab back to rehab and completed the sixty-day program, followed by two months in a halfway house. Her mother's sudden death had shortened her planned stay there and brought her home to Pine Bluff.

But she went to an AA meeting every day. Sometimes twice a day.

She'd almost relapsed after her mother's death, but with the support of Mae, Matt and Sammie, Angel, and her sponsor, she'd held on to her sobriety. In her purse she carried her list of people she needed to make amends to. Mark was the last apology left on the list, if her words to Harley counted. They probably didn't. She'd been hurried and acting out of shock.

"I'm such a chicken," she whispered as she parked.

Winston nudged her shoulder with his head, and she smiled and gave him a hug as she opened the car door. With the dog following, she once again surveyed the changes to the house she'd grown up in as she walked up the steps. Mae met her in the foyer with a wide smile.

Neither she nor Angel had a degree, but they both had money, and they'd agreed it best to put it to good use. Money and addiction didn't mix well. That's how The Phoenix Rising had been born. They were turning this big house into a refuge for kids in recovery from sexual abuse and addiction. Art therapy would be an integral part of the process.

"That was quick," Mae said. "Did you and Angel decide on the pale blue or a neutral color?"

Jinx followed her to the kitchen and accepted a glass of tea.

"Mark was there…" Her hand shook as she took a sip.

Mae crossed her arms and grinned. "Really? Well, imagine that. 'Bout time you two crossed paths again. It's destiny. You're meant to be. What was he doing there? Is he on his way over? I have a fresh pound cake, and I can start a pot of coffee."

Jinx shook her head. "I'm making my own destiny. And I don't know why he was there. But I can just about guarantee he won't be coming here. Harley was there too, and Angel's brother. It was all very confusing. I tried to make amends, but I did a bad job of it and ended up panicking and running out." She sighed and patted Winston's head. "Old habits are hard to unlearn."

"Don't beat yourself up." Mae tucked a stray hair behind her ear and gave her a kiss on the cheek. "You've come too far. This house is proof of that. After your mama died, I was sure you'd sell and never return. But you have, and you're turning this place into something good. Something you can be proud of. You stand tall and call your sponsor or Angel if you need them."

Jinx smiled and drew Mae in for a hug. "And you're my number-one cheerleader. Thank you. You've always been here for me."

Mae's face fell. "Not always…"

"Stop. We've talked about this. Daddy did things in secret. Punishments were doled out on Sundays, your day off. And you weren't there at night." She stepped back. "Remember how Karen and I used to beg you to let us spend the night? You were our haven, our safe place. I've never told you this, but when I was a little girl, I used to pretend you were my real mother and we were under a spell…"

Mae drew her close again. "Oh, Eugenia. I used to pretend you girls were mine, too. After Clarence was killed in the Gulf War, I didn't have anyone. I came to work for your parents, and you girls became my family. We *are* family where it matters, in our hearts."

"Thank you, Mae. I think I'll go for a walk. Maybe it'll clear my head a bit."

"All right. I'm going to put some work into these floors. Those contractor men just *think* they know how to clean." Taking the broom with her, she walked out of the kitchen.

Mae lived in the main house now, in a renovated suite on the main floor. Jinx had moved into the apartment Mae used to live in by the pool.

Jinx walked outside and took a deep breath of the cold, cleansing air. Feeling more centered, she tipped her head back to the gray sky. She looked forward to spring and the promise of hope and new life.

Winston ran off, chasing something in the woods, and she picked up her Big Book and followed him down the worn path. At her favorite spot—a large, flat rock overlooking the serene lake—she sat and wrapped her arms around her legs, feeling herself center immediately.

Opening her book, she worried again that her hasty apology to Harley hadn't really been good enough. She'd talk to her sponsor, Christy, about it. One thing for sure, she still owed Mark. Ava would know how to get in touch with him. After rehab, she'd canceled all social media and changed her phone number. But Ava remained her best friend and had been there with her at her mother's funeral. She'd often encouraged her to reach out to Mark, saying he'd asked about her.

Mark is here. Too many times to count, she'd thought about what she'd say, what she'd do when she saw him. But in her dreams and plans, it had always been *her* instigating the meeting—not stumbling upon him with his ex-wife. *Again.*

Winston came over and nuzzled her cheek before settling beside her. She yawned and curled on her side, using her dog as a pillow. *Why am I so weak?* This would have been her chance to come clean…

Listening to Winston's steady breathing and the lapping of the lake, she closed her eyes. *I might be a coward, but a nap sounds good…*

"Wake up, Lovey."

Not quite awake, she smiled, enjoying her dream. Mark was here; he'd come for her. As she stirred, her chest ached with the knowledge it wasn't real. Mark wouldn't come after her; she'd hurt him too many times.

A hand shook her shoulder.

"Come on, Jinx, it's too damn cold to be sleeping outside."

This wasn't a dream. *He's here.* Peeking from underneath her lashes, she whispered, "You're really here?"

Squatting next to her, he ran a hand over his face. "Until you run or pull a switchblade on me, yeah."

Though it was overcast, she felt as if she were staring into the sun. He was the light in her dark world and always had been.

His auburn hair was shorter but still long enough to blow in the breeze. His face was guarded, but at least it showed no revulsion.

"You never ran from the switchblade," she pointed out. "I like your hair shorter."

He chuckled and tucked a strand of her hair behind her ear. "True. Your hair is longer, softer." He stood and offered a hand, which she used to pull herself to her feet. To her surprise, his fingers interlaced with hers and squeezed gently.

"Y-Yes. It's part of my reinvention." She looked away. "I dunno if it's really me, though. I'm still trying to find myself." She shrugged.

At times she looked in the mirror and didn't recognize herself. She'd talked to her therapist, wondering if this was yet another mask she was hiding behind.

"Hmmm…It's nice. Different but nice." His fingers stroked through her hair, pulling out leaves.

Kiss me, kiss me, kiss me…

When his warm hand brushed her cold cheek, she turned into it, closing her eyes, wishing this moment would never end. How many times had she fantasized about kissing him again? At last his lips found hers, and she opened her eyes. He was hesitant, as if judging her response. When she didn't pull away, the kiss became sweet and tender, but not the least bit possessive. She opened her mouth, wanting more, but he pulled away.

Feeling self-conscious, she looked at the ground.

"I can't believe you're actually here." She choked on the words, her fear swimming close to the surface and threatening to spill down her now-hot cheeks.

He looked out over the lake. "This is what I do. Prince Chump to the rescue, remember?"

She lifted her gaze and gripped his arms. "No, you were never a chump. I-I'm an alcoholic, and I hurt so many with my selfishness. I promise I was going to talk to you, apologize for everything I've put you through. I just didn't know what to say…"

He picked up her book, took her hand in his, and started toward the house. "Don't. I don't want to play the blame game."

Winston ran ahead, chasing a falling leaf.

"But I need to —" she protested, trotting beside him to keep up.

Mark stopped so abruptly she ran into him. "Need to what? Do we really have to relive the past? Can't we just move on?" He pulled a cigarette from his pocket and lit it, offering her the pack.

"No, thank you. I quit. And yes, I have to relive some of the past. It's part of my program."

"You don't owe me a fuckin' apology."

"I do. I need to make amends."

"Amends?" He rubbed his brow with his thumb. "Geezus, Jinx. This is our problem. Everything about us is always so damn problematic. For once, can't we do simple?"

She bit her lip to keep from crying. And hated herself for being so emotional. Not numbing her problems with alcohol had flipped the switch on her inner crybaby. He was going to leave. Not that she could blame him. Her problems were too difficult to deal with, or she herself was…Her parents had told her that often enough. Even Ava had complained that she never let anyone get too close.

Pain echoed in the cavernous hole in her chest. *I will not drown my sorrow with booze.*

"Just once I'd like to go on a date—an honest to God, simple date. A movie, dinner, I don't care. I don't even want to complicate it with sex. Just a fuckin' date."

She blinked, taking in his words. *He isn't leaving?* "A fuckin' date with no sex?" She repeated, feeling a giggle rise.

He laughed. "You're right. That didn't make a helluva lot of sense. Make that just a date. No sex. What time should I pick you up?"

The cautious hope in his eyes made her smile. Despite the gray skies, her world brightened.

"Now." If he left, he might never come back.

"Now?" His blue eyes crinkled, and he gave her hand a squeeze. "I have to go back to Angel's and tell them I need to bunk down an extra night or two."

"You can stay here." She gripped his coat, not wanting him to leave.

His eyebrows lifted. "Slow down. This is just a date, remember?" He tapped her nose with his finger. "No sex. If I stay with you, sex will occur, no doubt about it."

"I don't live in the house. Mae does. You can stay upstairs in my old room. Unless you don't want to. I mean, I don't…Too many memories, even with the renovations we've started. But maybe someday. Jeepers, I'm running on and on. I'm sorry. I'll hush now."

"You don't live here? I ran into Mae at the mailbox. She told me you'd gone for a walk and pointed me down the path." He frowned. "Where do you live? What time should I pick you up?"

She let go and walked backward down the path toward home, not wanting to let him out of her sight. His smile now seemed relaxed and genuine, and it lifted the heaviness of her past off her shoulders.

A date! She was tempted to hold out her arms to see if she could fly. Or do a cartwheel.

"The pool house, six." With a laugh, she turned and ran toward home.

Impulsively, she did a cartwheel and promptly landed on her butt. She giggled, feeling silly but happy. Sometimes it was good to take a chance…And if you fall on your butt, you pick yourself back up and move on. A sharp whistle drew Winston out of the woods, but instead of joining her, he went to greet Mark.

Smart dog.

Five hours later, Mark stood at Jinx's door, taking a moment to gather his wits before ringing the doorbell. *What the hell am I doing?* Earlier, he'd driven toward New Orleans, only to do a U-turn and find himself at what used to be the Howell home. Mae had laughed and cried when she hugged him before practically shoving him toward the path into the woods.

Discovering Jinx sound asleep on Winston had been almost surreal. She'd looked and sounded different, but was she? She'd almost made it seem like they had a future, of some sort. But the fragile wall guarding his heart urged him to proceed with caution. Or were his old insecurities crippling him once again? If he expected honesty from Jinx, he'd have to acknowledge he'd never really dealt with his long-standing trust issues.

Only one way to find out, chickenshit. He pressed the doorbell and braced himself when he heard barking. Jinx opened the door and snapped her fingers. Winston sat with his tongue hanging out, tail swishing. She motioned him to enter.

Dressed in a pair of jeans and a soft pink sweater, she looked as inviting as the smells drifting from the kitchen. Her demeanor was so much softer than he remembered, and he liked it. He longed to run his fingers through the hair that now brushed her shoulders. She shoved her glasses up her nose, waiting on him.

When he didn't move, she asked, "Come in?"

Part of him still wanted to run, but the smell of dinner piqued his curiosity. The Jinx he was familiar with barely knew how to push the button to start the coffee pot.

"What's Mae cooking?" he blurted and then wanted to kick his own ass. *Way to go, MacGregor, insulting her before you even get a foot in the door.* He wasn't sure which version of Jinx this was. Maybe he should've brought flowers? Valentine's Day was coming up…Hell, he didn't date.

"She isn't. I am, if that's okay. It isn't anything fancy, but I thought it would beat anything we'd get at The Hamburger Shack. After we eat, I'd like to talk and maybe watch a movie or something. I mean, there isn't much to do on a date around here except hang out at The Roadside Tavern. And that's not an option with my recovery."

The "or something" brought quite a few possibilities to mind, but he shoved them all aside. *Slow down, motherfucker, slow down.*

"Sure, that's fine. I don't need to go to a bar; I still own one." He winked at her and liked the way she giggled. "I don't remember you being a cook." He followed her into the kitchen, Winston's nails clicking on the hardwood floor behind him. She'd painted the room a pale green with white curtains, but other than that it was much as he remembered.

"I'm not very good at it. This meal may be deadlier than my switchblade." She stopped to check whatever was in the oven, giving him an opportunity to admire the curve of her ass.

He definitely liked the pounds she'd gained.

"Quit staring at my butt," she commented without looking at him.

"I'm not," he protested.

She shut the oven door and turned around, one eyebrow lifted.

"Okay, so maybe I snuck a little peek," he admitted. Shit, he felt as nervous as a teenager.

"Some things never change." She laughed, but her cheeks bloomed the shade of her sweater.

Is she as nervous as I am?

"I, uh, obviously can't offer you anything alcoholic to drink. I'm sober."

"Just a glass of tea would be great, and congrats."

She busied herself pouring the tea. The clunk of ice cubes hitting the glass was all that broke the silence.

"Look," he said at the same time she said, "Here," and handed him his tea.

His fingertips brushed hers as he accepted the glass, and a current of electricity arced between them. She pulled her hand back as if burned and tucked it behind her. Her breasts rose and fell, and the movement mesmerized him until he realized he was staring. Reluctantly, he swept his gaze to the floor, the wall, the ceiling—anywhere but the face and body he wanted to memorize with his lips.

"So, uh, where did your mother move to? I guess living in the house was too much…"

"She died of a heart attack just before Christmas."

"Oh…I didn't know…I'm sorry." *Ava should've told me, dammit.*

"It's okay." She looked out the window. "We never fully resolved our issues, but she did come to a few family therapy sessions with me. And your family? Did you ever finish your master's?"

"Finished it in December. I've been looking for an accounting job since then and finalizing Derrick's buy out of the bar. Claire, my sister, is dating a great guy. My folks think he's a stoner, but he's just laid-back, which is what she needs. I was in Atlanta for my Dad's birthday party when Harley needed me…"

Jinx bit her lip.

"But she's with Damien, Angel's brother," he added quickly. "If the dumbass doesn't fuck it up. I know it looked weird back at Angel's. There wasn't time to explain…"

A few seconds of silence stretched into an uncomfortable minute.

"Wow. Do you feel as self-conscious as I do?" He placed his glass of tea on the counter.

"Yes. But please stay…at least hear what I have to say." She was staring at his lips. Her throat bobbled, and her breasts rose with her deep breath.

Does she feel this, too? He put his hands behind him and leaned against the counter to fight the urge to kiss her.

He wanted answers, but she'd never been honest with him before. He didn't want to get his hopes up.

Still, she stood before him now with a sense of quiet strength—not the fragile girl full of bravado he'd known before. This seemed to be a new Jinx in a lot of ways, though the sizzling chemistry between them would always be familiar.

"I'd like that. But if it's too hard right now, it's not necessary…" he began.

"It's necessary for *me*." She paused. "If you're willing, that is."

"Okay. Fine, I'll listen." He gave her what he hoped was a warm smile and refrained from drumming the counter with his thumbs, not wanting his anxiety to spread.

"Um, okay. Right then. Please, let's eat first and then talk. I'd hate to waste all this food. In case, you know…you run out the door screaming."

"The way this food smells? Not likely. I'll be too full to move."

"Or dead from botulism." She smiled and motioned for him to sit at the kitchen table. Winston settled at his feet with a loud sigh.

His stomach growled as he watched her finish whipping the potatoes. Whether it was hunger for food or the girl, he couldn't say. Her movements were sure and efficient as she readied the meal, but the soft pink glow remained on her cheeks. This quiet side of her was the polar opposite of what he was used to.

"So, when did you learn to cook, or have you just been holding out on me?" he teased as she placed a delicious-looking roast beef and mashed potatoes on the table.

Her laughter filled the kitchen. "I'm afraid it isn't much. Crockpot cooking is pretty easy. Mae's been trying to teach me. She swears I'm not hopeless, but we'll see."

Tossing the salad at the table, she served him and refreshed his tea before sitting across from him. It was all so homey and dreamlike; he could almost imagine two kids at the table along with the snoring dog at his feet. He smiled at his own ridiculousness.

"It looks great. Roast beef is my favorite." He picked up his fork.

"Oops, I forgot the vegetable." She jumped up and returned with a steaming bowl. Her eyes were bright, and there was a definite look of mischief on her face.

He raised his eyebrows and grinned back when he saw the green beans. "I'm glad it isn't eggplant."

She laughed and replied primly, "You hate eggplant."

"Yep." He winked at her.

"Perhaps we should say a prayer?"

"Huh?" He damn near dropped his fork. "Uh, sure." He took the hand she offered and watched as she closed her eyes.

"Please, God, let this be edible. Amen."

He laughed.

"Gotcha." She giggled in return, looking quite pleased with herself.

Picking up his glass of tea, he tapped hers for a toast. "To honesty and new beginnings."

Jinx propped her cheek on her hand, and he could feel her leg bouncing under the table. "To keeping it real. Do you wear the kilt job hunting?"

The first bite of roast melted in his mouth, just perfect with the creamy potatoes. He hummed his appreciation. "Nope, I'm an accountant-wannabe by day, kilt-wearing bartender by night. You'd be surprised to see how well I clean up in my nice starched shirt and tie when I'm pounding the pavement. My parents are holding out hope that I might actually get a 'real' job."

"Sounds like you stay busy. You've never talked much about yourself. I'm afraid my problems monopolized the attention when we were together. I mean when we weren't…"

"Frogging?" He laughed when she blushed.

"Um, yeah. So, tell me more about your family. I mean, I know about Harley of course…"

Jinx looked down at her plate, pushing the food around. When she noticed him watching her, she took a bite of salad.

"My parents are great," he said. "I don't see them much, but I try to call on Sundays. Mom's learned how to video chat, which can be annoying. I think she does it to see if I'm keeping my place clean." He laughed. "They pretty much rescued me from the foster-care system. I never knew my so-called real father; he died before I was born. My birth mother…" He put his fork down, his appetite waning. "She walked out on me when I was five to go 'find herself.' She was found dead a month later at a campsite, and her death remains unsolved. I shuffled around thirteen different foster homes after that, acting like a mean little shit until I ended up with the Lassiters. Kay and

Harold adopted me—that in and of itself was a miracle. Not many folks are willing to welcome a sullen, troubled teen."

He wanted to lick the glistening salad dressing off her lip, but her tongue took care of it, which made his jeans constrict.

"What's new with you?" he asked, picking his fork back up now that the focus of conversation was off of him.

"Aside from giving up being a drunken hot mess?" She grinned when he choked. "I went to rehab, but left after twenty-four hours and went on a two-day drinking binge. I woke up and realized my latest blackout spell couldn't be blamed on anything but my alcoholism. I admitted I had a problem, went back to rehab, buckled down, got clean, completed the program, and went to live in a halfway house." She looked out the window toward the main house, tears filling her eyes. "My stay was cut short when Mother died. I considered going back, but I decided to face my past here…I couldn't have done it without Mae."

She fiddled with her fork, flipping it over and over. "I'm trying to learn to let go of things that can't be changed. I'm active in a 12-step program and started therapy for the underlying issues that led to my drinking. I hope to finish my degree someday. I only lack a semester. And I spoil Matt's kids rotten, like any good aunt should. That's the Wikipedia version."

"Kids, plural?"

"Yup. Matt and Sammie have a little girl, Rayne. Luke wanted a boy, but he's okay with her now. I like to threaten Matt that I'm going to be like Auntie Mame. Sammie thinks it's funny; Matt, not so much."

Mark laughed. "I can imagine. Congrats on the new niece."

"My gift to the baby was a Velveteen Rabbit."

He laughed. "I bought Derrick Augustin Hebert, Jr. the same thing. Have you seen the baby yet? I'm still wondering how Ava talked Senior into a Junior, Derrick hates his middle name."

She shook her head. "Just tons of pictures."

After a moment, Mark turned the conversation back to her sobriety. "So rehab kinda fixed you, right? I feel like I should've intervened sooner, done something. I saw you spiraling—"

"Oh, Mark, I'm afraid you're terribly co-dependent. And rehab was only the beginning. The true battle started when I got home and faced everyday stressors. This is a disease, and currently, I guess you'd say I'm in remission."

He frowned. "When's the last time you thought about drinking?"

She shoved her mostly untouched food away and twisted her hands together. "Today, when I got home from Angel's."

He put his fork down again. "Shit. I'm sorry."

She shook her head. "No need for you to be sorry. I'm not your responsibility. This is my issue, and I'm dealing with it. The important fact is, I *didn't* drink. Sometimes I go days and don't think about it. Other days, it's a battle every minute. Angel calls it the 'nature of the beast.'"

Mark traced the rim of his glass, feeling helpless. "When we were together, I offered you alcohol just about every time I saw you. I didn't know…"

Reaching across the table, she grasped his hand and rubbed her thumb across his knuckles. "I didn't become an alcoholic overnight. You had no way of knowing. And a co-dependent is someone who cares too much and tries to rescue those around him. It isn't your job to save me. I have to save myself. This is *my* battle."

He sat still, pondering what she'd said. For as long as he could remember, he'd tried to save people. *And failed.* First his mother, then in high school he'd seen Angel—who was just a kid—spiraling out of control, but he'd gotten sidetracked by Harley and her broken heart. Which resulted in Analiese, who didn't even get a fair chance. And last, but not least, Jinx. This pattern had defined who he was, and yet it had done nothing but feed into his own trust and abandonment issues.

"So how do I stop? I can't just flip a switch and quit caring."

"I don't want you to. But I have to do this for myself. Let me put the food up, and we'll talk. I can put on a pot of coffee, and there's spice cake for dessert."

"You made a cake? Who is this domestic goddess and what's she done with my switchblade pixie?"

She laughed and stuck her tongue out. "Since we're being honest, Mae made the cake."

She removed their dishes, and he followed, scraping the plates and throwing Winston a tidbit of roast behind her back.

Dishes done and coffee brewed, she led him to the living area, where they sat on opposite ends of the couch. He looked around. The room was sparse, but he could see she was making it a home. A soft watercolor of the lake hung over the mantle. The walls were a soothing pale blue with white trim.

Slipping off her shoes, Jinx pulled her bare feet up to the couch and wrapped her arms around her knees.

"Lovey—"

She held up her hand. "Please, I have to do this, if you'll allow me."

"Go ahead."

"It goes without saying that I'm sorry for the pain I caused you. I put you in the impossible role of rescuer and then would blame you and run when you got too close. I can't do anything about the past, but I promise to be as truthful as possible in the future, no matter what our relationship is." She sighed and flicked paint off her nail. "I hope we can at least come out of this as f-friends, but I understand if that's not possible."

"You're not alone in this. I didn't give you the trust you needed, and I ran, too." He sighed. "I've got plenty of my own issues. Look, we're both fucked up, but we're kind of like different sides of the same coin, you know what I mean? I might want to kill you sometimes when we're together, but I miss the hell out of you when you're not around." He motioned to her. "C'mere. Maybe if we work at this together, we can salvage…something."

She moved beside him, and he pulled her into his shoulder and held her.

After a moment she said, "So we're good?"

"We'll never be *good*. We're more fun being bad." He chuckled and nudged her. "We're good. This is a side of you I've never seen. You're different, more sure of yourself." He stroked down her arm. "I like it." He gazed out the window at the inky darkness and pulled forth the courage to ask the question he'd wanted to ask since coming here. "So, ah, anyone special in your life?"

"Just one."

Mark wanted to kick himself. *Why did you ask?*

Jinx giggled. "Winston. He's the only constant in my life, you know that. And Mae, of course."

She pulled away from him and ran a hand through her hair. The smile on her face was infectious. "*Most* of my previous relationships were terrible, if you could even call them relationships. I want to do better going forward, and in recovery, it's advised that you learn to take care of yourself first. No relationships for a year."

"A year?" He felt himself blanch. "Like, *no* sex? Even as, say, a stress reliever?"

"That's what they say."

Mark rubbed his lower lip with his thumb, trying to decide if he should ask the next question — one that had burned forever. If he didn't, he'd always wonder, though he didn't relish the thought of being jealous of another Sinclair.

"What about Angel? Did you ever hook up with him?"

Jinx smiled sadly. "Never. I was hurt, and I used him to get back at you. Trust me, the day you came by and found him at my place, that boy was too sick to do anything but puke. He was in active withdrawal. It was gross. And now he's madly in love with Maggie. He talks about her *ad nauseam*. She's his new addiction."

She sighed and looked away. "I haven't always been discriminating about the men in my life. I've had meaningless hookups, but nothing serious. And most were douchebags. I seemed to attract guys who treated me the way I felt about myself — present company excluded. You…" She swallowed. "You were always a genuinely nice person and a true friend."

"Do you want to ask me the same question?" He smiled.

"Not really."

She made a move to get up, but he settled her into his lap. "Ask me."

"Okay, fine. How many girls have you been with, Two-Time MacGregor?"

Her false display of indifference thrilled him.

He leaned his head back, prolonging the moment, as if he had to take time to count. The huff of annoyance and roll of those amber eyes made him grin. Slowly and deliberately, he unfastened the buttons of his shirt.

The faux-bored look on her face faded. "W-What are you doing?"

"Answering your question." He pulled his shirt open, revealing his left pec, and waited.

Chapter Twenty-Two

Over his heart was a tattoo she'd never seen: a heart wrapped in chains with a banner across it that read *Jinxed.* She raised her gaze to his, covered her mouth, and giggled. Then she laughed long and deep. It was as if the chains shackling her heart—now portrayed on his chest—had fallen away.

He smiled. "Like it?"

"I-I, yes. But Ava says you're still a man-whore. I mean, you're a legend," she blurted.

The few times she'd mustered the courage to ask, Ava had told her Two-Time MacGregor's reputation was still going strong.

He raised his eyebrows and chuckled. "So you've asked about me, huh?"

Heat crept into her face, but she didn't answer.

"Well, the thing about having a reputation is, it's usually exaggerated. And what girl wants to go out with a known player and admit he didn't make a move on her? I'm not gonna lie and say I've been a saint, but really…The reputation is grossly exaggerated."

"You're awful!" She laughed.

"And for what it's worth, I've asked about you, too. But Ava…" He shook his head. "Man, it's like trying to crack a secret agent. She takes the girl code seriously. I didn't even know about your mom, and I'm sorry."

"She's a great friend."

Mark started to button his shirt, but she placed her hand on his and shook her head. He raised his eyebrows as she lifted her pink sweater over her head.

His shout of laughter when she'd finished made her giggle. Over her heart, just above her lace bra, was a tattoo of a broken heart with a sword splitting it in two. On the sword was the word *Marked*.

His index finger traced the sword and her nipples pebbled.

"I need to go," he whispered hoarsely, his eyes hooded. "Just a date…"

"But we haven't had dessert or watched a movie yet," she murmured.

"You said a year," he croaked.

She sighed. "I know, I know, stupid rules. I understand if you need to leave. Maybe it would be best…" She stood and pulled her sweater back on, taking the moment to catch her breath, reminding herself that the guidelines were there for a reason. When she poked her head through the neck, Mark was buttoning his shirt.

"No. I don't want to leave. We'll watch TV, but please, nothing with sex in it. Have mercy on me, Mistress Jinx." He winked and stood, adjusting himself.

Jinx covered her mouth, giggling. *He still wants me. Maybe there's hope.*

"I promise."

Mark nodded. "Okay, then. You choose. I'll be back in a minute. I've still got this nasty habit." He pulled out a cigarette and stepped outside, with Winston following.

After overindulging in cake and catching up on people they both knew, Mark yawned. Without either saying a word, they stretched out, spoon style, on the couch to watch TV. He said it had been forever since he'd seen anyone with a DVD player. He laughed until tears ran down his face when *Gilligan's Island* came on. His arm draped around her waist, pulling her closer. It felt right, and she smiled when his steady breathing ruffled her hair. Uninterested in the show, she closed her eyes and settled in to sleep, knowing the nightmares that often visited her would not do so tonight.

"G'night, Thurston," she whispered.

"Night, Lovey," he mumbled back sleepily.

She smiled, at peace.

She was safe.

She was home, in his arms.

His right hand numb and heavy, and Mark wiggled to try to get some circulation going. His left hand was in better shape, cradling a soft, sweater-clad breast. He resisted the urge to squeeze, still unsure where the switchblade was hidden. Jinx's hair tickled his nose, and her warm scent comforted him like no other. Despite the terrible crick in his neck, he couldn't think of anywhere he'd rather be than snuggled into Jinx Howell. He could tell by her breathing she was awake, so he nuzzled her neck.

"Morning," he growled in her ear, knowing she had to be fully aware of the morning wood pressing into her ass.

"Oh, thank God you're awake. My back is killing me," she grumbled in return, struggling to sit up and elbowing him in the ribs in the process.

"Ow, shit, watch out. Geezus, I'm too old to sleep on a couch." He sat up and shook his arm, which prickled as feeling returned.

Jinx stumbled toward the kitchen, mumbling about coffee as he and Winston followed. She opened the back door to let the dog out, and cold air swooshed in. They stood in the doorway as Winston scoured the yard for the perfect tree.

"The old boy must like it here, lots of room to run and play," Mark mused, not watching the dog at all.

"He does, but he's slowing down."

Mark laughed and rubbed his morning scruff. "Aren't we all? Pretty soon I'll have gray in my muzzle, too."

Closing her eyes, Jinx lifted her face toward the early-morning sunlight, and a smile danced on her lips.

With her tousled hair and flushed cheeks, she looked like a pixie again, but the minute she opened her eyes, it was gone. Reality returned, and she closed the door, busying herself with making coffee.

The ensuing silence was uncomfortable as she retrieved two earthen mugs from the cupboard. The smell of the brewing coffee filled the air.

"Can I ask a personal question?" he asked, leaning against the counter.

"Before coffee?"

"I'm just curious; I couldn't read it last night."

"Read what?"

"The tattoo on your ribs. I noticed it when you showed me the other one, and I wondered what it said."

Haunted eyes—the ones he remembered so well—met his curious gaze, and he almost regretted asking. After a moment she pulled her sweater up and turned so he could read the script.

> *Death freed me, and freedom killed me.*
> *Drowning, suffocating, struggling to survive.*
> *I'm here. I'm alive. The phoenix will rise.*

He turned away, attempting to swallow the damn knot lodged in his throat.

The back door opened, and when he turned around, she was gone.

Goddammit, did she run again? Grabbing a cigarette, he stepped out onto the back porch and found her kneeling by Winston, looking into the face that stared back at her with doggy adoration.

"Quit chasing the bunnies, silly old dog; they aren't bothering you," she chided. She glanced at him over her shoulder. "Winston loves to chase the rabbits, but I don't like him to…What if it's the Velveteen Rabbit?" She stood and smiled. "My tat isn't complete. I want to add a phoenix. I'm thinking of getting Angel to design it; he's doing the logo for The Phoenix Rising. Ready for some breakfast?"

She hadn't run. She was being real. It was his own insecurities fucking with his head. He nodded, still unable to speak as emotions swirled in his head. Winston licked her face, and for a brief moment she relaxed, laughing.

It was the most beautiful sound in the world, a reassuring reminder of promises and hope, a sound he wanted to hear every day for the rest of his damn life. But he'd have to work on himself, too. And he wanted to. He wanted this more than anything else.

He ditched his unlit cigarette and hauled Jinx to her feet, cupping her cold, pink cheeks in his hands. "Sweet pixie, what magic have you used to cast your spell on me?"

"Waxing poetic? I thought you were a numbers guy." Her eyes twinkled. "I dunno about casting spells, unless it's the allure of morning coffee. But the one thing I do know, we both have the breath of dragons. Don't kiss me."

He threw his head back and laughed, draping an arm around her shoulders and escorting her back into the warm kitchen.

"Go brush your teeth, woman. I want to kiss you until you're breathless."

"I really need to shower." She looked at him from underneath her lashes.

"You're trying to kill me, aren't you? I thought we agreed to take things slow."

Her fingers walked up his arm. "You're the one who just said you wanted to kiss me breathless."

He clasped her hands in his and kissed her forehead. "Kiss you, not frog you."

"I'm not froggable anymore?" she pouted.

He groaned. "That isn't what I said. Look, I'm going back to my room in the big house to grab a shower and endure the wrath of Mae. I'm sure she's well aware I didn't come home last night. If she doesn't kill me, I'll be back in forty-five minutes for breakfast."

"You're a lot surer of my cooking skills than I am," Jinx grumbled.

"True. That could be what does me in, but I have faith in you. The roast last night was delicious." As he left, he kissed the top of her head and smacked her on the butt hard enough to make her rub it.

Winston followed him around the pool. "What do ya think, Winston? Can she cook breakfast?"

The dog snorted. Mae met him at the back door, but instead of the tongue-lashing he expected, she folded him into her arms.

"It's about time you two hard-headed kids got together. How's Eugenia? Did she wake up with a smile as wide as the Grand Canyon this morning?"

Heat rose up the back of his neck. Sometimes he really missed long hair. "Mae, a gentleman doesn't speak of such things," he replied, gratefully accepting a cup of hot coffee.

Mae's eyes narrowed. "That's a good non-answer. What are you doing back here? Are you taking your things to Eugenia's?"

"Aren't you the one who fussed about me staying in her room when we first met?"

"Well, yes, but I didn't know you then."

He kissed her cheek. "Admit it, I've grown on you. I came to shower and shave before breakfast. Jinx is cooking."

Mae chuckled. "Oh, Lord. You'll be lucky to get a bowl of cereal out of her. She's not a morning person. How was your dinner last night? Did she remember to add sour cream to the mashed potatoes?"

"Yes, ma'am, she did. It was delicious."

"You go get cleaned up, and I'll make you some eggs and toast. It'll be our little secret."

"You're the best." Whistling, he took the stairs two at a time, anxious to get back and see what Jinx had in mind for the day.

After showering and brushing her teeth, Jinx raced to the kitchen and stood with her hands on her hips, looking in the sad refrigerator. *What was I thinking offering breakfast?*

She never had more than a cup of coffee and a protein bar. Checking in the pantry, she found the empty box and threw it away. There was a box of cornflakes that were God knows how old. She checked the date and tossed it in the garbage. Aside from last night's leftovers, the fridge held a carton of milk and a jar of Mae's strawberry jam. In the freezer were half a dozen frozen dinners, a frozen pizza, and a carton of vanilla ice cream. *I don't even have a loaf of bread for toast.*

The knock at the door came sooner than expected. She gave an exasperated sigh as she weighed her options. She could go borrow some eggs from Mae, they could go out for breakfast, or he could eat leftovers.

When she opened the door, Winston trotted in, shaking off the morning dew before heading to his food bowl. Mark stamped his feet and rubbed his hands together. His hair was damp from his shower, and she fought the urge to finger-style the waves into submission.

"Where's your coat?"

"Real men don't need coats." Pounding his Tulane sweatshirt with his fist, he grinned.

"You have two breakfast options."

"Oh yeah?"

"Leftovers or vanilla ice cream."

He looked at the floor as if pondering his decision and let out a slow breath. "You know, I've never done the boyfriend shtick. And I want to do it right and not fuck this up. You're important to me—"

"But?" *Is he regretting being back here?*

She turned away, still leaning on the counter for support. *I will not drink today.*

"What? There is no but." He turned her to face him and tilted her chin up. "Look at me."

Confused, she looked into his smiling face.

"I've already had breakfast. A damn good one, in fact. Mae fed me. How am I doing? I'm trying this honesty thing, so we can move forward."

"That's it?" She laughed nervously. "Holy shitake, Mark. I thought you were going to tell me goodbye."

He pulled her into a hug, kissing the top of her head. "I'm not going anywhere for a couple of days. I don't have any interviews scheduled until the end of the week. I've already let Derrick know."

As she listened to the steady beat of his heart, she relaxed and tightened her hold on his waist.

"I once told you I wanted to make love to you, slowly, gently. I still do—exploring every inch of your body."

"But the year thing—and I have issues…I'm still working on them…"

"I don't mean today. I'm not going anywhere. I'm a man who strives to accomplish his goals. I'm simply telling you, that's one of my goals."

She didn't know how to respond. Sure, she was clean, but she still struggled. Therapy was helping, but she had barely touched the subject of Mark. As co-dependent as they might be, he could easily become the healthiest part of her life—or the worst. Sadly, an actual healthy relationship was uncharted waters. She was terrified of drowning.

"I'm scared."

"Me, too."

Pulling away, she looked up at him. "Why?"

"I don't want to hurt you, or risk getting hurt myself. I don't know how to do this. Should we see a therapist? I mean—"

She attempted to lighten the situation. "Scared I'll knife you?"

"No." He paused and grinned. "Well, maybe. I'm terrified I'll push you too hard and end up doing more damage."

Looking into his eyes, she felt herself drawn in by the love she saw there. Taking his face in her hands, she whispered, "How about I promise to let you know if it's too much? And if you really mean it, yes, I'd like us to go to therapy together, if we're going to give this a go."

His eyes crinkled as a devastating grin took over the face she'd memorized years ago.

"Yeah?"

"Yeah." She took his hand in hers, interlacing their fingers. "Follow me."

Leading him outside and then to what used to be a six-car garage, she opened the door to her newly renovated studio.

"I have more I need to tell you, and I'd kinda like to do it where I feel safe, where you can get a glimpse of the real me through my art, because sometimes I struggle with words. Is that okay?"

"Of course." He busied himself looking around the studio.

He stood before a canvas with his hands on his hips, staring. In a self-portrait, the whiskey-colored eyes of the little girl, faintly seen on the canvas, seemed to follow him around the room from behind a wash of angry black strokes. It was almost as if the paint had stabbed the canvas.

Jinx rocked on her feet as he moved to another picture. She'd painted a stuffed rabbit lying in a pool of blood with the stuffing ripped from its chest. He stood still for a moment and blew out a deep breath.

Mark moved to the next canvas. This one was more whimsical, a black-ink line drawing colored in soft pastels of a pixie peeking over the shoulder of a Celtic warrior, her arms wrapped around his neck. In one hand he held a sword; the other grasped the sprite's arm.

A look of assurance and a hint of a smile played on his face.

He pointed at the painting. "That one. I want it."

She laughed. "Isn't it a little too girlie with the pastel colors?"

"Don't judge me." He chuckled, his eyes locking with hers.

Sitting on the couch, he pulled her onto his lap, wrapping his arms around her waist. She curled into him, soothing herself with the sound of his steady heartbeat.

It took her five minutes to work up the courage. But she did.

"It started when I was seven. Mother was away—having a nervous breakdown or drying out, whatever. Karen had escaped to spend the night with a friend. Daddy came into my room to kiss me good night. He was my daddy…"

Mark's hand stopped mid-stroke. Her body tightened, and the ticking clock was the only sound in the room.

"I'm not going to go into the details, mainly because I don't remember. I've just pieced some of it together from my nightmares, phobias, and Karen's notebook. My father was a sexual predator. I'm pretty sure he drugged me. He'd always bring me hot cocoa. I can't stomach anything chocolate, and now I think I know why. It makes me gag—" Her stomach lurched, and crossing her arms over her gut, she squeezed her eyes shut. "He was my father; he was supposed to protect me, not hurt me…" Silent tears streaked down her cheeks.

Mark pulled her into his chest, stroking her back and her hair. "I've got you, Lovey."

She wanted to vomit.

She wanted to curl up in a ball and die.

She wanted a drink.

Mark sat still, forcing the bile back down his throat. He'd suspected this after reading her sister's diary and thought he was prepared to hear it. He was so damn wrong.

Anger coursed through his veins, but he had to retain control, for Jinx's sake. He stroked her hair and held her tear-stained face in his hands.

"You're safe. Let it go, Jinx."

Taking a deep breath, she leaned in, whispering her confession. "I have these huge gaps in my memory. I didn't understand why I wasn't *normal* when it came to sex…Huge chunks of my memory just seemed to be on the periphery. I was scared of the dark, but I didn't know why. I was afraid of my father, but I didn't know why. I felt like such a disappointment to him…I thought Karen was his favorite. He did it to her first…"

Her lip trembled, and she looked away, her cheeks flushed.

"I hate him. I have for a long time, even before I knew why. And God help me, I have moments where I hate Karen, and my mother, even Mae, for not protecting me. After the pieces fell into place, I was so filled with rage it burned me from the inside. When my father put that bullet through his brain, I wished I'd done it. And then I felt guilty. Because despite everything, I loved him. Afterward, I drank to put the fire out, to numb the feelings."

"Oh, Jinx…" He held her, his tears mixing with hers.

"When I was around eight, I remember telling my parents I couldn't remember things. I felt anxious all the time. My father told me I was mentally ill like my 'crazy grandmother.' I thought he'd send me away. My grandmother had severe depression and was institutionalized. Mother did, too. They both had shock therapy, and the thought of it terrified me. So when I got older, I hid my fear behind my wigs, my makeup, and I presented myself as a badass, but inside I was a quivering, scared little girl." She sagged against him, her fingers clutching his shirt so hard her knuckles went white.

Dear God in heaven, if James Howell wasn't already dead, he'd kill him for sure. He held Jinx tight as she wept in his arms. Her tears bathed his neck for what seemed an eternity, but not a sound came from her throat. She fell apart just as she had suffered as a child: in total silence.

"It's okay, my love. It's okay," he repeated over and over, trying to comfort her.

What an asinine thing to say. It wasn't okay. It was so far from okay it was off the fucking charts. James Howell was a monster who should've been tortured before dying a slow, painful death.

Jinx sat up, wiping her eyes and staring at the floor. "I honestly didn't want to tell you any of this. I don't want you to see me as a victim. But I can't continue to let him have that power over me."

"I don't know what to say." He tightened his arms around her. His heart pounded as her pain seeped into him, infusing his very being. Never in his life had he felt so helpless.

"I've wondered if I'm bipolar, but my therapist says no, that these mixed feelings are normal. I loved him. I hated him. I feared him. I needed him. I have one spotty memory of him calling me *baby*, touching me where no father should, and telling me he loved me…"

His breathing felt like steam escaping a valve, and his vision went red. Like a movie playing backward, he thought about all the times she'd stopped him from touching her, the way she'd freaked out when he called her *baby*. It all made sense now. *That goddamned, motherfucking sonofabitch.*

"What your father did was disgusting, cruel, and criminal. It wasn't your fault."

"I know."

"You deserve to be happy. You deserve nothing but the best. You can't let that bastard win. You fight for this, do you hear me?" He wiped tears away and reiterated hoarsely, "You fight for this."

She nodded. "I am."

He kissed her forehead. "We'll fight it together. I'll get some counseling, too. Together we can do this, Jinx."

"Y-You'd do this for me?"

"Not just for you." He tapped her heart and then his own. "You and me. Together. We're going to do this for *us.*"

Her eyes sparkled like polished amber, and her timid smile filled the hole in his jinxed heart.

"So how do we do this? Where do we start?" Her eyes searched for answers he didn't have.

"Uh, well…Hell if I know. What do normal people do?"

"Heck if I know."

They laughed. He wanted to baptize himself within her and resurface with their past washed away. But the past would always be part of them. He had to take this slow. He refused to hurt her. She'd been through too much, and she mattered too much.

"Jinx?"

"Yes?"

"Is kissing okay? Just a kiss."

She answered with the sweetest kiss of his life.

Chapter
Twenty-Three

Three months later

Thwack! The sound of the ax splitting wood echoed through the woods. Plugged into his phone, Mark didn't hear her approach. She leaned against a tree and watched him swing back in a fluid motion before letting the blade fall, splitting the log. He'd been working since sunrise, and sweat dripped off his brow. The muscles of his arms and back rippled as he swung, spilt, and tossed rhythmically.

The sight dangled before her like forbidden fruit.

And it was her own damn fault.

And her therapist's.

And her sponsor's.

And anyone else who had ever told her she needed to take care of herself first.

Dammit, she was tired of "taking care of herself." She wanted Mark. That *was* taking care of herself, wasn't it?

It was his fault, too. Who would've thought Two-Time would be so damn noble?

For the past three months, Mark had treated her with nothing but solicitous respect. He'd come up to visit whenever he wasn't working at the bar or job hunting. And she'd made a couple of trips back to New Orleans, staying with Derrick and Ava. Either way, she and Mark spent daytime hours together, but at night they parted. And she was beyond frustrated.

He'd arrived in Pine Bluff two days ago for his latest visit. As usual, he was bunking with Mae. Yesterday he'd agreed to look over the books for The Phoenix Rising, and his advice had proven invaluable. She and Angel couldn't balance a checkbook between them, and recognizing his expertise, they'd offered him a job. He'd hedged and asked for a few days to think about it, which to her, signaled a red flag in their fledgling relationship.

Two days ago, when he'd arrived, their date had been him driving her to her 12-step meeting while he attended Al-Anon. The kiss afterward had been hot, but shortened by his hurried "good night." Yesterday, they'd met with her therapist. This was their sixth session together, and while it wasn't as awkward as the first one, Mark still sat on the edge of the couch, cracking his knuckles and looking like he might take off running at any moment.

He played the role of the perfect boyfriend: attentive, kind, funny, involved in her life—right up to the point where things *should have* turned more physical. She'd teased him last night as he left and asked if he and Mae were having a torrid affair. He'd said any woman who could make a coconut cake had his heart. She was now determined to get Mae's recipe.

She shifted where she stood in the forest, and the snap of a twig woke Winston from his nap by the woodpile. He trotted over to her, tail wagging. She petted her dog, aware of the intense blue eyes now trained on her. But that wasn't anything new. Mark had always stared at her. Only now, where his eyes used to smolder with passion, fear lurked in their depths. He watched her every move, as if afraid she'd disappear into thin air or shatter into a million pieces.

When he didn't think she was looking, a deep sadness etched his face, tugging at her heart. She didn't want to see worry lines around those eyes. Ever since she'd told him what she could remember about her childhood, he'd treated her like she was a broken toy, no longer able to be played with.

And did she ever need to be played with. She wanted him to see her as a real woman, a woman with needs. She wished she'd never mentioned the stupid relationship recommendation. How long would he stick around, knowing sex was off the table? Anyway, she couldn't continue to live like this, unable to breathe without him asking if she was okay. Now she wondered if perhaps her past was too much for him to handle, and he just didn't know how to get out of things with her. Sobriety was difficult—especially with the added layer of her childhood abuse—and sometimes her struggles were reflected in her mood swings. There was a good chance she was just too complicated to love.

His eyes met hers for a moment. His actions said he still cared about her.

But he hadn't *said* so since she'd left him at the bus station, when she thought they were meaningless words. *Was I right?*

Maybe she should tell him she loved him. But Two-Time Mac-Gregor could very well take off if she did. Love was a commitment.

Her greatest fear was that he stayed out of pity. Like the man who can't leave a woman because she's dying with cancer. As a couple, they were drowning, weighted down by their past. Perhaps one of them needed to cut the ties and save them both.

He pulled the earbuds out of his ears and smiled the smile that never quite reached his anxious eyes. "You okay?"

"Yeah," she replied, as her soul screamed, *No!* "I brought you some water and trail mix."

"Thank you." There it was again: the solicitous politeness that was driving her crazy.

All thoughts of rational conversation fled as her anger simmered and boiled. He'd told her to fight for this. Why wasn't she? The suffocating civility between them was like a blackout shade on the light of their true emotions. He'd spoken of truth between them, of being real, and yet they were living a lie, or at least half-truths. And she was at fault, scared of jumping off the ledge into honesty. She feared rejection, not being good enough.

He shrugged into his shirt, buttoning it up like a shield against her. She handed him the water and trail mix. His eyes didn't meet hers as he collapsed on the woodpile, brushing the sweat off his brow with his sleeve. When he finally glanced at her, he gave a timid, worried smile and motioned for her to sit.

Ignoring the invitation, she paced rather than hit him. The urge to drink washed over her like a tsunami. Maybe she should just leave and call her sponsor. No, she refused to take the coward's way out.

She needed to speak her truth and go after what she wanted, whatever the outcome might be.

Jinx clasped her hands behind her and swallowed, trying to speak around what felt like dry cotton in her mouth. "I, uh…"

His eyebrow rose, and he paused with the bottle of water halfway to his perfect lips. "Yes?"

"When you first came back, you spoke about being honest," she blurted, throwing her arms out with frustration.

He frowned and shifted, his gaze leaving hers for a fraction of a second.

Words were inadequate to describe the bubbling exasperation in the pit of her stomach. Closing her eyes, she slowly inhaled, trying to remain calm and rational.

She failed.

"You…you…" she gasped, until finally she stomped her foot and screamed, "Stop being so nice to me!"

His mouth twitched, and he raised a brow. "Stop being nice to you? That doesn't make any sense."

"Shut up." Trudging back and forth in front of him, she muttered every curse word she could think of.

For a good portion of her tirade, he sat with his mouth hanging open. Then he started to chuckle.

"I'm a motherfuckingsonofabitch? Why? What the hell is going on? You never cuss." He was laughing so hard tears streamed down his scruffy face.

She glared. "Quit laughing."

His look sobered. "Hey, just tell me what's going on. You're being just a tad irrational." He hesitated before adding softly, "Are…are you drinking?" He stood and stepped toward her.

"No! But believe me, the thought has crossed my mind." She laced her fingers around the back of her neck. "I can't do this anymore."

He looked sucker-punched.

The urge to drink began looping through her brain. It hadn't been this bad since her second month of sobriety, after the high of being clean had worn off and she'd been left dealing with the fragmented pieces of her life.

Just one drink. Numb the pain. You can quit any time you want…

"What do you mean you can't do *this?*" Mark sank back onto the woodpile, his shoulders sagging.

Typical co-dependent.

"*This.*" She motioned between them.

"What the hell are you talking about?" He put the bottle of water down and gave her his now-patented patient smile. "Let's call your therapist, or your sponsor. Or what about Angel?" He dug in his pocket for his phone.

Argh! She threw her weight into a shove that flipped him backward off the woodpile. His phone flew out of his hand. He sprang to his feet and his eyes burned like the center of a lit match as he marched toward her. Her heart pounded in her ears as she backed away. He reached out to grab her, but she anticipated it, darted to the left, and took off running.

"Goddammit," he swore behind her.

Heavy footsteps followed her, and she didn't dare look back as she pushed herself to run faster, ignoring the brush that scratched and snagged at her clothing.

Her side hurt, and her breathing sawed, but she pushed harder, the burst of endorphins making her feel good for the first time in days. Winston ran after them, barking. His four feet outran her two, and he jumped in front of her eager to join the game. As she stumbled, she felt Mark grab her shoulder, but Winston tripped him as well. They all tumbled to the ground, panting. Mark's arm wrapped around her as she struggled to catch her breath.

He rolled onto his back, laboring for air as he held her hand. "Fuck, I'm out of shape." He turned to look at her, and his eyes sparkled as he smiled. Rolling on his side, he plucked a leaf from her hair.

"Me, too," she gasped, when she could finally speak. "You need to quit smoking."

"Yes, dear. Damn." His smile faded, and a shadow crossed his eyes. "Why did you run? What's going on, Lovey?" he asked, rubbing her hand with his thumb.

"Stop it." She pulled her hand from his and struggled to her feet. "Stop treating me like I'm made of glass. I won't break."

He sat up, rubbing a hand over his face. "Jinx —"

"See? You're doing it."

Mark leapt to his feet. "What? What the hell am I doing?" he roared. "Goddammit, Jinx, quit acting like a girl and just fuckin' tell me what crawled up your ass this time."

Jinx grinned. "That's more like it. And by the way, I *am* a girl—not that you've even *noticed* the past three months, ya clueless jackass. And why are you chopping wood in May? It isn't like we'll need it until November."

"Because wood has to season before being burned—and I have to do *something!*" He pulled a cigarette from his pocket and searched for his lighter. "Fuck! Fuck, fuck, fuck." Clomping around like a crazed bear, he pulled her back toward the woodpile.

"What are you doing?" She struggled to get away, but he tightened his grip and kept walking.

"You're not running away again, and I need a smoke."

"You just admitted you needed to quit—"

"Shut up, Jinx."

Winston leapt in front of him, his hackles up and teeth bared as he growled. Mark let go, smiling at the dog. "Good boy. You protect your mama, because right now, I want to kill her."

Winston gave him a doggy grin and wagged his tail, allowing Mark to scratch behind his ears. Jinx rolled her eyes. Fickle dog.

"At least you're showing some emotion," she mumbled, patting Winston to assure him she was okay.

Mark stopped so suddenly she ran into his back. He turned and ground out, "What do you mean *at least I'm showing some emotion?* I've been nothing but patient and understanding with you. You said we had to wait a year, so I resigned myself to cold showers and beating off and *chopping wood* for three hundred and sixty-five days."

"That's just it—I don't want or need that." She paused and did a mental check on her feelings. "Actually, that's not true. I *do* need some of that. But, Mark, I need your passion, too. I'm not some fragile keepsake to put away on the shelf. I don't want to feel like a victim. And I've made progress. Now I want you to fuck me."

His eyebrows shot up. "Fuck you?"

He stared at her for a full minute. Then without saying a word, he found his lighter, lit a cigarette, and inhaled deeply.

She crossed her arms in front of her chest and waited.

"For God's sake, cut me some slack. I'm at a loss. I don't know what to do. I love you, goddammit, but you've always been the Mistress of Mixed Signals. As I just pointed out, you said a year. That means twelve long damn months. That's great that you think you're ready now, but are you sure? After everything you've told me, I'm terrified of triggering some horrible memory. I've done it before without even knowing it. Now I *do* know, and I want to protect you."

He took a deep breath. "Don't you get it? I *love* you, and the thought of hurting you…I hate sounding like some preteen girl, but *I just can't*. I'd rather rip my own heart out or cut off my left nut. I want to love you the way you deserve to be loved—cherished, adored, hell, placed on that goddamned pedestal. You and I are one, Jinx. If you hurt, I hurt. If you're happy, I'm happy. I don't care what the therapist or 12-step meetings say about being co-dependent. It doesn't apply to love."

"You still love me? You still want me?" She grinned as her joy slipped down her cheeks in hot, happy tears.

"Hey now. Don't cry." His voice softened, and his face creased with worry as he stamped out his cigarette. "Shit, see? I've made you cry." He pulled her into his arms. "I'm Two-Time MacGregor. Would I keep coming back if I didn't love you?"

"Then frog the one-year rule. When have we ever followed the rules?"

The shirt soaked up her tears as he stroked her back.

His chuckle rumbled in his chest. "Well, that's true."

He smelled of tobacco, the woods, honest sweat, and Mark—comforting and enticing.

Dashing the tears from her face, she looked up at him and smiled. "Green bean."

His mouth crashed onto hers. With shaking fingers, she unbuttoned his shirt, needing to feel his warm, bare skin. Impatient, she popped the last two buttons. She'd buy him a new shirt.

His lips caressed her jaw as he murmured unintelligibly. One hand crept under her shirt onto her back, his fingers branding her skin.

Mark pulled back to gaze into her eyes. She smiled at his lust-filled, hungry face and, standing on tiptoe, bit his lower lip.

He growled in the back of his throat. "I'm going to fuck you like you've never been fucked, just the way you like it. But eventually, I'm going to love you like you've never been loved, my way. Understand?"

"I understand. But first…I want to do something."

"Yeah?" His eyes lit with interest.

"Yeah. Follow me and don't think about it, okay?"

"What do you have in mind?"

She giggled and grabbed his hand. "Come on!" Taking off at a run, she hustled him toward the lake.

At the top of the bluff, Mark pulled back, shaking his head, his eyes wide. "Oh, hell no! This is right up there with spiders." He stared down at the lake below them. "How high are we?"

"Can you swim?"

"Yes, but—"

"Trust me?"

"Yes, but—"

"Hold my hand. We're going to take a literal leap of faith. And I've got something to say to you."

He stared at her for a moment, then looked back at the water below them.

"Are you Butch Cassidy or the Kid?" he joked. "And can't you say whatever you need to say here?"

She laughed and shook her head.

He sighed, took her hand, and nodded he was ready. They jumped.

And as they fell, Jinx screamed, "I love you, Mark MacGregor."

For a split second it felt like flying—until they hit the water, feet first. She was the first to surface and dog paddled. Mark jettisoned up through the water, spitting out a mouthful. His wet hair dripped down his face. She swam to him and kissed him.

"Fuck, Lovey. That was insane."

"I know."

"You really love me?"

"Yes, I love you." She giggled.

"Goddammit, woman, that's a helluva way to tell me." He dunked her. They played in the water for a few minutes and then climbed back up the bluff toward her house.

As they arrived, he swooped her over his shoulder. When she squirmed, he spanked her butt and moved to put her down.

She smacked his butt. "Don't you dare stop."

He chuckled and opened the front door. Then he kicked it shut with his foot and locked it.

"You can put me down now."

"Shut up. You're not in charge at the moment."

He carried her to the bedroom and tossed her onto the bed. Before she could move, he was on top of her, tossing her wet shirt to the floor. Her bra soon followed, and she managed to toe her shoes and socks off.

His mouth found her nipple, his teeth tugging the hard peak as he fumbled with the button and zipper on her jeans.

"Wait," she gasped, tugging at his hair.

He pinned her arms beside her head, his eyes searching hers.

"Take off your clothes," she instructed.

His lips quirked. "Didn't I tell you you're not in charge at the moment?"

She nodded. "But—"

"I realize you have control issues. So for now, we're using safe words. Otherwise, you keep your damn mouth shut unless it's busy, understand?"

"Busy?"

"Busy working. And you know what I mean."

She giggled and squirmed but was unable to move the mountain of man holding her down.

"Tell me your safe word to stop." He burrowed his face in her neck.

"Eggplant."

"And if you want me to slow down?" He nipped her ear.

She smiled, knowing he'd protect her.

"We never set one. I guess a yellow vegetable? Squash."

"That'll work, and where are we now, Lovey?" He kissed her, sucking in her lower lip, teasing her mouth with his tongue.

"Green bean, chef." She giggled against his smiling lips, wiggling her hands in his iron grasp, thrilled at being at his mercy.

He winked at her. "Good girl."

She rolled her eyes.

He laughed, and his hair dipped over his forehead in an unkempt mess as he worked the zipper of her jeans. The scruff of his unshaven beard rubbed her belly in a delicious way as he kissed her stomach, moving lower and stopping just short of the part of her that throbbed for more. One final tug and her wet jeans and panties went flying through the air.

Mark shrugged out of his shirt, giving her a hungry look. Jinx licked her lips and smiled.

"I'm gonna let you put that tongue to work in a few minutes."

"Promises, promises."

His smiled widened. "God, do you know how much I've missed you?"

"I dunno. Lemme see." Jinx reached out and unbuttoned his jeans, pulling down the zipper in slow motion. His abs danced as his breathing became ragged. When his erection sprang free into her greedy hands, she looked up at him and coyly said, "Judging by this, I'd say you missed me a little." She ran a finger from the base to the tip and circled the crown.

"That's cruel. Never use the word *little* in reference to my cock." He somehow managed to kick off his boots, socks, jeans, and underwear with the speed of a Talladega pit crew.

"It's an impressive sword. That better?"

Her body thrummed with awareness of the naked man standing before her; her mind cried out for him to relieve the desperate need within her.

"Mark…please. My way…"

"Okay." He tore open the condom, and she rolled it down his length. They tumbled into bed, and Mark positioned her on top, giving her the control.

Mark watched her with a lazy smile. "I love you," he whispered. "Promise you'll never leave me."

"I won't. I'm tired of running. Besides…" She pressed against him, raining his face with kisses. "You always find me…"

"I always will." He took her face in his hands and pressed a kiss to her lips. In his eyes she saw her reflection—and love. She lowered herself onto him and moved slowly at first, savoring the feel of everything being right in her world.

He rubbed up her thighs and grabbed her ass. His mouth found hers, and lightness overtook her mind and body. It was like flying and drowning at the same time. Drowning in his love.

"I love you," she gasped as he guided her into the age-old rhythm.

His breathing was ragged and a faint sheen of sweat dotted his brow.

She wanted more, needed relief from this pleasurable torture.

"Yessss," he hissed.

Jinx ground against him as she slid up and down his length, finding the spot that would relieve the pressure building inside her. As she moved faster and harder, he pumped inside of her. It only took a few seconds before she shattered, collapsing on top of him. He followed, his hands gripping her for dear life.

The sound of their breathing mixed with the silly snores of her dog, and the smell of their sex hung in the air. His taste lingered in her mouth, and the feel of his body beneath hers was the best of sensory overload. He hummed in the back of his throat.

"I'm sorry. I must be heavy." She moved to roll off, but he held her tight.

"No. Not yet." There was desperation in his voice.

She traced his lips with her finger and gazed into eyes that flashed fear before he shuttered his feelings. Leaning forward, she kissed him tenderly, secure in his love.

"I'm not going anywhere, and neither are you." Reaching into the nightstand, she fumbled for a moment. With a grin, she pulled out her switchblade and flicked it open. "Don't make me cut you."

Mark laughed. "I wondered where it was." He took it from her hand, closed it, and tossed it back in the drawer. "Let's shower."

"Do I have to move? I promised not to leave, and the fact is, my limbs feel like Jell-O." She giggled. "Green Jell-O."

"Yum. I love you."

"Back at ya," she murmured. "I love you, and you're stuck with me."

"And in you." A wide grin crossed his handsome face. "I have a very serious question for you."

She swallowed and steeled herself. "Yes?"

"How many condoms do you have? I've got three left."

Grinning, she raised up and peeked in her bedside drawer. "Six."

"Perfect. I guarantee you won't be able to walk by this time tomorrow."

She laughed. "Is that a threat or a promise?"

Hours later, Jinx traced the outline of Mark's Jinxed tattoo. "I need to call my sponsor and Angel."

"Why? I don't want to share," he pouted. "Besides Christy's old enough to be my mom, and Angel…just no."

She chuckled. "You're so crazy. Not to come over. To explain why I won't be at AA tonight."

"I'll take you." Mark moved to get up, but she pushed him back.

"No. You made good on your promise. I don't think I can walk," she replied.

"I always keep my promises. What time is it?" He trailed a finger up her spine.

She shivered. "It's time for you to tell me your story. You know mine. I understand why you're afraid I'll leave. And I know about Harley…" She kissed his right wrist tattoo. "But who is Analiese? And why didn't you take the Lassiters' last name if they adopted you?"

After a moment, Mark nodded. "I was thirteen when I met Claire at a soup kitchen. I'd run away from an abusive foster home and was hungry. She was volunteering there and took me home, insisting her parents do something." He grinned at the memory. "God knows why, but they jumped through the hoops and fostered me, eventually adopted me."

"But you kept your last name?"

"Yeah. Harold and Kay, my parents, convinced me it was up to me to change who I was. They said a name change didn't mean shit without behavior change. So although I had a few missteps in high school—some of them involving Angel—I eventually buckled down and tried to make Mark MacGregor someone worthwhile. I didn't want to let my mom and dad down. They took a chance on me, and I wanted to prove to myself and the rest of the world that they hadn't made a mistake. That's why it took me so long to get through school. I did it on my own."

He rolled onto his side, facing her. Jinx smiled and brushed his cheek with the back of her fingers. "You could never be a mistake. You're a good man, Mark."

"I've made plenty of mistakes. Harley for one."

Jinx swallowed, doing her best to keep her face neutral. "Go on."

"Harley's parents worked for Angel and Damien's folks. At one time, Damien and I were good friends, and she was always around any time I was over at his house. I fell for her, hard. But she loved Damien. She always has. For whatever reason, he had blinders on where she was concerned. He came home from college for spring break and broke her heart her senior year in high school. I jumped at the chance to pick up the pieces. We were careless, and she got pregnant. We married, trying to do the right thing, but then we stayed together for all the wrong reasons. Maybe if we'd been older, more mature, and able to deal with the shit life throws at you, we could've made a go of it. It wasn't like we married intending to end it."

He paused, his face reflective. When pain filled his eyes, she interlaced her fingers with his and kissed his hand.

"Harley's pregnancy wasn't easy, and Analiese arrived prematurely." His voice choked. "She was beautiful. Her tiny hand would clasp my finger…But she was born too soon and didn't make it."

Jinx kissed the tattoo commemorating his daughter.

"After that, our relationship fell apart," he continued after a moment. "It wasn't a sudden thing; there was no fight. We were just too damn young to deal with the hand life had dealt us. It took us a while to legally end things, as you know. I can't really explain why, except that finalizing the divorce seemed almost like negating our love for our daughter. Like, if we ended things, her precious, too-short life didn't matter."

He paused, staring at the ceiling. "Harley and I have remained close, and we always will be. You can't go through the birth and death of a child and not feel a connection. But as Harley has said, we make much better friends than spouses."

Jinx kissed him. "Thank you for telling me. If you think you can put up with my messed-up past and alcoholism, I can learn to live with Harley in your life."

Mark turned toward her. "I, uh, have some news. I was going to take you to dinner and tell you, but a naked pixie sidetracked me…"

"Tell me what?"

"I have a new job—in my field."

"So you're not going to work for me and Angel?" She bit her lip to contain her disappointment.

"I don't think that's wise. If we're moving forward in our relationship, working together could add a whole new level of stress that we don't need to deal with."

She blinked back her tears. "But just seeing you two or three times a month…"

"My job's in Harrisville."

"Alabama?" she squealed.

"Yup. It's not that far to commute from here. I'm no longer an owner of the Hangout. But…"

"But?"

"I need a place to stay."

Without batting an eye, she replied, "I'm sure Mae will love having you live with her." She gave him a resounding kiss, laughing at the same time.

"Works for me. That woman sure can cook." He tweaked her nose.

"Thank you, Mark."

"For?"

"Sticking with me and loving me, hang-ups and all."

He grinned and rolled on top of her. "I'm always up for a challenge."

She laughed and bucked against his erection. "I noticed."

Chapter
Twenty-Four

Five months later

Mark looked at his watch and sighed, unleashing his tobacco-free frustration on the hapless dog. "Dammit, Winston, quit dragging your shit out. I just picked it up two minutes ago."

Winston snorted and collapsed on his bed, leaving the chew toy in the middle of the floor. Mark tossed it toward him.

From the bathroom Jinx called, "Don't pick on Winston. He's old."

"Well, I'll be ninety by the time you're ready. Lovey, we're going to be late."

"No, we're not."

She'd been in the bathroom for over an hour getting ready. This was the girl who could be up and out the door in five minutes since giving up her heavy makeup and wigs. He didn't miss that edgy, hard girl. The new Jinx was much softer, though she still had her taut sense of awareness, rarely letting her guard down around others.

The past five months had not been easy. Both set in their ways, they'd found adjusting to life together to be a challenge. Yet despite fights that lasted for days, they'd persevered — talking endlessly and opening up about their feelings and hang-ups. Quite frankly, at times he was sick of talking so much, but it was worth it. He no longer worried she'd leave him for no reason. And sometimes, after being fucked to hell and back, she'd look at him, and he'd literally stop breathing with happiness. With tousled hair and swollen lips and a dreamy satisfaction in her eyes, she was open and vulnerable, and it pleased him to be so trusted.

The bedroom door opened, and Jinx stepped out in a pink tulle skirt and black and white striped T-shirt. The outfit was perfect, edgy but softly feminine at the same time—like the new Jinx. Nervously, she fingered the pearls around her neck.

"Do I look okay? Are the pearls too much? They were my mother's."

Understanding dawned. "No to the pearls," he told her. "You look beautiful."

She unfastened the pearls, and immediately her countenance lifted, as if the necklace had been a choke collar. He'd bet money her father had given them to her mom.

"Mae insisted I buy the outfit. She said it was more wedding appropriate than red or black. She's gonna be mad that I ditched the spaghetti-strap top that came with it, though. But it was just too much." She wrinkled her nose. "Anyway, I can't believe the wedding day is finally here for Maggie and Angel. They did things right, taking it slow."

Mark laughed. "Black, red, pink—it doesn't matter what you wear. My favorite color on you is *nude*." He pulled her back to the bedroom and picked up the sterling silver heart necklace off her dresser—the one he'd thrown at her door the Christmas he'd thought she was lost to him forever.

Jinx grinned. "I like you nude, too."

He fastened the necklace and leaned over to kiss her collarbone. "This necklace looks better. I'm glad you cut your hair again. Better access to your neck. Now you're perfect."

"As are you." She turned and straightened his collar. "This is one of my favorite outfits on you." Her hand crept under his kilt, and he instantly hardened.

"So I remember."

He glanced over at her dresser and picked up a feathered Mardi Gras mask. "When did you get this?"

"Today. It came in the mail with these." She held up a strand of beads and a squooshed, stale MoonPie. "Ava sent them. This is her not-so-subtle hint that she wants me to visit New Orleans."

He grinned. "You once said we were Mardi Gras people, hiding behind our masks…You were right, but not anymore. And I like where we are."

"Me, too. Ready to go?"

"Yes—"

"Wait!"

Puzzled, he watched as she tore open the MoonPie.

"I want to do something first. With you." She picked up the MoonPie. "Kind of a symbolic communion?" She bit her lip. "This is crazy, never mind. It's October, and this is probably left over from one of the Mardi Gras parades."

"No, let's do it." He took the confection from her and took a bite. Tearing off a tiny piece, he popped it in her mouth.

Her eyes held his as she swallowed. "I did it. I ate chocolate," she said, a look of wonder on her face.

"You did. I'm proud of you." He kissed her forehead.

"I'm proud of me, too. But I still don't think I like chocolate."

He grinned. "These aren't my favorite even when they aren't stale. I can think of better ways to eat chocolate."

She laughed. "Me too. Maybe we'll explore different ways…later." She looked damn pleased with herself.

A zing of electricity shot through him.

He held his hand out, and she placed hers in it. His thumb brushed her empty ring finger. *Soon.* Her eyes narrowed, and he pulled her hand to his lips, kissing it, hoping he hadn't blown his surprise for later.

"What are you up to?" she murmured as he escorted her to the car.

Thankfully he didn't have to answer. The kids loading into The Phoenix Rising's van greeted them with shouts of excitement. They were attending the wedding, too.

"Wow! Jinx, you look pretty."

"Hey, Mark, you look cute in a skirt. You got lipstick in your purse?"

"It's a kilt and a sporran," he shouted, clutching his heart, pretending to be horrified.

The kid laughed. Mark and Jinx smiled, a knowing look passing between them. The teasing from this troubled kid was a breakthrough.

Three weeks ago, the teen had arrived with track marks, self-inflicted cigarette burns, and a vacant look in his eyes.

Mae fussed as she badgered the kids to hurry and buckle up. Jinx waved, looking at ease and happy. Her smiles and laughter came easier these days and were more frequent than the sad looks and nightmares.

The urge that had been growing stronger each day tugged at his heart. He wanted to cement their relationship and start a family. So far, she'd resisted any mention of marriage, and after a few hints, he'd quit trying to bring it up.

He'd finally discussed it with Mae. Her advice was to pop the question after Angel and Maggie's wedding. She said nothing put a woman in the mood for roots like weddings and babies. So just in case the opportunity presented itself, he had a ring in his sporran.

Misreading his silent reflection, Jinx patted his arm as she stepped into the car. "They're just kids teasing you. Get in the car, you handsome, skirt-wearing man."

He leaned in and kissed her soundly to the applause of the kids before closing her door.

"You're in a strange mood today," Jinx commented as they drove the short distance to Maggie and Angel's bed and breakfast.

"Am I?" he hedged. "I need a cigarette."

She handed him a piece of nicotine gum.

"Not the same, but thanks."

"It gets easier."

They arrived and made their way to the back of the bed and breakfast. The yard had been raked, but red and gold leaves fell like confetti. Chairs surrounded the front of a white gazebo. He and Jinx greeted the guests they knew, and Harley ran toward them in a pale blue dress, a bright smile on her face.

"Mark, Jinx! It's been forever." She kissed them both on the cheek and held their hands.

"Hey, Harley." Mark kept it casual and loose, feeling Jinx's tension at his side.

"Can you believe Angel's getting married? Who'd of ever thought he'd be the first of us to the altar." Her mouth dropped. "Shoot, Mark, you know what I mean — now that we're halfway grown up and somewhat sane, I'm not sure ours counted."

He laughed and looked at Jinx. "Did she just insult me?"

Jinx shrugged, her wall of protection high and damn near impenetrable. He didn't blame her. Harley had no filters and bounced around like a hyperactive kid on a sugar high. He pulled Jinx closer, kissing her temple and keeping his arm securely around her waist.

Harley cocked her head to the side. "Mind if I steal Jinx just for a minute? We can go check on Maggie. Wait until you see her dress; it's gorgeous." She held her hand out to Jinx, who looked less than thrilled.

"Go," Mark urged her. "You can *ooh* and *aah* over Maggie, and Harley can tell you all sorts of stories about me. Don't believe half of them; she's been known to exaggerate."

"I live with you; surely I know most of them," Jinx commented with an aggrieved sniff.

Mark grinned. *Was that a hint of jealousy?* It delighted him to think so.

Jinx's standoffish attitude didn't seem to faze Harley one bit. "I'm sure you do. It's been years since I had to put up with his arse. Even when we were married, we didn't live together for long. If we had, I have no doubt I'd be in prison for killing him. Come, let's compare gross man habits. Even my OCD boyfriend has some. Has Mark learned to put the toilet seat down? If not, let me tell you how I broke Damien." Harley looped her arm through Jinx's and pulled her toward the house.

Mark frowned. Maybe his ex-wife talking to his future wife wasn't such a good idea. But he changed his mind when Jinx's shoulders relaxed, and she laughed as they walked away.

"No, he hasn't, and my dog, Winston, likes to drink out of the toilet. It makes a huge mess. I swear, we need two bathrooms…"

Mark went in search of Angel and ran into a grim looking Mr. Sinclair, who nodded brusquely and strode past without speaking. Mark winced, knowing Angel was probably not in the best of humor. He and his father had always had a tempestuous relationship. Mark could remember plenty of knock-down drag-outs between them when he was over visiting. Mark peeked in the guestroom and suppressed a laugh. Angel paced while Damien stood leaning against the wall, arms crossed in front of his chest, smirking.

"Quit running your hand through your hair. You look like an unmade bed," Damien commented.

"Shut the fuck up, asshole. Just wait, your turn is coming, and I'm going to pay Harley to make your life a living hell."

"Ah, the brotherly love. It warms my heart to see some things never change," Mark said as he entered.

"This isn't what I signed up for. I mean, look at me. *I'm wearing a suit and tie*," Angel replied. "It feels like a goddamned noose. When Maggie said a small wedding, I figured it would be jeans, a nice shirt, a preacher, and a few friends—you know, like a picnic. Not all this." He waved his hands above his head.

"You can always call it off and go back to sleeping under a bridge," Damien offered. "You agreed to this. And it really is a small wedding compared to what my darling Bridezilla is planning."

Mark laughed. "Uh, you two aren't very encouraging. Here I am trying to get the balls to ask Jinx to marry me." He pulled the ring box from his sporran and flipped it open. Inside was a Scottish Luckenbooth ring with a ruby.

"Turn back! Run!" Damien replied with mock horror.

Angel grinned. "Hey, congrats. Maybe this marriage will take, unlike the last fiasco with Harley."

Damien punched his brother. "Have some consideration. You're talking about his ex and my fiancée."

"Ouch, dammit. I was joking, kind of. I mean, everyone knows Harley's always loved you, Damien."

Damien sighed. "Well, not everyone."

Mark laughed. "No, it took both of us a while to figure it out. But I think it's clear now."

Harley took her into an empty guest room and closed the door. Jinx took a deep breath, refusing to cower before Mark's ex-wife.

"If this makes you too uncomfortable, stop me," Harley said, grasping both of her hands in hers.

Jinx raised her chin and forced herself not to snatch her hands away and hide them behind her back like a child. "I'm fine, but I thought we were going to see Maggie." She tried to suppress the little green monster of jealousy that always appeared around Mark's ex-wife.

"We are. I just…" Harley paused. "I wanted to tell you how excited I am to see Mark so happy. He's crazy about you." Harley dropped her hands and walked away for a moment, looking out the window. "It never should have happened—our marriage. We were young, stupid, and foolish. I loved him, but not the way he deserved to be loved. I hurt him, and because of our tangled, strange relationship, I've hurt you." She turned back. "I want to apologize and offer my friendship, if you'll accept it."

Jinx stared into her eyes and saw truth and kindness. She took her time to answer. Feelings were sometimes hard for her to process. She still struggled to not suppress them with alcohol. Stopping to do a mental check, she realized with surprise she had no desire to drink.

Harley sighed. "I understand if you can't."

"N-No."

Harley's face fell, but she nodded and moved to leave. Jinx detained her with a hand, giving her a tentative smile.

"Wait. I meant there's no need to apologize. I'm just as much at fault, for jumping to conclusions. I'm sorry for all the misunderstandings between us, and I'd like to put the past to rest." She smiled. "And I have to confess, it's easier now, knowing you're with Damien."

"He's a wanker, but I love him." She raised her eyebrow. "Has Mark proposed to you yet?"

"No. I'm still working on me. I'm not sure I'm marriage material. I don't think I'm ready. I mean, I don't think *we're* ready, yet." Heat crept up her neck. Secretly, she sometimes dreamed about a happily ever after with Mark…

Harley smiled. "No? From the way the two of you look at each other, I'd double down that you're both ready. You're perfect for him, Jinx. Don't sell yourself short and deny yourselves the happiness you deserve. We're all a work in progress. Part of the fun is working and growing together. I mean, look at Damien and me and all the time *he* wasted. It took him twenty-four years to realize we belong together."

Jinx laughed. "You fell for him when you were five?"

Harley grabbed her hand. "Yep. I've loved him that long. Now, let's go see how pretty Maggie looks. She's wearing an emerald green dress that's to die for…"

Jinx followed Harley, wondering if a happily-ever-after was in her future. Down the hall she saw Mark in the corner, talking to one of the boys from The Phoenix Rising. The boy had a look of awe as he listened. He nodded, and Mark patted him on the back as they turned to rejoin the guests. When Mark spotted her, he winked, and his warm smile assured her everything was okay. He was honestly the best thing in her life. A kernel of longing and hope took root in what used to be a barren heart, a heart now filled with love for Mark.

Jinx held her strappy sandals in one hand and gripped Mark's with the other. "It was such a pretty wedding."

"Yeah, it was. Angel and Maggie are perfect for each other." Mark opened the front door, and Winston came running out, happy to be loose.

He tilted her chin up. "Know my favorite part?"

"The cake? It was divine. I love buttercream frosting. Harley said Maggie made it."

"Not the cake, Lovey." His gaze was inscrutable as he leaned over and kissed her on the lips.

"No?" Nervous anticipation combined with a hyperawareness of her feelings. Harley's gentle admonishment to not deny happiness played like a tape on a loop in her mind.

"Dancing with you," he murmured, taking her in his arms and swaying as he hummed.

"Mark?" She gripped his arms as if he were her lifeline.

He stopped swaying and his brows knit together. "You okay?"

"I, uh…" Could she do this? She had to. It was the next step. If she didn't move forward now, their relationship was doomed. A black wave of anxiety washed over her. "Squash," she said, her voice trembling.

"What?"

"Squash." Her breathing sputtered, and her vision tunneled.

Taking deep breaths, she focused on Mark's blue eyes, full of concern—and more importantly, love. It had been months since she'd had a panic attack. As always, he was here for her. He wouldn't hurt her. This was a proven truth.

"Just hold me?"

"Of course." He didn't press her to say anything else.

Allowing his strength to shore her flagging bravado, she held him tight.

"I love you," she whispered into his shirt.

"I love you, too. Always. Remember that." He stroked her back, and as she listened to his steady heartbeat, she relaxed, her panic ebbing. He picked her up and carried her to their bedroom, placing her on the bed.

Winston scratched at the front door. Kissing her brow, he said, "I'll let Winston in and be back in a minute."

She nodded. The front door opened, and he called to Winston.

"That's a good boy. Yes, Daddy has a treat for you. Come on." Winston's claws clacked as he followed Mark to the kitchen. "Here you go. Don't tell Mama."

She smiled, knowing Mark was sneaking the dog a piece of ham from yesterday's dinner. Their children would be so spoiled…

Their children? Jinx sat up, startled by the thought. Mark as a daddy wasn't hard to picture. He loved kids and had an affinity for them. The times he'd interacted with the kids at The Phoenix Rising was proof of that. They loved the weekends he visited. He'd help them with homework, play ball, and listen to them.

But her, a mother? Memories of holding Elizabeth and Luke when they were babies brought a smile to her face. Despite her problems, Karen had been a good mom. Was that a possibility for her?

Mark returned and sat on the bed beside her. He stroked her hair and kissed her cheek. Jinx stretched out on the bed and patted it. He joined her, kissing the tip of her nose. "I love this. Just being with you."

"If I ask you to do something for me, would you?" she whispered.

"If at all humanly possible, of course." He brushed her hair from her eyes. "Your wish is my command, Mistress."

She rose above him and stared into eyes that gazed at her with a love so deep she was sure she could drown in it. "Make love to me."

"My way?"

She nodded. "I trust you to take care of me. I want you to touch my soul—and me. Bathe me with your love; make me clean again."

"You were never dirty, Jinx. *Never.* I want all of you. Your past, your present, and your future. Everything."

"I want that, too." Her hand crept down his kilt, across the soft fur of his sporran. He was hard and ready for her. She frowned. That wasn't all him, there was something in there.

"What's this?" She sat up.

"I, uh…nothing. It can wait."

"No, show me. What about honesty? No secrets."

He sighed and sat up, pulling something out. She peered over his shoulder, curious.

"Don't look. You're spoiling the surprise," he teased, shrugging to block her view.

She gasped when he knelt before her, a black velvet box in his hand.

"Trust me?" he asked with a grin.

She squealed and threw her arms around his neck.

"Whoa, wait. I haven't said anything yet," he protested, pushing her back to sit before him. He frowned. "Place your hands on your thighs, where I can see them."

Puzzled, she knit her brows together. "Why?"

"So I can watch for the switchblade."

She giggled. "It's in the drawer of my dresser." She hadn't even thought about it.

"Good." He popped the box open to reveal a ring with two hearts and a ruby. It was simple and perfect. "Jinx, would you do me the honor of being my girl, and when you're ready, my wife? Will you trust me to be here for you, to be your rock, your soft pillow, your sounding board, even your punching bag, if needed. And to love you, argue with you, laugh with you, and keep you safe to the best of my ability for the rest of our lives?"

"You forgot something," she whispered, his face swimming before hers.

"What?"

"To frog me on a routine basis." She wiggled her eyebrows and grinned.

He laughed. "Absofuckinlutely. To frog your brains out as needed. But also to make love to you slowly and deliciously until you're purring like a kitten."

She bit her lip and took her time answering. "All my life, I've wanted to connect with someone. I didn't know how, and I made some stupid mistakes. I'm not easy to love—"

He started to protest, but she put a finger over his lips.

"Let me finish."

He smiled but remained silent.

"You, Mark MacGregor, broke through my walls. Every time I put them up, you crash through until all that's left are teeny tiny pieces I can no longer put back in place, nor do I want to. I promise not to leave. If we have to handcuff ourselves together until we talk and work things out, we'll do it. I love you, and yes, I'd very much like to be your girl, forever."

She wrapped her arms around his neck and kissed him soundly. He placed the ring on her finger and then kissed it. Smiling impishly, she crept her other hand under his kilt, finding him still hard and ready.

"We've come full circle. Isn't this how we met?" He smiled into her ear.

"Want me to get my switchblade?"

"Not tonight, Lovey. Tonight, we're making love."

"Sounds perfect to me, Thurston."

Quietly, they shed their clothes. He gazed into her eyes. "This."

"This?" She kept her eyes on his, knowing she was safe with him.

"This is how I want you. No masks. Naked, vulnerable, and trusting me to take care of you."

"Okay."

"I love you," he murmured against her lips.

She smiled. "Love you, too."

"Ready for it?" Kissing up the column of her neck, his warm breath tickled her ear.

Nodding, she held her breath, waiting.

"Sure?" he asked, nipping her earlobe, his hand caressing her breast.

She made a conscious effort to relax her limbs. "Uh-huh…"

"Sweet nothing," he whispered in her ear.

She laughed outright and shoved his shoulder.

"See? That wasn't so awful, was it?" he teased.

"Not bad at all. I-I think I'm ready for more."

"Good. Me, too."

With a chuckle, he made his way down her body, his warm breath fanning over her before his mouth followed, licking, nibbling, and kissing. He rubbed soothing circles on her stomach and hip, gentling her skittishness.

He paused. "Where are we, Jinx?"

"Green bean. Definitely green bean, you son of a sea cook."

"My favorite vegetable."

He lowered his mouth to her clitoris, and as he lapped, sucked, and took her to the precipice, he watched her. Under his gentle care, she relaxed, closing her eyes and giving in to the moment. And when she came, it was his name she cried out.

He made love to her not once but three times that night.

Finally, when they were both sated, he lay on top of her. She held him, her fingers running through his auburn waves.

"G'night, Thurston," she whispered, feeling a peace she'd never imagined.

"'Night, Lovey."

The End

The series will continue with Matt and Sammie's story in
The Reintroduction of Sammie Morgan.

Author's Note

If you, or someone you love, has been sexually assaulted, there is help. The National Sexual Assault Hotline is available via telephone (1-800-656-HOPE) and online (online.rainn.org), 24/7.

Telephone

When you call 1-800-656-HOPE (4673), you'll be routed to the sexual assault service provider that serves your community.

Online

Visit online.rainn.org to chat one-on-one with a trained RAINN support specialist. It's simple to use — it's just like instant messaging, only much more secure. The chat is completely confidential and you will not be asked for any personally identifying information.

Both the telephone and online services are available 24/7
and are completely free.

If you need more information about **alcoholism**, please visit
https://www.aa.org/

You are not alone.
Do not suffer in silence.
Don't be afraid to reach out for help.

Acknowledgments

As always, to my family, thank you for putting up with me and supporting me on this crazy journey as an author. Without your love and support, I'd never make it.

Jessica Royer Ocken, many say editing is the worst part of writing. For me, it's the most fun, even when you make me dig deep and work hard. I can't imagine working with anyone else.

Shannon Lumetta, you always guide me and then get the cover perfect in spite of my insane suggestions.

Coreen Montagna, you fine tune and format the book after I've read it so many times that I miss the little stuff and you never yell at me for last minute corrections.

Thank you to Stephanie Phillips of SBR Media for being my friend as well as my agent. You listen to my rants and pick me up, dust me off and put me back on the right path.

Christina Santos, PA Extraordinaire, you're the Bosslady who keeps me organized. I couldn't do it without you.

Cain Raisers, you are my "chosen family" and I love that we can have fun, talk books and be silly without judgment. You are the best, ever. I especially want to thank the Cain Girls who read and review my books.

To all the bloggers who have taken an interest in my books and helped spread the word, I couldn't do it without you. You truly are unsung heroes/heroines.

And to my SLOBS, you keep me honest, you make me laugh and you lift me up.

Gel of Tempting Illustrations, you always bring my story to life with your beautiful teasers, thank you.

About the Author

During the day, Nancee works as a counselor/nurse in the field of addiction to support her coffee and reading habit. Nights are spent writing paranormal and contemporary romances with a serrated edge. Authors are her rock stars, and she's been known to stalk a few for an autograph, but not in a scary, Stephen King way. Her husband swears her To-Be-Read list on her e-reader qualifies her as a certifiable book hoarder. Always looking to try something new, she dreams of being an extra in a Bollywood film, or a tattoo artist. (Her lack of rhythm and artistic ability may put a damper on both of these dreams.)

Website: nanceecain.com
Blog: nanceecain.com/blog
Goodreads: goodreads.com/Nancee_Cain
Facebook: facebook.com/NanceeCainAuthor
Reader's Group (Cain Raisers): facebook.com/groups/Cain.Raisers
Twitter: twitter.com/Nancee_Cain
Pinterest: pinterest.com/nanceecain
Instagram: instagram.com/nanceecain
BookBub: bookbub.com/authors/nancee-cain
Newsletter: eepurl.com/bhFMtX
YouTube Channel: bit.ly/2xsU6Ad
Spotify Playlists: open.spotify.com/user/12184539074

Books by Nancee Cain:

Paranormal Romance (Angels)
Saving Evangeline
Tempting Jo
Loving Lili (novella)

Contemporary Romance (Pine Bluff Novels)
The Resurrection of Dylan McAthie
The Redemption of Emma Devine
The Rehabilitation of Angel Sinclair
The Redirection of Damien Sinclair
The Reinvention of Jinx Howell
The Reintroduction of Sammie Morgan
The Realization of Grayson Deschanelle

The Redirection of Damien Sinclair
A Pine Bluff Novel

Sometimes You Get What You Need

Acclaimed divorce attorney Damien Sinclair has witnessed more than his share of love's ugly aftermath. He keeps things black and white, preventing anyone from getting too close. But his illusion of control fades when an attempt on his life leaves him struggling with PTSD.

Enter Damien's childhood friend, the free-spirited Harley Taylor. Shrugging off the awkwardness of their teenaged fling and her broken heart, she appoints herself his caregiver. The man needs to learn not to take himself so seriously, and she's hellbent on snapping him out of his brooding funk.

After a decade apart, Harley and Damien find their attraction is stronger than ever. Could Harley's sunny disposition be the bright spot Damien needs in his life? Or will their differences overshadow any hopes of a future together?

Paranormal Angel Romances

Although each of the titles in this series can be read as standalone stories, this is the preferred reading order:

Saving Evangeline

Tempting Jo

Loving Lili (novella)

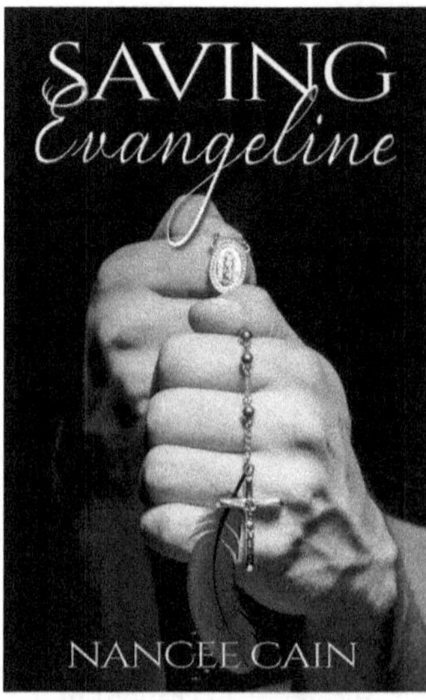

Evangeline is the town pariah. Everyone knows she's crazy and was responsible for the death of her last boyfriend. Even her mother left her and moved cross-country. Lonely and desperate, Evie decides to end her life.

Rogue angel Remiel longs to return to Earth, but there's just one problem. He tends to invite trouble and hasn't been allowed back since Woodstock. The Boss sends him to save Evangeline, but there's a catch: he can't reveal his angelic nature, and he must complete the task as *Father* Remiel Blackson.

Forced together on a cross-country trip, a forbidden romance ignites and love unfolds. A host of heavenly messengers tries to intervene, but Remiel and Evangeline are headed on a collision course to disaster. Will his love save her, or will they both be lost forever?

Forbidden love is hell...

Confident and quirky, Jo Sanford thinks her boss is God's gift to women—and she couldn't be further from the truth. Devilishly handsome, Luc DeVille will stop at nothing to lure his administrative assistant right into his arms—and bed.

Over Rafe Goodman's dead body...

Rafe, Jo's best friend, refuses to sit by and watch as Luc tries to win the heart of the woman he's always protected. After all, Rafe is her guardian angel. Suddenly, Jo's caught in the middle of a battle between good and evil. But the closer she gets to the fire, the hotter it burns. Now, Jo's going to learn that when love battles lust, Heaven and Hell collide.

Loving Lili (novella)

Their lovemaking is hot and dirty. Their break ups are nasty and epic.

Tired of taking the blame for every wicked thing that happens on Earth, fallen angel Luc DeVille decides to write a tell-all-book exposing The Boss.

Sharing a long and passionate history, Luc is shocked when Lili Nix arrives to interview for the job as editor. Immediately the verbal sparring begins, but the sexual chemistry remains combustible. Fascinated by this heavenly creature, Luc changes his game plan. After all, she's the only angel who has ever held his attention and understood his intentions.

Being in this world, but not of this world, is a lonely business. Can two lost angels connect and make it last this time?